AMBULANCE ONE

BY

JOHN EDWARDS

NEW MILLENNIUM

292 KENNINGTON ROAD, LONDON SE11 4LD

British Library in publication data.
A catalogue record for this book is
obtainable from The British Library.

Printed and bound by Watkiss Studios Ltd.
Biggleswade, Beds.
Issued by New Millennium*
Set in 12 point Times New Roman Typeface
ISBN 1 85845 317 8
* An imprint of The Professional Authors' & Publishers' Association

ii

To my ex-partners John and Teresa

First Edition Run

John Edwards

INTRODUCTION

This features one of the many dedicated professionals that work on the emergency ambulance service. Jason is fifty-eight years of age, has five children, all girls, and two failed marriages tucked under his belt. He joined the service in 1976 when it was more a question of scoop and run rather that treating the patient on the scene and stabilising before transporting to the nearest casualty unit.

Paramedics had not been much more than a topic of conversation prior to the 1989/90 dispute. This was the largest national strike action ever undertaken by ambulance crews in the history of the service. What had started as a face-saving battle by the Thatcher government turned into the finest advancement seen to date. No longer were these men and women classed as glorified van drivers; they were afforded the credit that they had long since deserved. This was indeed the turning point for advanced training that was so long overdue, bringing the ambulance service in line with other emergency professionals.

Jason and his partner Tom both took their exams at the end of 1990 and qualified as full time paramedics.

Jason was constantly recounting the difficulties and horrors of his work, making himself suppress his own feelings and incapability; forced to hide away emotions that tore him apart. He started to find that he was being crushed by the hardships of others from their need for sympathy or compassion.

No one knows what awaits him or her behind a closed door, the simple job could turn into a nightmare at any time and you just have to be prepared to face any unseen danger. They could walk into a domestic argument, a drunk armed with a weapon, or even a frail little old lady with a sheaf knife strapped to her walking stick to stop a crew taking her to a place of safety.

However, who could this paramedic turn to? How would he explain away the horrific screams of those in agony that constantly came into his sleeping dreams? His eyes had witnessed their piercing cries and contorted bodies as they are caught in death's last spasm. Many times he had tried to put up barricades, hoping that he could hold back those nightmarish emotions. But he was one man alone, influenced by the fact that, should he make a simple mistake, it could cost a life!

FOREWORD

An Ambulance is like a 'Ghost'. Invisible to most, just another white van until the Blues and Twos are switched on. They are often seen and rarely heeded, until the day comes that you need one yourself.

They scream up and down the road by day and by night. The only seeing eyes that are wide and bright are those of a child's.

They tend to the sick, the dying, and the fearful consequences of daily accidents: they are always on call twenty four hours a day.

When the time comes that you are in need, you will think that you are the "Only One."

This is the time that you remember all the previous occasions that you have seen and heard the Ambulance pass. Now your brain is saying, why is it taking so long? There are lots of them out there, so why am I being kept waiting? But the fact is that there are not that many at all: after certain hours most areas drop down to one or two; depending on the size of the town that you live in.

The men and women that crew the front line Emergency Ambulances are praised by some, but are abused by others; it is a sad fact that the later is all to often the case. Many crews are assaulted while carrying out their duties to serve the general public, both verbally and physically, although they are slightly better off than the hospital staff, for the crews can try and tactfully withdraw or call for Police backup.

PROLOGUE

There was an eerie silence along the corridors of Southsea hospital; in a few hours there would be a complete change as vast numbers of patients and hospital staff hurry backwards and forwards along the stark tunnels. Hundreds would be seen and treated in yet another busy day. But for now all was quiet, just the occasional stretcher being wheeled to and from the casualty department. The corridors are endless at night and the echoing sounds of a door being closed in the stillness seem to be amplified. Behind each ward door the nursing staff are busy while patients sleep soundly in their beds; the nurses work quietly trying not to disturb the patients restless dreams.

This is just one part of a hospital at night. But in the casualty department it is a totally different story. This is the department within the hospital that never sleeps; it can be just as busy at night as the corridors during the day. This is where the distressed and fearful public find themselves when they or their loved ones suddenly become traumatised.

Along the dozen or so cubicles lay the sick and injured waiting their turn to be seen by the casualty Doctor: The confused old gentleman busy pulling out the intravenous line from his arm, spraying the cubicle with blood, while a drug addict in need of a fix is threatening staff to spread his contaminated HIV blood all over the department. A drunken man paces back and forth between the cubicles, his nostrils flaring like an enraged bull. He glares angrily at the nurse who is trying to pacify him, while blood from a head wound drips slowly down his chin and onto the polished floor. Suddenly a strong smell rose up, filling the air with a distinctive fragrance as the patient in cubicle six vacates her bowels.

Constant bleeps of the monitors go unnoticed except by the staff that tends them.

Cubicles one, two and three are set aside for cardiac and respiratory problems. There is a large obese man in cubicle one, his skin is grey and the sweat oozes from out of his body like raindrops. His breathing, is laboured making him puff like a tired steam engine; he is struggling to regain stability while fighting against the pain and the fear. The leads of the electrocardiogram attached to his chest show unnatural waves on the monitor screen as the pain kicks in and shoots across his chest in uncontrolled waves. His treatment is urgent and the need to stabilise the condition has now become paramount.

Likewise in cubicle two, an asthmatic fights to control her breathing with the help of a nebuliser, her chest is heaving with the effort it takes to breathe. Eyes start bulging as the panic takes hold, because the medication has not worked instantly. This lady shakes with fear believing that she cannot breathe at all and that she is going to die.

In cubicle three, puffing quietly, a frail old lady, her chest infection, which had been neglected, has developed into pneumonia. A nurse takes a tissue from out of its box and dabs the old woman's mouth, absorbing the sticky wetness dribbling down her chin. Now in a semi-conscious state she is no longer aware of the serious condition her body is in.

These three cubicles would continuously be in use all through the twenty-four hours of each day. As soon as one trolley is vacated it will be replaced with another new patient within minutes.

The aftermath of most trauma end in a department like this; road traffic accidents, fights, accidents in the home, knife attacks or even the odd shooting incident. All will be treated in hospitals all over the country; each day and night the constant fight continues in an ever-endless battle.

Some of these many stories are in these pages. But this is not about a casualty unit but about the front line trauma witnessed by the 'Emergency Ambulance Services' throughout England ...

x

CHAPTER ONE

Jason drove into the ambulance station for the start of his second duty of the week parked his car and entered the crew room.

"Morning, Pop, how is the 'Jinx' this morning? We have just been looking through your paperwork for yesterday. You really are one unlucky son of a bitch!" said Phil one of the night crew.

Jason had been working on front line vehicles for the past twenty odd years and he had a knack of always being in the wrong place at the right time.

From this he had earned the nick name of 'Jinx'; it had become common for crews to throw their arms in the air with dismay on learning that it was Jason that partnered them on a shift.

It was almost certain that it would be a busy duty and if there were any bad jobs waiting out there, Jason would draw them in like a magnet.

His mind slipped back to the day before: he and his partner Tom had just walked into the station when the alarm sounded for an emergency call. It was a call for a child with a serious head injury that was to be conveyed as a nil delay to Great Ormond Street, Hospital, London.

This was a transfer from one hospital to another, and with nil delay requirements it implied that the child's condition was not very stable and all haste would be needed once mobile.

Jason and his partner threw their personal belongings and equipment into the back of the ambulance, then set off at high speed towards the local hospital's Intensive Care Unit. Whilst on route, the alarm from the cab radio sounded and the controller passed the following message.

"The child is unconscious and has been intubated, you will have a doctor and a nurse as escorts. The doctor has requested that you get there as quickly as possible, but go easy on the bends and also the brakes. Control out."

1

Tom turned to Jason. "This looks like being another fun shift. You just seem to draw them in all the time. I will lay you odds that when you retire my working days will be much quieter."

"Don't you bet on it, someone will take over where I left off," replied Jason.

Tom shifted into top gear and pushed the throttle pedal down hard. Blue lights mounted on the roof of the vehicle flashed, giving warning to other road users. The traffic was heavy and progress was much slower than they would have liked.

Driving under these conditions always puts the pressure on the man behind the wheel. The fact that he has to drive at high speeds through slower moving traffic, through red lights and other law-breaking functions puts an enormous stress on the designated driver. He has to think faster, be aware of the implications and also try and anticipate every other driver's moves before they make them.

Gripping the door handle, Jason held on like grim death as his partner swung the steering wheel vigorously to avoid traffic on either side of the road.

Darkening clouds were building just off the shore and the cold water looked grey and menacing. Inclement weather had been forecast for later and it looked as if they had got it right for a change. Today could see the first snow of the season and that could create all kinds of problems for the emergency services.

They arrived at the local hospital and made their way towards the Intensive Care unit. The usual hustle and bustle of hospital life was in full swing as patients and staff hurried between their assigned clinics or wards. It was like standing in the centre of 'Kings Cross' railway station waiting for your train to arrive, the station announcer being replaced by ward clerks calling to patients to follow them to their designed locations.

As Tom and Jason wheeled their trolley along the corridor, they passed many members of staff who were known to them

2

and exchanged the occasional word or greeting. They stopped in the corridor outside the Intensive Care unit and waited to be waved into the ward.

The ward sister was sitting just inside behind a long desk used by the doctors to read their patient notes or write up treatments they had carried out.

She was wearing her uniform to show off her hourglass figure; this immediately caught Tom's eye with interest.

"Oh good, you are here in plenty of time," she smiled, "he is stable at the moment so you can start making arrangements to move him as soon as you are ready. He seems to be doing very well considering his condition." She gave them an up-date on the history leading up to the child's admission into hospital and the present treatments being given. Then she introduced them to a Doctor Smith, the ward consultant and a male nurse called Robin; they would be coming with them to escort the child.

The doctor asked them if they had been made aware of the type of journey that was required?

"Yes, we have been given our instructions and if there is anything you need or any problems, just give a shout and we will do our best to assist," said Jason.

"Alright, then lets get going. Have we everything that we need for the journey, Oxygen alright? Right, we will move off," said the doctor.

Tom had checked the oxygen supplies and found that they had more than enough to get them up to London.

They carefully loaded the stretcher into the rear of the vehicle and after securing the patient, stowed away the equipment required to see the boy safely to London.

During the journey and a lull in the conversation the doctor had asked if they might get a look at the 'Millennium Dome' on the way back from London. It would require a small detour, but Jason had agreed that if they did not get sent on anywhere else after this job that they would indeed go and take a look ...

The radio alarm suddenly screamed through the Ambulance Station, snapping Jason back from his thoughts of yesterday.

Almost as soon as Tom answered the radio, the control operator started giving out details. "We have a doctor's urgent case to transfer to the local casualty, no other instructions yet."

"Here we go again. It never seems to stop these days," said Tom.

They both climbed aboard the vehicle and took off down the road heading towards the location given to them by the control operator; but at this time in the morning roads were packed with people trying to get to work. It made the driving slow, but short of flying over the top of the traffic they just had to make the best speed possible ...

Once again Jason's thoughts slipped back to the previous day. They had made good time getting to London with the child, in fact it had been an easy job: the child's head injury had not caused them any real problems on route, plus the pressure had been taken away by the doctor and the nurse doing all the work.

They had wheeled the trolley along to the ward to find the child's parents sitting awaiting their arrival. The handover was completed swiftly and they said their farewells to the child's parents before making a discreet exit.

Everything was stowed away in the vehicle and they all climbed aboard, the doctor still requesting that they went to look at the new 'Millennium Dome' on route back home. They decided to make a slight change of direction via the river sites on their way back to base, so that the doctor could have his wish.

After this was accomplished and the doctor had reviewed the magnitude of the dome they found a filling station to refuel the vehicle. While Tom started pumping diesel fuel into the tank, the doctor and nurse stocked up with light refreshments from the garage shop. Once this was done they set off again to complete the trip home.

Fate now took over, for the next turn of the steering wheel was to change the whole pace of the shift. As they joined the duel carriage they came across a large formation of traffic.

Everything came to a sudden standstill.

"Something seems to be going on up ahead. I hope it's not an incident, but we had better try and get a closer look," said Tom. He flicked the two switches on the top of the instrument panel setting the blues and twos into action and forced the vehicle forwards.

The cars in front eased over to form a pathway through the middle of the road, allowing the ambulance to creep between them until they came across the cause of the hold-up. What they had found was a 'six car pile up' and they were the only emergency vehicle in sight ...

Wrecked cars and their owners were all over the road, some just walking around not knowing what to do, others were laying or sitting by the road side.

The crew of the Ambulance bailed out of the front doors and the doctor and nurse left by the back, each seeking somewhere to start.

Jason found himself alongside a man who introduced himself as an off duty police officer who was just about to smash the back window of a car. The car driver was slumped across the steering wheel and was not moving. Both the two off-side doors had been damaged in the crash and the policeman had been unable to get them open.

With one swift downward blow the policeman smashed the window with a crowbar; he reached in and lifted the catch of the back door, then did the same with the front.

"Thanks," said Jason as he quickly opened the car door and spoke to the driver. "Are you ok? Can you here me?" he shouted.

But the driver made no response.

Just then the face of the male nurse appeared at the doorway. "Do you need any help here?" he asked.

5

"Yes, please, can you get hold of my partner, and ask him for a Low neck collar and the Back Splint?" Jason replied. He then started to go over the injuries that he could see without moving the driver. Most of the surface injuries were minor cuts, although the head always tends to bleed a lot.

The male nurse Robin returned with the equipment before positioning himself behind the driver's seat to keep the injured man's head still. Then Jason very gently eased the rigid collar around the driver's neck and made it secure.

Robin then slid the 'Back Splint' down so that its base was touching the seat. Now came the tricky part: slowly and very carefully they eased the driver into the contours of the Splint, this was the danger point, for if they had not taken care at this time then his injuries could have been increased.

Once strapped and secured the injured man was given oxygen to help with blood loss, shock and to reduce any swelling within the skull should any head injury exist. This was standard procedure, but from Jason's initial examination he had suspected a possible neck fracture or back injury because of the position of the driver when found. Also the fact that he had wounds to the head could imply that he might have suffered bruising to the inside of the skull. Because of the position and the damage to the vehicle, the next part of the operation was going to cause them problems. Both the near side doors were wrapped around and buried into the crash barrier. The impact had been so severe that the front had come back into the cab space; torn and twisted metal had wrapped itself around the driver's lower leg, causing entrapment. This was going to be a long, slow removal, hampered by the sharp metal all around the trapped driver. Although the crews carry rescue equipment, this only covers small jobs; this was going to need the expertise of the Fire Brigade to extract the patient from the vehicle.

Slowly the driver started to recover; he made a choking, gagging sound, then coughed up a large measure of phlegm and spat it out. It missed Jason by a fraction, sticking to the dashboard of the car.

"Don't bloody mind me," exclaimed Jason in annoyance.

The driver turned to look at the paramedic by his side, while still trying to clear his throat. "Bugger off! Don't start on me. I hurt," he said with a slurred tone.

The paramedic glared at him in disbelief; he could feel his calmness dissolving and it was obvious from the smell of this guy's breath that he had been drinking. Insults were common, he was used to this type of abuse but it still took him by surprise. Anyone that needed help would get his full attention, but the pay was not enough to keep taking abuse from big apes like this.

The driver's recovery was short lived; he soon slipped back into a state of unconsciousness, which in one respect was just as well. Fortunately the doctor appeared outside the car and they both set to work feverishly trying to stabilise the injured man. The doctor set up two wide bore intravenous drips with a Hartmann's solution while Jason maintained the guy's airway. His Glasgow coma scale had dropped to five and this made the doctor concerned. This is the measurement to describe levels of unconsciousness in trauma injuries, fifteen being the highest level of consciousness and three being the lower; this is considered to be moribund.

Once again the patient started to respond: his colour, blood pressure and awareness all started to improve. Just then Tom appeared along with a London Ambulance Officer. "All of the other patients have been taken care of, mostly walking wounded. The London crews have shipped them off to hospital and that just leaves this one." Tom went on to assist the doctor with equipment from the off side of the vehicle.

The London Ambulance Officer leaned forward to talk to Jason. "Are you happy to carry on and remain with the driver or do you want to hand over to his people as it was on their ground?"

"No, that's not a problem. I am fine with things the way they are; we have gone this far so we will stay with it," replied Jason.

"Good, thank you for what you have done! Looks like the 'Fire Brigade' have arrived. I will have a word with the police before I leave and ask them to give you an escort when you are ready to go to the local hospital," continued the London ambulance officer.

Tom meanwhile had been talking to the fire officer in charge and was bringing him up to date on the requirements needed to extract the driver and to the extent of his injuries. In situations of this nature Jason always left the talking to his partner, for he was lucky that Tom was also a part time retained fire fighter and knew the routine backwards when it came to jobs like this.

The fireman asked Jason to make sure that he kept his safety helmet on and to try and shield the driver's face with a blanket whilst they took off the car roof. Jason knew only to well what it felt like to be in a vehicle with cutting gear eating into metal and glass; the sound alone was harrowing, plus the splintering and shattering of glass makes it feel much worse.

Through all of this Jason was aware that it was his job to look calm and to keep on reassuring the patient beside him. He kept a close eye on the patient's GCS, checking the airway and the blood pressure constantly for any change.

Suddenly the driver started to yelp in pain. "My leg, oh, my leg; please give me something for the pain," he screamed.

Jason quickly looked down into the foot well of the car. "Stop!" he cried out.

As the spreaders and cutting equipment started taking out the roof and some of the side panels of the vehicle, it began twisting the metal floor around the man's lower leg, trapping the foot. Once the movement caused by the cutting equipment was at a standstill the pain eased off. This forced them to concentrate more on the legs being released before they moved onto the roof again.

The doctor gave the driver something for the pain while they eased the leg free from the jagged metal. Once released, his leg was dressed and secured before the firemen restarted on the removal of the roof.

It was at this time that the weather decided to change for the worst. Sleet, followed by a north-easterly wind that was almost at gale force, made the working conditions more difficult. It was at least six degrees colder as the biting wind cut into the rescue workers.

At long last the roof was cut off and they could now start to extract the driver from the car. Everyone prepared for the execution of the rescue, all acting as one. This was done with the help of a rescue board and many pairs of fireman's hands. Very slowly and with the minimal discomfort to the patient they eased him out inch by inch onto the waiting stretcher.

On the trip into hospital the condition of the driver improved to almost normal. His behaviour unfortunately did not; he continued to throw his insults at anyone that got too close.

Jason wondered how this blustering bag of wind would feel later after he finds out the police have booked him for drunk driving. They had treated him for the very worse scenario and it had made vast improvements to his condition. The diagnosis made on the spinal injury was confirmed almost immediately when they arrived at the hospital. The casualty Doctor soon found a fracture in the Lumber four area of his lower back. This created problems for the crew as they had to leave the rescue board with the patient; getting it back from the London area would be a nightmare job for one of their officers.

By the time they had helped themselves to a drink and completed the hand over, two hours had passed. Jason got in touch with his control via the landline; he gave them a complete up-date on the job along with the news about the equipment that they were leaving behind. They were not very happy about the loss of the rescue board for the next call that came in might also need it, although this would not be the first time that crews had run on 'front line' without the full range of equipment. Their vehicles and the equipment inside them were the tools of the trade, without it they reverted back to basics.

Some of the Management seemed to worry more about a BSI kite mark on the back of Ambulances than they did about them being fully equipped. In fact, a lot of the time, instead of being up to the standards set, the vehicles were running light on essential life-saving equipment because of a lack of spares to back them up.

The BSI Standards created problems because they wanted the equipment to conform to the criteria set down. Management required that any equipment that recorded measurements would need to be calibrated on a regular basis.

This included Blood Pressure cuffs, ECG Monitors, Defibrillators or any type of Flow Meters, such as found on Oxygen Bottles.

There were times when the equipment had to go away for re-calibration, meaning that vehicles were forced to run without life- saving items on board. On arrival at an incident the crews were then put in the position of either calling for a second ambulance causing a delay on departure or making a run for the nearest hospital. This put added stress onto the crews and the patients ...

Chapter Two

They arrived at the first call of the day which was to transfer to the casualty department a lady of eighty years, suffering with diarrhoea and vomiting, who needed to be re-assessed on her mobility status. Arriving at the lady's address, Jason recognised the patient as being one of the regulars that they had frequently conveyed to the outpatient clinic some years previous. Jason remembered that when he first meet Lily she used to be a sprightly lady, with a wicked tongue full of witty remarks. He was amazed at the condition he saw her in now, the deterioration had been swift and unmerciful, and this once sprightly woman was a pitiful sight to behold.

The interior of her house was just as incredible; the bodily smells of neglect hung in the air and hit their nostrils as they entered the room. Because of her weakness she had slipped into this state and like most old folk she was too proud and would not ask for help from anyone. Unable to fend for herself her age and body had both worked against her, preventing the basic routines from being accomplished.

Her condition had slowly deteriorated and her Doctor was forced eventually to request that she be taken into hospital for assessment; she could no longer live in this way and would need long term care, a sad but necessary conclusion. The two paramedics were convinced that she had not realised just how bad her self-cleanliness had declined.

Her quick wit still remained and her mind was as sharp as a razor. "How quickly people and things change in such a short space of time," Jason thought to himself as he looked at the dried faeces that were caked on her skin from the top of her thighs to her ankles.

At that moment Lily gave a little cough along with an explosion of wind, the force of expressed air flooded the bedding and

11

diarrhoea ran away from her. The poor soul was very apologetic, feeling a little ashamed at creating extra work for the two paramedics.

"I am sorry lads, just can't help myself, when I cough I 'fart' then it just runs away from me," said Lily. This remark brought smiles all round.

They did their best to clean Lily up before moving her but the diarrhoea had its own ideas, causing them to abandon the operation and look towards other means to keep the mess contained. Both men had noticed her prodigious toes that finished in yellowing curled nails; they reminded Jason of the claws of the sloth.

"I wish I was young again, its been a long time since I had a young man give me a cuddle," said Lily with a cheeky grin.

Tom gave Lily a body lift into the carry chair. "What a lovely bum!" she exclaimed as she gave Tom's backside a playful squeeze.

"Behave yourself, woman," he responded, taken by surprise at her boldness. Tom had been used to this sort of behaviour and it was taken as part of the job, but Lily had caught him unprepared, making him blush.

These were the calls that paid for the daily bread; sixty per cent of all ambulance work carried out was on jobs like this. Jason enjoyed doing urgent cases; there was no pressure and he had time to have a laugh and a joke with the patients. Some of these older people were interesting if you had the time to listen.

Most forget that the older generation were young once and they have a lot of history behind them. Just get them to open up and sit back, they will astound you with a complete way of life as it was when they were young.

Lily was no exception; once Jason got her to talk about her life; it was like walking through a time warp. Her stories held him spellbound, commanding strict attention to detail as she unveiled the secrets of her past life.

"Sounds to me you were a bit of a girl in your time," said Jason.

"I have had more than my share of special moments," she laughed. There was a definite twinkle in her eye as she spoke.

Jason had listened to her tell about the war years and how she had survived the bombs falling on Stratford, east London, about her brothers who went to war as young men and returned with much older outlooks, their youth stolen away from them by the horrors that they had been forced to witness. She told of the terrible things that happened during those air raids. How they had managed to survive the relentless bombings and how everyone surveyed the traumas of dismembered corpses found in the streets when they finally surfaced from their shelters. These were the unlucky souls that did not escape the intensified bombing raids by the German Luftwaffe.

The co-ordinated blanket bombing raids on England's cities was designed to demoralise the British people. Hitler wanted to crush the population of this small Island into submission, but all he succeeded in doing was reuniting them into a reinforced nation, with a renewed determination to fight harder. The whole country was motivated by the will to keep their freedom reorganised and found a spirit to strengthen the attack on the German invaders.

Young women like Lily worked hard to replace the men that had joined the armed forces, becoming factory workers, farmers, drivers and nurses in fact filling any gap that was required. They worked hard and they played hard, living only for the moment and never making long-term commitments. None of them could plan for a future, for they had no guarantees that there would even be a tomorrow, let alone a future life.

She would tell the stories of her marriage and her children, the struggles of trying three times to set up home only to be bombed out and forced to start all over again.

When Lily had given birth to her son it was decided that for their safety it would be advisable to move them into the country away from the fear of bombs and destruction. The evacuation from the streets of London to the green fields of the English countryside had already been put into action.

It was like moving into a complete New World for Lily. The village where she was placed was set in the very heart of England with miles of green pastured meadows. Smells of sweet grass, flowers and fresh cut hay were all part of the newly found magic, a complete contradiction to the pungent smells of the streets of London. Luscious fields filled with delightful wild flowers were full of discoveries and In the spring the meadows would fill with fat yellow buttercups and the warming sun would produce the cowslips and carpets of bluebells.

The quaint little cottage that she rented had an abundant vegetable garden where she was able to grow enough home produce to feed them for the year. Living in this small community with its few houses and single chapel was a most genteel time for Lily and she blended into village life with ease. She had been given an insight to a lifestyle that she had only ever been able to read or dream of in the past. Finding this fresh, tranquil world away from the noise and hustle of the city was a joyful adventure full of abundant discoveries. Embracing each sweet taste and smell, learning the simple ways of country folk and the wonders of its wildlife was like being 'Alice' in wonderland. Her education was vast, finding out that there were more birds than the common house sparrow or pigeon was amazing. All kinds of feathered species would congregate in her small garden to peck away at the fruit trees and vegetables and she was happy to share with these graceful creatures. She would relax watching the parent birds feeding the young fledglings and observe as they inspected their first flight of wing before leaving the nest. After a while Lily had almost forgotten that her beloved England was still at war.

For, apart from the odd reminder on the radio or the occasional dog-fight over the village sky, she lived those days not in fear but in a peaceful relaxed existence.

If there had been more time spent with her, Jason could have written a book on Lily's life. But like most of their calls it is very rare that they got that involved.

Tom and Jason had a regular banter that they used; "If we drop you call for an Ambulance." "I can't stand the sight of blood especially if its mine." "Don't scream too loudly; its only pain and we can't feel a thing." "Are you allergic to anything other than the wife?"

All of these verbal phrases were designed to take the patient's mind away from the pain or discomfort that they were experiencing at the time. Making them laugh was the best way to combat pain, although there was always someone that would take exception. But you can't win them all.

When asked about blood risk from the job, he replied with the standard joke, "Don't worry, mate, you only get it once." He had dipped his hands into other folk's blood more times than he cared to remember.

During the first twelve years of service no one worried much about wearing rubber gloves. After all, they were not much good when crawling around in a car wreck full of broken glass and sharp metal. The paper-thin latex used to disintegrate once holed, very quickly. It was only in the later part of his service that blood-borne diseases were emphasised: Hepatitis 'B' and AIDS being the most talked about, causing the use of protective gloves to become more wide spread amongst ambulance crews.

Suddenly, without warning, Lily leaned over the side of the trolley and spewed. Erupting vomit splattered to the floor, forming a puddle of vile green liquid as she expelled her stomach contents. The smell of vomit rose up filling the air with its acrid fragrance.

Jason breathed through his mouth taking only shallow breaths to avoid the full impact of the pungent vomit. That smell was so strong it hit him full on, making him fight the urges of his heaving stomach as his own acid hit the back of his throat.

'Oh Christ, I'm so sorry,' Lily cried. She looked pitiful, the pallor of her skin showing a china - white sheen and her body still heaving as if the vomiting wanted to continue.

Behaving in a professional and dignified manner, he pushed aside his own feelings and tried to clean her up, but with just tissue paper and water he could only make a token gesture. He took the tissue from the roll fixed to the side of the saloon wall and dabbed her mouth, absorbing the sticky wetness of her vomit.

When they arrived at the hospital; Tom opened the rear doors and quickly took a step backwards as the smell from inside hit his nostrils. He made no comment; his facial expressions said it all ...

The emergency department was like any other hospital casualty: a steady flow of ambulance stretchers were constantly in and out of the unit, phones were ringing and the staff were busying themselves sorting patients. The air in the department was heavy with the smell of stale body odours, strong urine and of course vomit.

The usual humour was passed. "Trying out a new brand of After-Shave again, are we?"

They dropped Lily off at the casualty observation ward and made their way back to the vehicle. On returning to the ambulance they found that the distinctive smell still lingered in the saloon. Tom grabbed the Fresh Air Spray from the dash locker and emptied half its contents around the interior.

"Don't know what is worse, the vomit or the lemon smell," exclaimed Jason.

They managed to fit in three more calls, two doctor's transfers and an uneventful road traffic accident, before the next emergency landed on their laps ...

After a night of heavy drinking Dave Parsons arrived ready

16

for work on the building site. They had almost finished half of the fifty-six houses on the site of the old fair ground.

Dave was not feeling on top form this morning; in fact he felt like crap, this being brought about by a self-inflicted hangover from the late night drinking binge that was to make him struggle through the rest of the day.

When lunchtime arrived, his work mates headed off as usual for the nearest public house. Normally he would have been at the front of the queue leading the way to the pub door eager for that first taste of the golden nectar as it slipped down his throat. But today Dave declined the offer to go because he still felt hung over from the previous night and did not wish to rekindle his alcoholic intake.

Sitting down on the edge of a newly built wall some ten feet off the ground he opened his tuck box carefully prepared by his loving wife, drew out a large thick cheese sandwich and bit deep. His wife spoilt him when if came to food, she always put too much in the lunchbox but he would never complain about that.

After a while he began to relax and because of his dulled senses from drinking too much beer, he was not fully alert. He turned, forgetting his surroundings, and lent backward expecting to find a solid support not an empty space. Somersaulting backwards he fell onto the hard ground below, landing on his backside, a sharp pain shot through his body and he was sure that he had damaged his spine.

After a few minutes he realised that he had landed on one of the concrete reinforcing rods that stuck upright from the ground and that it had penetrated the soft flesh of his buttocks. The pain was indescribable; it made him catch his breath and the waves of nausea swept over him. He knew that he had to remain conscious; if he did not, he would sink down further onto the metal spike that had impaled him. Dave also knew that his work mates would not rush back from the pub and somehow he would have to hold on until they returned. It was only at that moment that he noticed the dark red bloodstains on the earthy ground; placing a hand carefully to the seat of his trousers, he felt the wet sticky liquid oozing out of the wound.

The pain that was deep into his buttocks felt like hell! He tried to lift himself off the twisted spike but it held him fast. Once more the pain tore through his body this time causing him to vomit.

Vile smelling liquid shot forward and cascaded onto the ground in front him; dizziness caused him to sway a little, and he fought against the urge to drop to his knees. If he collapsed now it could be the end.

Time passed and after what seemed like hours he heard the rest of his mates returning from the pub. The steady sounds of laughter grew nearer, interrupted by raised voices that had noticed that Dave was in trouble.

Laughter died away as they realised that he had been impaled on the spike and this was not a matter to make jokes about.

Some of the language used was educational when they saw what had happened. "For fuck sake, one of you get an ambulance," shouted a builder.

"Don't panic, Dave, we'll get you help," said another.

Dave was getting weaker through the loss of blood and did not think he could stay conscious for much longer.

"For God's sake, don't let me pass out, lads, or I'll fall back on that bloody thing."

They did their best to keep him alert but the loss of blood was making him weaker by the minute.

His mates attempted to set him free by pulling him off the spike, but it caused so much pain they had to abandon the idea. Each did their best to try and take his mind off his entrapment by talking and cracking the odd joke. Both the fire and ambulance services had been called and would hopefully soon be able to get Dave some relief from his pain.

In the mean time he would just have to grin and bear it ...

Tiny teardrops of rain splashed gently against the windscreen as they sat awaiting the controller's instruction. They had been outside the casualty department for the past fifteen minutes on stand-by and were starting to get bored. The rain increased its output and began to fall in torrents. A cold whining wind sprang up from nowhere and tore through the air searching for upright structures to bite into. A collection of trees bent forwards on their stout trunks in its wake, bearing testimonials to its demonstrable power.

"God, where did this lot spring from?" questioned Tom.

"I have no idea, but I hope that it goes as quickly as it arrived."

The radio bleeped and interrupted their conversation. "I have a call for you, can you make your way to the old funfair site." Believed to be an industrial injury. Fire brigade are also on route."

"Sod it, that's just our luck in weather like this, the last thing I want to be doing is crawling about on a bloody building site," exploded Tom. He turned on the warning devices and pointed the vehicle in the direction of the coast road.

When the paramedics arrived they were astounded when it was realised what the difficulties were going to be. They both studied the situation giving it serious though before making a move.

After falling off the wall Dave had landed onto a metal reinforcing rod used to strengthen the concrete footings. These were set, leaving approximately fifteen inches of exposed spiralled metal above ground level. The rod appeared to have entered the fleshy part of the buttocks and sliced its way upward alongside the rectum. Jason was concerned that it could be touching the spinal column and if this was the case getting him free of the metal spike could be a daunting task.

The builders had come up with the clever idea of packing sandbags around and under Dave's backside to stop him slipping down further onto the spike. Just as well, for Dave was in a weakened state, caused mainly by the loss of blood and shock.

19

"I wish this bloody rain would ease off, it's making conditions almost impossible to work in."

The lads put up a makeshift shelter to keep the rain off while the paramedics worked on their mate.

Tom worked in unison with the firemen, who started to cut carefully through the protruding metal while Jason set about stabilising Dave's vital signs and trying his best to control his pain.

Drips were set up to administer fluids to replace the blood volume and Nubain (Nalbuphine Hydrochloride) given for the pain; the wound was packed and dressed and Oxygen administered to help with the circulation and breathing.

All the while they reassured Dave, keeping him aware of everything that was going on around him.

Slowly he started to respond and after a short while the rescue workers were pleased to hear him crack the odd joke. But Jason had no idea if his patient had suffered any internal injuries and he knew that they would have to treat for the worst scenario. They positioned three electrodes on Dave's chest and began to monitor his heart rate. The electrocardiogram would give them an early warning if there were any cardiac arrhythmia's present. All the while it showed a regular activity Jason would be happy, although he knew well enough from past experience that the electrocardiogram alone could not determine the overall condition and he would have to remain vigilant at all times. Detaching the metal rod from the ground was not easy; every movement of the cutting saw vibrated up the shaft and transmitted pain into Dave's body. Fearful that the vibrations could cause extra problems, Tom paid close attention to the operation and the patient's reactions. If there was any possibility that the rod was indeed touching the spine, just the slightest movement might have devastating results. If they got this wrong, Dave could spend the rest of his days in a wheelchair.

Eventually the painstakingly slow procedure was over, the rod was cut free from its concrete base and very carefully they lifted

Dave away. The spike was still protruding from out of his backside, giving them no option but to lay him face down onto the stretcher.

Dave was coming back to his old self and full of wit, he had both paramedics in stitches with his curt remarks. "First time I've had a foreign body that big shoved up my arse."

There were no problems on route to hospital and when they arrived at the casualty department they wheeled Dave into the cubicle covered by a blanket, to hide the two inches of metal still sticking out of his rear.

Unfortunately the story had reached the department in advance and there were many inquisitive members of staff that wanted to see for themselves. They could see that the spike was indeed embedded deep into the rectal area and this produced a lot of black humour. Dave took this with a few wise cracks of his own, but in good humour.

The casualty doctor took control very quickly to avoid any more embarrassment to the builder, although Jason was sure that he observed a faint smile on the doctor's face. Jason gave the doctor a brief but detailed account of the cause of the injury and the treatment that he had received so far.

Before they could do anything about removal, he needed x-rays to determine just how far and in what direction the metal rod had travelled into Dave's body. The doctor's fear was that at least one or more of the patient's vital organs had suffered some kind of damage.

Once the wound had a temporary dressing place around the entry to stem the bleeding and keep it clean, he was moved off to the x-ray department to have the whole area scanned.

The paramedics hung around hoping to find out the results and to witness the removal.

Fifteen minutes later the results were in and inspected by the doctor. Dave was to be lucky, his x-rays had shown that the spike had entered the buttocks and run alongside the rectum as suspected, but had missed all the vital organs and had embedded itself into soft tissue.

The casualty doctor smiled as he put the films back into their envelope and congratulated his patient, for now the removal should be simple.

Jason and Tom could not wait around for the final outcome; they had to get back on the road.

Before they had reached the door one of the nurses stopped them. "Your control is on the phone, can you take another call?"

"Oh shit, are we the only bleeding vehicle at work today?" ...

The call that was passed came from the patient's husband, whose wife was having an 'epileptic' fit. She had been fitting continuously for over five minutes.

Tom started the engine and set off in the direction given by the controller. There was a huge amount of traffic on the road making progress slower than they would have liked. Trying to push his way through the busy traffic was harrowing. The sound of the sirens blaring made little difference and even the blue lights flashing like a disco's special effects did not make the slightest change, they just did not get the response they should have had. Jason sensed his partner's frustration, but short of putting wings on the side of the vehicle Tom would just have to live with the situation. It took them just over six minutes to travel the couple of miles to the address given.

The lady, who was in her late thirties, was still fitting and was sweaty and turning blue. They managed to obtain a brief history from the husband while they worked and he informed them that she was a known epileptic and had been suffering these kinds of attacks for many years.

She had had three fits since this morning; her last being the present fit that was still in progress and it had been a 'Grand Mal' (continuously fitting). Their first priority was to maintain the woman's airway, because the danger from this kind of attack

22

was that the tongue would occlude the airway preventing normal breathing.

Once they had secured the breathing they concentrated on getting the fit under control. In the past there was not a lot that ambulance crews could have done, except to try and protect patients from causing any damage to themselves while they thrashed about. The only option used to be the removal of all objects that could cause them injuries and wait until the fit subsided. Thankfully 'paramedics' now carry a drug that relaxes the central nervous system and normally eases the fits. Giving 'Diazepam' used to create problems of it's own when it was first introduced, because of the way that it was administered, 'rectally'. It was not too bad if the fit took place at the patient's house, but caused all kinds of problems if fitting took place in the streets or at the workplace. Removing personal under garments and stuffing a tube of diazemuls up their rectum can cause all sorts of questions from family and friends.

Jason had once performed this technique in the presence of two police officers in an alleyway at the back of the high street. The shocked female officer had tried to stop him not realising what he was trying to achieve. Things are far better now, as they only use the rectal method on young children; even then you have to be careful and explain your intentions. Adults are given the drug intravenously these days, but that has draw backs, trying to get a needle into a suitable vein while someone is in the throes of a status epileptic fit is not an easy task.

Jason started to talk softly and reassured the woman that she had nothing to fear and that she had suffered another fit. The oxygen mask was gently removed; they needed to keep her calm for her body had gone through a terrifying experience. Both men were aware that she could start fitting again without warning.

Her condition slowly returned to normal as the medication started to take effect. The next problem they had was to persuade her to go with them to hospital. Her first reaction was to refuse point blank to go with them, but when Jason explained gently that because she had three recurring fits with at least one being a 'Grand Mal' she really did need to talk to a doctor urgently in case her medication needed to be altered, she reluctantly agreed to go with them and see the hospital doctor.

Many long-term 'epileptics' can carry on with normal life styles, providing they remember to take regular medication. They have some restrictions such as not being allowed to drive or work machinery unless the epilepsy is controlled. But these people are no different to anyone else; it is not a reason to be shunned by others that have no understanding of epilepsy. Yes, it can be a terrifying sight and very unsettling to someone seeing a fit for the first time but an epileptic needs help just the same as the person who suffers a heart attack or a stroke.

On route to the hospital the lady was stable and she was improving all the time; their aim now was to keep her like that. The woman's husband asked Jason some questions concerning his wife's condition, as he was very worried about the day's turn of events. "She has never had fits this bad before; normally I can handle them myself but not when she gets this bad."

Jason tried to explain that normally it's just a matter of changing the medication but there could be underlying reasons that needed to be eliminated.

When they arrived at the accident department, Jane, one of the staff nurses on duty, greeted them and she directed them into cubicle five. As they wheeled the trolley into the unit Jason gave the nurse a brief outline of the problem.

"Have you been busy?" Tom asked the nurse.

She raised her eyes skyward as she replied. "It's been hell, we have not stopped since you were last here. What is the weather like out there now, are the roads clear?" she asked.

Tom told her that the weather had improved a little but did not know for how long.

Jason went across to have a word with the nursing sister about Dave, the builder. The news on their builder was good; the metal spike was successfully removed with out any problems. They were shown the object that had caused them such concern. It was eleven inches long and still bearing the wet stain where it had penetrated deep into the man's flesh. At least nine of those inches had entered his body; nine inches and no damage it was unbelievable. The half-inch thickness of metal rod that they used to reinforce concrete had missed vital areas by a whisker, passing upward with out actually puncturing the rectal wall and abdominal region. Both paramedics popped their heads into the cubicle being used by the builder.

"Just checking on your progress," said Jason.

Dave still had an amazing sense of humour. "Bit of a pain in the bum, I'll be sitting on the bog a bit easier from now on,"

Tom struggled to maintain his composure, but could not hold back his laughter. They had to make a move and made their excuses to Dave before turning to leave.

"I thank you both for what you did out there, lads; without you, Christ knows what would have happened."

Once the administration side was completed they collected up their equipment and made for the door and the waiting ambulance, the sound of Dave's words still ringing in their ears.

It did not take long for the story to get out and spread around the other crews. The black humour came thick and fast as the word started to circulate, but all of them were amazed when they heard the full story, for they could not believe the man's luck.

CHAPTER THREE

He arrived home tired and drawn from the effort of the day. The shift had produced nine calls and most required lifting heavy weights.

"You look as if you had a bad day," said Jason's wife as she shuffled the place mats around the kitchen table, then laid the cutlery alongside each one in turn. "Just waiting for the peas to finish off, your dinner won't be long."

Still no words left Jason's mouth; he sat in a chair looking upwards, his eyes fixed firmly on the ceiling above. The silence was not at all normal.

"Are you all right? Has something upset you at work?" she enquired.

Finally he spoke, his eyes still firmly fixed in a stare towards the ceiling. "I'm fine. Just need some time to unwind a little, that's all."

She sat back on a kitchen chair and sighed. 'This was not doing him any good. He might say that he felt alright but the work was causing him to constantly come home totally wrecked.

Jason shifted his gaze and moved towards her, smiling wearily. "I am sorry, its just been one of those days, its not you that's done anything wrong, sometimes things get me down and lately it seems worse."

"I know, don't worry, I do understand," she replied.

He sat and shook his head, trying to clear the memories of the day from his muddled brain.

"Come on, your dinner is ready, you will feel a lot better once your belly is full." She leaned forward and kissed him lightly on his cheek before turning her attention to putting the meal on the table.

It was pointless trying to get Jason to talk about anything when he was like this. When he was good and ready he would offer up the information voluntarily. She knew that it would not have taken much to send him over the edge while he was in this state.

He worked his way through the meal without a single word being spoken and when finished he made his way into the lounge and sank himself into a soft armchair. His eyelids were heavy and once closed, he drifted off quickly into a sleep.

Two hours later he woke with a start as his wife shook him vigorously. "Come on, you get yourself to bed." He could never understand why she would wake him up to go to bed to sleep, when he already was asleep.

Once Jason's head touched the pillow he was gone, drifting into a heavy restless sleep. He tossed and turned; his eyelids were closed but the eyes were fully mobile in their sockets. Legs kicked and thrashed at the bed covers; his deep mumbling broke the stillness of the room.

The nightmare was full of screaming vivid images beckoning and pleading with him for help. Their hands open and close as if to entice him forwards. There was not one dominant group or direction to the dream; each figure tumbled into the next until they were jumbled up into a mixture of human flesh in its putrid state.

His subconscious searched through the mass of swirling bodies looking for— well, that was the problem, he just did not have any idea what he was looking for.

The dream was total confusion, everything mangled and twisted, dismembered bodies with limbs like freshly slaughtered meat dripping their bloody output. Crushed and rusting metal spread out with sharp edges formed unnatural structures. Hair-raising screams lifted up into full voice from the twisted mouths. Suddenly the muddle cleared and he was back in the ambulance turning into a street full of light. He could see the flames licking around the windows of a house fire; red and amber glows mixed with the blue – grey of the smoke creating a mixture of colours.

27

The Fire Brigade is already in attendance, working flat out to extinguish the blaze while others are putting on their breathing apparatus. A man in a white helmet stands alongside the fire appliance screaming out orders and points towards the front bedroom window.

A woman rushes forward and shouts at the fire officer, 'that's my child inside, oh god please get him out he is all that I have left.' The officer is waving Jason forwards, but he cannot move, he is frozen to the spot. He can see the distraught woman's face as she stands imploring him to do something, but still his legs will not take instruction from his brain and he remains firmly rooted to the ground.

This scene vanishes and sounds of moaning, crying faces ring shrilly in his ears. Their eyes are just dark holes where once bright lenses caught life's special moments like the recordings of a camera.

His back arches and he kicks out again against the sheets, as once again he realises he is back at the fire, but this time he is inside the house. The exploding heat knocks him backwards; flames consume the oxygen as the increasing heat sucks the air out of his lungs, making breathing harder. He scrambles amongst the burning building, searching, then suddenly he catches sight of the lost child, small arms searching for someone to reach out to and hold. The black acrid smoke wants to smother the small child, to render him helpless so that the flames can take their own sweet time to consume his tiny structure.

The child puts his arms out to Jason and screams in pain. Jason tries to rush forward to help but once again he cannot move a muscle. All he can do is look in horror as the flesh on the small child starts to melt; the child screams then screams again and again.

Jason wakes with a long, drawn out undistinguished sound, 'No-o-o-o-o.'

His wife switched on the bedside lamp to find Jason drenched with perspiration and the bed linen damp from his wet body; his eyes were fixed and wide with fear, his breathing was rapid and sounded like worn out bellows.

"Are you all right? Was it another bad dream?" Asked his wife as she gently stroked his brow. She tried to make a joke of the state of the bed, but secretly she was deeply worried; this was not good for him. Why did his sleep punish him so much. It was as if he held himself responsible for all the traumatic cases that he had dealt with.

Sometimes we all see things in our dreams that we can't explain: Images that enter the mind through veiling mist leave you trying to analyse the cause. Confusion had left Jason in a state of turmoil as he tried to eliminate those hellish nightmares and so seek redemption. No matter how much Jason tried to escape the tragedy and the pain, the scenes and thoughts would not leave him. He relived them in his dreams and the thoughts of other people's sadness raced across his brain during the day. His only relief was on days when he could spend time with his wife or some other member of the family.

When these images had first caused an intrusion into his subconscious or from where they had materialised, he could not remember. All he wanted was to revert back to normal and let the hallucinations return to their own dimensions...

Jason's wife climbed up the bank at the side of the lake, reached down and touched the cold water. She did things now that she had not done for a very long time. Picking up stones and skipping them across the surface of the water, she wondered how deep it was and if it would be possible to wade across to the large boulder on the other side. From this point she would be able to have a clear view of the whole lake.

She heard the sound of Jason coming towards her, looked up and smiled as he bent forward to take her hand. He helped her up and gave her hand a little squeeze as if to show his pleasure at the sight of his wife. Since her retirement the change in her personality was unmistakable, full of life with eyes that once again sparkled like stars.

No longer was the rush of danger felt, the stress of driving through heavy traffic to the next call, or the push of Adrenaline pulsing through her veins because she held someone's life in the palm of her hands. This was the peace that they both craved as they walked hand in hand in the frosty sunlight.

The ripples on the water as fish surfaced caught the sun's reflective light. How peaceful to stand and watch the ducks glide across the still water, spreading their wings, making the ripples circle outwards, then continuing with the effortless swim across the clear sparkling lake.

Yes, he thought to himself, this was the peace that they both needed, no work or worries, just the rays of the sun shining down kissing the skin gently. How different this was from chasing around in an ambulance all day. Tired of the crashes on the motorways, the fights, drunks and the daily stream of illnesses that stalked him.

Jason moved a bit closer to his wife. Placing his arm around her waist he gave her a gentle hug. There must be more to life he thought to himself. If only he had the time to stop and look around, it was all here ...

CHAPTER FOUR

Gordon Brown was a very successful businessman; he started with nothing but with grit and determination he had realised the rewards that long hours and personal sacrifices bring.

The money had started to flow into his bank accounts and the business thrived. He had courted, then married his secretary, a stunning creature whose beauty had caused him to fall in love almost from the start of her employment. Gordon Brown was a lucky man who was set to live life to its fulfilment.

He had a passion for fast cars and although he would not admit to it openly, felt that at times they gave him more excitement than sex with his wife. To feel the surge of power as he pushed the accelerator pedal to the floor on a good stretch of road gave him a rush of adrenaline before starting his day at the office. With his veins full and pumping he had the edge over his colleagues; it was like a kick-start to get him rolling.

He woke a little later than usual this morning, causing him to curse under his breath as he rushed through the house with a purpose trying to regain the lost time. Gordon had a big deal going down, a kind of deal you get once in a lifetime, the reward would be a cool £250,000, if he could pull it off. The meeting was set for ten o'clock and these people represented a large corporate company. 'He could not afford to be late.

Removing a whisky flask from his briefcase, he took two large gulps before making his way down the stairs to the kitchen. Making a final adjustment to his tie, he snatched up his briefcase kissed his wife goodbye and stepped out to the garage, he opened the door of the TVR and slid behind the wheel.

The weather was the last thing on his mind as he moved out of his driveway; focusing only on the ten o'clock appointment, he pushed down the accelerator and drove the car towards the motorway. He had made this journey so many times his body acted automatically, changing gears and steering through the bends in the road.

His brain was fully engrossed with the details of the pending deal: £250.000 would lift him into a higher league; this was the big one, this deal could set him on the ladder to fame and fortune, the once-in-a-lifetime opportunity.

The road ahead was like a giant white blanket; the council lorries had not started their gritting operation yet, and everything was clean and unused. Snow flakes started to fall from the sky like small white feathers floating downwards until they made contact with solid objects; they fell against the windscreen of the speeding car making vision difficult. Gordon set the wipers into action and cursed; he had to make this appointment at all cost for so much depended on this meeting ...

Jason sat watching the snowflakes fall silently to the ground; the trees hung heavy with the snowy caps that they bore. Icicles hovered above the ground waiting to fall and birds huddled together quietly on the window ledge, trying to keep warm. He took comfort from the hot drink of coffee as he prepared for the shift that lay in front of him.

Tom was sorting out his snow boots for it was too deep for normal shoes, and he knew that it would not be long before they were turned out.

How different it was from yesterday when he had walked in the park with his wife. The sun had come out briefly in its magnificence, creating a warm feeling to everything that it reached out and touched. Although the chill of winter had been present, it did not seem forceful. He wished that all days were like those to soak up the peace and serenity of a walk in the park with his beloved Olive.

Outside the snow was increasing its hold and the feathery particles started to build up the mounds of white. Silent gusts of wind picked them up and moved them to form small drifts as they encountered a solid object.

Remembering the ducks on the lake and how they glided across the water leaving ripples in their wake, he thought that today it would be frozen, solidified into a single mass upon its surface.

Tom broke the spell of his partner's daydreams. "I don't like the look of that weather. We could be in for another bad period like last year."

Jason recalled that all too well: digging the snow away from the wheels of the vehicle, placing clean blankets under the wheels just to get them free of the iced surface, trying to get through to a young baby with breathing difficulties, only to be turned back by blocked roads.

His temper had got hold of him that day. In places snow had drifted to sixteen feet and the snowploughs were just not equipped to cope with that kind of blockage. He had no wish to experience those conditions again and hoped that he would never have to repeat the frustration he had felt trying to reach that child. The shrill sound of the emergency alarm shocked him back to reality; it was time to start earning their wages.

"No peace for the wicked, and, boy, one of us must have been," exclaimed Tom ...

Wind began to pick up and force the snow into driving sheets; this was not normal snowfall but more like blizzard conditions. Even the trees, standing upright and defiant, had to acknowledge the awesome power by bowing to its might. There was no water, just snow and ice.

The speeding vehicle caught the bend too fast, car tyres tried hard to find a grip but they could not hold onto the icy surface. Control was lost and the inevitable happened. Twisted and torn metal fights with the concrete road surface, crashing into objects all around, then spinning on the ice until the unmoving tree brings everything to a sudden stop. He lay amongst the tangled mass of twisted metal; the car smelt hot and burning.

Gordon was dazed and bewildered trying to adjust to these strange surroundings. His legs hurt as the pain flowed through to his brain; the weird silence surrounded him muffled by the snow. "I'm trapped and cannot move. Sod it, something is crushing my legs." He struggled to break free but the crippling pain shot up his legs and he could feel a warm sticky fluid running from open wounds; he felt faint and wanted to be sick; his body began to shake and tremble. "I'm so cold, please, is there someone who can get me out of this mess?"

Sounds coming from outside the car caught his ear, creating a feeling of confidence as he detected the movement outside. "Thank God, I am going to be alright. Oh Jesus, please hurry and get me out. Wait. The car is burning, the flames are licking around me and the smoke is suffocating. I can't breathe God, help me, I can't take a breath and the pain is all over me now." Fear rushed through his brain as the terror started to take hold of him.

He felt strong arms tugging and pulling at his clothes, trying to lift him clear; the pain ripped into his brain like a fruit saw. Suddenly he popped out like a cork from a wine bottle as many hands pulled him from the burning wreck.

Calm warm voices were all around him, working with fast determination their caring hands to eased his pain. The voices started to turn into human forms, these were real people this was not a dream. Those strong arms that lifted him out were now easing him onto the waiting stretcher. He knew that these people had saved him, but for them he would be most certainly dead by now.

His pain decreases into a dull ache but he felt strange, almost as if he was outside of his own body and observing the hurried action that was taking place ...

"He has lost consciousness. Those burns are really bad; I don't like the look of him," said Tom.

Jason quickly gave him a brief examination; his medical observations were low and Tom had been correct in his judgement of the situation. The need to move was now vital, if this man's condition continued to decline he would not make the journey into hospital. Jason finished setting up a drip to help replace the lost fluids, while Tom placed wet sterile dressings over the burns. They recruited the assistance of two police officers to help them to lift him gently into the ambulance. Once inside Jason changed over to the main oxygen bottle and pushed the flow meter to maximum.

The police had offered to give them an escort to the hospital, which they gratefully excepted. Speed was paramount and with the weather conditions slowing them down they needed any form of help they could get. Jason examined the patient in closer detail: the burns were deeper than he had imagined and the extent of area was at least thirty per cent full thickness burns. He was worried about the interference to the patient's breathing, due to soft tissue swelling complicating the airway but, as luck would have it, the tissue oedema was restricted to the outer extremities. There was still the problem with smoke inhalation but that was being dealt with.

The next move was to try and gain a second access to a peripheral vein and set up another drip sight; this was hampered by the severity of the injuries. After a couple of failed attempts, Jason managed to get the second line into position. He rigged up another bag of crystalloid to replace some of the plasma loss.

There seemed so much to do in such a short period of time; he was constantly on the look out for changes for there was so many things that could bring this man's life to a swift conclusion. The airway, burns, circulatory failure leading onto renal failure, all this without the injuries sustained in the crash. Everything was stacked against this poor chap; his chances of survival were slim. Jason had the job of keeping him alive until they reached the hospital, which had much more equipment at its disposal than him.

Slowly Gordon showed signs of regaining consciousness. At least that was a small weight off Jason's shoulders; if he could keep cool for a few more minutes they would reach the safety of the hospital and he could relax once more.

Gordon opened his eyes and looked around this strange new environment, with the face of Jason smiling down at him. Bewildered and confused he found himself in the back of the ambulance speeding its way towards the hospital, where many more pairs of helping hands waited to make him comfortable.

On arrival doctors in white coats appeared from every direction, nurses in pressed uniforms all worked quickly and apart from the odd command the only sound was the bleeping of the monitoring machines ...

Gordon realised that it was getting darker and the sounds seem to be fading away; the voices were talking in whispers but the pain was almost gone, just a warm feeling and gentle kisses on his body. There was a bright light before him and he could see a figure beckoning to come forward; there was no more pain, no more worries as he floated towards the light ...

The doctors and paramedics were working flat out, their hands everywhere, all doing their very best with one resolve to come up with the right result.

"Let's try adrenaline again, thank you," said one of the consultants.

"Still the same, Doctor," said a voice in the crowd.

"Right. Give him another 360 joules shock and if that won't work we will have to call it a day."

"Stand clear, shocking now," boomed the voice of the charge nurse holding the paddles of the defibrillator over the patient's chest.

Once again they shocked the patient. But the result remained the same; everything that they could possibly do had been tried. They had known from the start that the burns were much too intense for anyone to survive.

"Death pronounced at 09.02. Thank you all for a good effort." Said the consultant in charge of the accident unit.

"The police said that he had been drinking and the car was driven at high speed, until he lost control. There was evidence that he tried to brake but the black ice on the road stopped the tyres contact with the road surface," said Jason.

"Yes, I am afraid that he will just go down as another victim of the weather," stated the consultant.

Tom and Jason collected their equipment and made for the accident unit door. It took them ten minutes to put the vehicle back to order ready to go out on the next call.

"I hate losing them like that," said Tom.

Jason just nodded his head for he had known right from the time that they arrived that the odds were against them,

They radioed their control and were told to return to station for stand-by. Jason frowned, it was cold this morning even though the snow had warmed the air slightly.

On route back to station they observed four vehicles nosed into the kerb; an ageless VW Golf, a muddy old ford van, two year old Rover and a battered old Viva. All had succumbed to the winter weather.

"The cold always picks up on any faults."

Tom started to talk about his work-out at his sports club the night before, knowing full well that Jason had no interest in sports. Then, because Jason did not bite back, he tried his usual form of sarcasm to wind him up.

Jason was forced to listen to his mate's precocious banter about how he should spend more time getting fit. But he could give back just as good as he got; with calm temperament he would wait for the moment and then drop the hammer. There was no animosity between them, it passed the time to play the game and they never held a grudge against each other. Back on station they fell into the chairs in the rest room, clutching their hot drinks and making the most of the short break. When the weather turns bad they knew that the workload was going to be hard.

Tom flicked the switch on the television set hoping to catch the morning news broadcast. They discussed the last call in some detail. It did not sit well when the patient loses the fight for life.

Crews always seem to blame themselves, dissecting every move they made to make sure that everything was done by the book.

Jason thought about the way the man had been burnt and an iced chill ran up the length of his spine. The burns had been really deep in places and the pain that the man must have felt was beyond imagination. He said a little prayer to himself: "God take him into your care."...

Rose had left the club alone after a row with her boyfriend Roy. In a fit of rage and hurt pride she had stormed out of the club with just one intention, to get home as quickly as she possibly could. "How dare he treat her this way, who did he think he was anyway?" She looked around for a taxi but the rank was empty; standing in the cold night air with no sign of a cab, she decided to walk. 'It's only a few of miles and she had made the journey many times before: besides, it would keep her warm,' she thought to herself.

Hoping to catch sight of a cab along the way, she set off in the direction of home. It was a good forty-five minutes walk to her parent's house but Rose was used to hiking and she loved to exercise, often testing herself to the limit.

She was a pretty girl in her early twenties, who was much liked and respected by all in the general store where she worked hard and diligently. Her cheerful outlook on life coupled with a generous smile and polite manner made her very popular with the customers. Her employers at the store thought very highly of her attractive modesty and determined ambition.

Rose had picked herself up after a bout of deep depression some years previous and had improved her life.

The journey home was into its first twenty minutes when the snow started to fall, fine like powder covering the pavement, then turning into small fluffy flakes floating down on the wind and settling on the thick grassy banks. Rose started to wish she had not run out of the club before she had rung for a taxi. 'It was a bit silly really,' she thought to herself. The snow fell heavier covering the ground like a giant shroud.

She turned off the road and decided to take a short cut across the field; this would save at least fifteen minutes off the journey. There was a little panic starting to build up inside her; she took comfort by remembering this same field as a small child, and her father, who had often taken her this way to school.

Her mind drifted as she walked and she thought of the field in spring when there would be rabbits frolicking in the long grass, the buttercups and bluebells in their thousands covering the green field, turning their faces towards the sun. She remembered how safe it used to feel holding onto her father's large hand as she skipped joyfully by his side.

Rose stopped! Her brain snapped back to reality once more. 'There it was again,' the sound of a cracking branch sent an iced cold shiver down her spine.

She called out loud "Is there anyone there? Dad, is that you?" but her voice was taken by the wind and lost in it's whisper.

The shadows formed grotesque shapes, was there someone skulking in the darkness?

Eventuality her imagination gave way to stark fear, followed closely by panic as one of those shapes moved towards her...

The silence was shattered by the sound of the phone ringing in the crew room. Jason picked up the receiver in one hand, pen poised in the other, knowing full well that the call was from the control room. A call had come in via the police, with a request that they made a silent approach. This normally suggested that the police had a siege, hostage, a jumper or an attempted suicide call. Crews would still make their way to the call in the same way but turn off the warning devices a mile or so before arriving at the incident.

Muffled by the snow all around, the mournful cry of the siren made an eerie sound. The same snow that was making the journey so slow. Six wheels were far better than the normal four, but in these conditions caution was the way forward.

The roads were deserted, most people had remained behind their own front doors. Only the sound of the engine and the tyres crunching into the snow-packed surface filled the ghostly silence.

They approached by a winding lane that would give them easier access to the field. A lone policeman stood by his patrol car to deny entry to anyone that was not authorised to be there. He directed Tom towards a farm gate at the end of the lane, advising him not to drive beyond that point.

Branches whipped across the ambulance windscreen as it lumbered along the narrow, unmade track, screeching as they scratched its structure. Jason was rocked from side to side as the vehicle lurched violently. Tom seemed to enjoy the thrill of crashing the motor through the thickening hedgerows and bouncing over the potholes. Jason could not understand how he managed to get a quick thrill out of something like this. The extensive shaking he received sitting in the passenger seat was most unpleasant and caused him much discomfort.

Tom stopped the vehicle, turned off the engine, opened the door and slid out of the driver's seat. Jason grabbed his medical bag and disembarked from the other side. He immediately cursed out loud as his foot sank into a large watery hole. "You have bloody done it again!" he exploded. If ever there was a patch of uneven ground or water Tom would always find it 'on Jason's side'.

"Sorry mate, it was the largest puddle I could find," he laughed.

The weather started to turn nasty again: snow, sleet, hail and wind all struck at the same time.

"That's all we needed," exclaimed Tom as he opened the gate and they both passed through. The gate led them onto a narrow track opening into the field.

Jason scuffed the pathway as they hurried awkwardly along the frozen ground, he stumbled over a rut, and stretching himself forward, he fought to keep his balance and not lose his grip on the medical bag. He fell on the ground hard, and grunted.

"Bloody hell, sod this," he cried out as he scrambled back to his knees. He felt the wetness of the mud and snow seeping through his uniform trousers and he quickly brushed himself down before setting off once more. Hail whipped up by the wind was driven against their faces like tiny stinging insects; it sent minute objects directly into Jason's eyes causing his vision to become blurred.

On arrival they both approached the ring of men in black uniforms standing looking downward at the form on the ground. One of the police officers gave them a brief update on the situation. It was obvious that there was nothing anyone could do to help this patient. Jason stood mesmerised, stomach heaving, jaw dropped and overpowered by the sight before him. He was looking down at the lifeless form of a young female. Her young, slender body lay contorted on the ground with a look of surprise still held on her breathtaking face.

Pulling himself together, he surveyed her long bare legs and widely spaced breasts, her hair was matted with snowy dew mixed with clotted blood, as was the ground around her. She was wearing a smart outfit, chunky shoes, short black skirt, and a fancy white blouse under a red three-quarter-length topcoat. Her hair was matted with clotted blood, as was the ground all around her pale body. She had three deep stab wounds, two to the chest and one to the side of her neck. Anyone of these could have been the cause of death, but that would be up to the coroner's inquest to decide. There were also superficial cuts to her hands and both thighs, closer observation had shown old lacerations on her wrist, almost certainly self-inflicted. He had no way of knowing what had caused or understood why she had tried self-mutilation in the past. He tried to picture what sort of a person would do something like this to another. Thoughts of his own daughters came to mind and he felt sick inside. Unfortunately there was nothing that anyone could do for this poor girl. Her life had been snatched away by some totally sick bastard, playing out his elaborate fantasies. He must have searched for his unsuspecting prey, looking for the easy target. Waited for the kill to come into sight and then struck!

To end any life before it reached a natural conclusion distressed Jason.

His medical knowledge made him visualise all of the systems that make the human body function; then suddenly being shut down by someone with a knife.

In his mind he had a vision of the murderer leaning over her with the blade in his hand. Then a thought of the soft flesh parting as the knife slid into her body and the blood gushing from the wounds. Jason was chillingly aware of these kinds of attacks, by sick and twisted maniacs that stalked and preyed on these helpless females. They commit these crimes only to release their warped desires. Rapes and bloody assaults are all to common, depraved madmen looking for the target and once found, the innocent woman becomes yet another tragic victim. The families are left empty and distraught with only fond memories of their loved ones, while the cowardly attacker slinks away, leaving the victim for others to care for, already planning his next attempt, until hopefully he is finally caught and punished. They are like the Jackal, crafty in the ways of life.

In the cold, sharp morning air the thoughts made him want to vomit; he was so sickened that he felt confused by what lay before him. But this was not the time to think; he had a job to do. Nothing could be done for this poor woman now, except to cover up her lifeless body until the coroner arrived. Jason lay a red blanket over the body to keep prying eyes from witnessing the wicked sight on the ground before him.

A police officer turned towards him. Somehow he had sensed what Jason was feeling or did he see it in his face? "Are you going to be alright, you are looking bloody rough, mate?" he said.

"Yes, just can't get to grips with something like this. I don't think I ever will and I have been doing this for more years than I care to recall," Jason replied. He jammed his hands into his coat pockets as he walked back with his partner across the grass towards the waiting vehicle, his face showing emotional anger.

"Don't dwell on the circumstances of her death, the guilty party will pay, I'm sure of that," said Tom.

Jason snapped round. "I'm bloody fifty-eight years old, and I really am trying to make a big effort to keep myself from going under. I'm not neurotic, just pissing angry over that young girl's death. Call me a sentimental old fool, but that was just a pure fucking catastrophe."

Briefly he looked back before mounting the seat in the cab of the Ambulance. "They say men don't cry. BUT SOME DO ..."

He had put aside the thoughts of the last job; to dwell on the sights that they had just witnessed would have made no difference at all to Rose.

There are not many ambulance personnel that manage to escape the bloody awful sights that come with the job they do.

43

Often Jason and Tom, when faced with senseless death, would stoop to black humour, this being the only way they could cope with the complete chaos, death and heartache that all emergency crews have to face on a daily basis. Without this type of humour they found it impossible to continue; this was their only safety valve against the harrowing scenes they had to contend with. Jason had felt inwardly hysterical during times such as these, but had always kept the lid on his emotions, allowing his professional behaviour to create stability among the people that relied on him. Because of his pent up feelings, Jason suffered many sleepless nights and had become distanced with the act of death.

Some of the patients were sad, lonely or just plain old. Depressed people locked away with no visitors, slowly losing their self-respect and the will to take care of themselves. Lying in bed for long periods without movement created ulcerated flesh that would stick firmly to the bedding. There were layers and layers of clothing to keep themselves warm, forgetting the last time they had been removed for washing. Pungent smells of stale urine and perspiration make a mixture of the most unpleasant aromas that could turn the strongest stomachs.

Rose was not given a choice to live, Tom and Jason would put her down as another sad statistic, another innocent victim who was in the wrong place at the wrong time. But it would be a long while before Jason forgot the captured image of that young girl's body laying on the cold ground like a discarded rag doll ...

Control instructed them to return to station to see the divisional commander who was waiting for them.

"What the bloody hell is wrong now?" asked Tom.

"I have no idea, can't think of anything we have done to cause his displeasure," replied Jason.

The two paramedics spent the whole journey back to station worrying about what it was that they had done wrong; normally, if the divisional commander wanted to see someone, it was not good news. They arrived back on base, made sure that the vehicle was parked in the correct manner and walked into the crew room.

As they walked through the door they were greeted by the DC Tony Walsh, a big beaming smile on his face, which was a fairly good sign. "Sit, down and relax, lads, you are not in any trouble; well, not that I am aware of anyway," announced Tony.

"Thank the Lord for that; we thought we were in the crap pot again," responded Jason.

He started to explain his presence and why he needed to talk to them. "As both of you are aware, we have put up with the pair of you for over twenty years, I don't know how you managed to get away with it for this amount of time but you have." There was a broad smile on his face the whole time. "It must be about forty four years of service between the two of you? Seriously, you have managed to do a fairly good job over the years and we would like to invite you both along with your wives to an open evening up at Headquarters to present you both with the Queen's Long Service Medal."

He had paused for a moment before continuing. "It states here that it is also for good conduct but I am not to sure about that part. Do you think the two of you can make your presence felt on the third of March, then?" he finished.

Both Jason and Tom were lost for words, but not for long. They had known Tony for the past eighteen years; in fact Jason had taken him out on his first week as a trainee paramedic. Although they were miles apart in rank, it did not stop their social activities or friendship, for they had been good mates before Tony started to climb the promotions ladder.

They both agreed to accept the offer of the invitation, then settled down for a drink and half an hour of catch up on all the latest news that was going around the service. There was always something or someone to talk about just because of the very nature of the work; either the excitement of the job or a juicy bit of gossip kept tongues wagging sometimes for weeks.

Tom was not satisfied with one exciting job, he had to have two, being also a part time retained fireman. Jason could not understand how his partner managed to keep the two jobs going. Often he would arrive to start work on an early shift after spending three or four hours fighting a fire in the middle of the night. His fire-fighting duties gave him a large subject to talk about, from practice sessions once a week to adventure and bravery of actually fighting fires. Jason would look at his partner in astonishment when he talked of training sessions. That, after twelve gruelling hours on the ambulance, he would attend drill nights where they would simulate fire-fighting tasks such as dragging an eighty pound dummy out of a smoke filled room, or running with a sixty pound hose reel up the ladder of the practice tower.

The physical standards that Tom and his mates were expected to maintain were beyond Jason's understanding. What made his colleague drive himself this way? It was not as if he was still a young man, for he, like Jason, was close to retirement age. His job on the Fire Brigade did not consist of fighting fires all the time, the work also involved, people locked out of their houses, burst water pipes causing flooding, road traffic accidents and the most common of all, 'false alarm calls'. Each call, like the ambulance service, had to be responded to just the same any emergency call.

Jason never told Tom, but he was proud to have a partner in the fire service and knew that having a trained fireman along side him at a road accident or a house fire was extremely useful.

The fire crews accepted Jason as 'Tom's mate'. Divisional Commander Tony Walsh was fully aware of Tom's other occupation and although he had been given management permission, they were not really happy with the conflict of interests.

The D.C. left the station, leaving Tom and Jason to talk about the 'Medal Presentation'.

After the excitement subsided they both settled down and tried to relax before the next call changed the mood. Warmth from the central heating soon had an effect on Tom and within minutes he was softly snoring from the back of his throat. Jason closed his eyes and reflected that at fifty – eight years of age he had found that he was no longer able to attend to the demands of his job the way he used to. Nor had he the desire to match the younger crews with their macho bullshit and brinkmanship to gain a quick promotion. He had witnessed every type of emergency in his time and felt that he did not have to prove himself any more.

His eyes opened to the click from the station radio and he was up and switching off the alarm before it had a chance to ring the bell. Swiftly writing the details onto scrap paper he responded to the controller with a 'Roger,' then moving quickly across the crew room floor, he called out to his sleeping partner. "Tom."

He stirred, but did not respond immediately. Jason shook him gently. Tom finally opened his eyes and quickly turned away from the lights above his head.

"We have a red call. Come on, shift yourself," said Jason raising his voice slightly.

Tom grabbed his belt with the hand radio and 'Maglight' attached and made for the garage door, still trying to clear the sleepy mist from his eyes.

Tom hammered the ambulance towards the destination, swinging the steering wheel wildly as he fought to avoid some of the homicidal drivers that tried to race him. He was weaving his way in and out of the lines of cars in front of them, trying to judge what they were going to do before them.

Driving through town was a real pain at the best of times, the stop, go, slow crawl made everyone irritable, but Tom would become consumed with anger.

One day the whole world would grind to a halt, the gridlock would cause total collapse.

Suddenly Tom cursed loudly as a lorry pulled out of a side street, causing him to apply the brakes harder than he would have wished. The veins in his temples pulsated with anger, causing them to swell up and look as though they were about to explode, like lava from an erupting volcano.

The look on his face radiated from deep within his gut as he glared at the driver of the lorry, who in responsive defiance raised his stiff middle finger as they passed ...

Victor Evans was almost eighty years old; he lived with his wife Mary in a three bedroom semi-detached house sitting close to the sea. As a young man Victor had served with the Royal Air Force as a gunner in Lancaster bombers; he had flown many missions over Germany, being twice shot down over enemy lines and managing to survive the war, unlike a lot of his comrades.

He married his wife Mary in 1946, having just one son, Harry, between them. They lived a simple life and had got on extremely well, until seven years ago when things started to go very wrong.

Mary had noticed that Victor was becoming depressed and could not explain why. As time passed, she was aware that his memory was not to good and would be most forgetful of the little things. He had a few falls, nothing too serious, and was unable to concentrate for any long periods.

Mary was frightened; she could not understand what was happening to her husband. She struggled to cope with the situation until the stress got the better of her. With difficulty she was able to get Victor along to their Doctor, who noted the problems and sent him along to the Psychiatrist at the local hospital. He was diagnosed as having Alzheimer's Dementia, medication was organised and the Doctor arranged for him to visit a community centre twice a week to keep a check on his condition.

Sadly, the Alzheimer's progressed over the years and the medicine did not help any more. Mary was frightened to leave him alone even for the shortest period, worried what she might find on her return, for he was a danger to himself and to others.

She started to feel guilty, unable to cope with him and feeling useless because she was unable to help the man that she loved so much. Her Doctor could see the stress that Mary was under and he had suggested that Victor might be better off in a nursing home for a while to give them both a break. Mary immediately became tearful and broke down; she loved him and could not come to terms with the thought of her man sitting unhappy in some strange home. No, she would cope with help; Victor must stay with her ...

Victor woke in the middle of the morning. He looked around the room, bewildered and confused, unable to remember where he was. Although it was his own bedroom, everything seemed strange and unfamiliar, distressing him deeply.

Mary had taken the chance to do some quick shopping, feeling sure that her husband would sleep for some time.

Victor moved towards the kitchen almost as if some sixth sense had directed him. He felt dry after his long sleep and instinctively turned in the direction of the gas cooker; he turned on the tap to its full maximum, ignited the gas and reached out for the kettle.

At that precise moment he felt a warm wetness spreading from his crotch and bifurcating down his legs. He looked down at the puddle forming at his feet and became irritated and restless.

He kicked out in a state of frustrated anger, forcefully knocking over the forgotten bottle of solvent solution and dislodging its cap. The contents spewed out onto the kitchen floor, but were ignored. His physical and mental abilities were diminished and did not enable him to react normally. Being unsteady on his feet, Victor lost his balance and crashed forward, hitting the front of his head as he fell; he lay still.

When he regained his senses, he had forgotten the task that he had set out to do and went upstairs to change his soiled clothing.

Once this was completed, equipped with fresh clothes, he remembered the kettle had not been put on the stove and made his way back to the kitchen once more.

The blue flame from the gas cooker flared next to the open chip pan; close by, the oil was quietly heating until reaching boiling point. Victor placed the kettle on the still flaming ring and sat down to wait for it to come to the boil.

His mind wandered as he sat in the chair day-dreaming of good times long ago flying over Germany on one of his many missions. It was strange how his memory could recall the events that happened fifty years ago, but he could forget things that had taken place within hours. His incoherent mumbling, not recognised as normal conversation, caused frustration as each tried to gain acknowledgement from the other. Although Mary loved him, the stressful life that she had to endure caused extreme agitation as she tried to cope with the demented antics of her husband.

Meanwhile, the kettle now boiling, spat steam and droplets of water towards the bubbling oil. The water seemed to intensify the heat from the hot oil, and then suddenly there was a ball of flames that engulfed the top of the cooker. Bubbling oil hit the naked flames from the gas ring and sent them higher until there was a 'whoosh' and the whole kitchen seemed to be burning, then the flames found the fumes from the spilled solvent hanging heavy in the air.

Hot blue and yellow flames licked at the painted surfaces, the intense heat sucking the oxygen from out of the room causing the air to be thick and acrid.

Burning timbers began making loud cracks like a starting pistol as the heat expanded the wood.

Victor was confused and agitated; the heat and smoke seemed to be everywhere; he knew instinctively that he had to get away from the fire and make his escape. His distressed state of mind caused him to run back upstairs. His poor, bewildered brain told him to go up when it should have directed him out of the back door to safety.

Locking himself in the bedroom he crouched in the corner of the room like a frightened child trying to hide away from the fire. The fear swept through his body as the smoke started to creep under the door, forced its way up through floorboards and slowly filled the room with a thick black acrid cloud.

Shivering with anxiety, this poor bewildered soul tried to scream but his voice and movements were becoming weaker as death drew him near. It was only then that it occurred to him, as his last gasp of air was squeezed from his lungs that this was the final breath he would ever take. He made a funny gurgling noise as he collapsed, falling forwards onto his face as the flames started to lick at the soft muscled flesh. The corpse twisted, its limbs flexing in their deathly dance as the skin shrivelled and stretched. Hands turned to claws, caused by the involuntary muscles closing, gripped by shrinking flesh. Purple and orange flames engulfed the luckless cadaver, turning it into a blackened mass of sizzling meat, its contortion created involuntary twisting movements as the muscles cooked over the bones.

Flames torched the window drapes, turning the lush colours into charcoal black. The blazing inferno created tiny explosions sending the flames leaping up from out of the centres.

Firemen worked as one, unrolling hose reels, playing them out before connecting them to hydrants that would supply the thousands of gallons needed to extinguish the roaring flames. Ladders were removed from the appliance and laid against the upper windows. Then they moved towards the seat of the fire, each man working as part of a well-oiled team, for there is no room for independent action in the fire brigade. They watched each other's backs and mimicked the movements of the guy in front. The first to enter faced the real dangers, their main communications maintained by hand signals.

The smoke was noxious thick and acrid, making their progress slow. Sounds of cracking timbers filled the air as the fire billowed and spread its flame. Thirty-pound BA sets that were strapped to their backs made each movement laborious.

The hallway was narrow and smoky. As they moved forward, the lead fireman caught his leg on something hard in the darkness and cursed. They continued searching every room in turn hampered by the heat and thick black smoke that brought their vision almost down to zero. They reached out in the blackness, using the backs of their hands in case live electrical cables were present. By using the back of the hand it saves serious injuries; electricity touching the back combined with reflex action will take the limb away. If they touched a live cable with the palm, the fingers would close and grip onto the cable, causing electrocution.

For a while the fire seemed to be getting a stronger hold on the lower part of the building, it was engulfed in orange and red flames that seemed to be like a living predator devouring everything in its path. The water jets hit the hot fire, turning cold liquid into steam and even their protective clothing could not hold back the searing heat. The firemen felt the scolding moisture burning the surface of their skin, but they were winning and the fire was being beaten back and little by little the water smothered the flames.

"Tread carefully, there are sharp objects and broken glass everywhere," the lead fireman told his companions. He traced the torch beam, sweeping the ground, looking for unseen hazards.

The crews were aware that their air supply was diminishing; the effort of dragging the heavy hose and the BA units on their backs had made them use air at a rapid rate.

If the warning bleepers sounded off, they knew that there could be no hesitations, it would be retreat time. They must stop and get the hell out as fast as they could run.

They were looking for anything that resembled human form, even though there would be little chance of survival. Life would have expired within minutes due to smoke inhalation

When they finally located Victor, his body was burned beyond recognition. No hair, eyes or skin; all that remained was a blackened mass that once resembled human form. His life had been extinguished, not by the flames but the smoke and intolerable heat.

Fire has a terrifying appetite and will, if left unguarded, consume everything in its path. Whatever the outcome they had to extract the corpse from the building, for it needed to be presented to the coroner's office for an autopsy; he would hold a inquest into the full cause of death ...

As the ambulance stopped outside the address they noticed the smoke still trickling from out of the upper windows. Jason had jumped off his seat; his feet touching the pavement before the vehicle had even stopped. A policeman was restraining a screaming woman from running into the house, black smoke still spewing from its open doorway.

"Please let me go, my husband is still inside," she pleaded.

Tom went over to the fire officer to get an assessment update. When they arrived at the front door, the fire brigade was still working to finish extinguishing the fire although it was mostly under control. They were directed to a charcoal covered entrance that was once a door leading into a smoke blackened room. The strong smell of burnt timbers, still thick, filled the air. There was fire damage all around and the reek of burnt timbers was prevalent. Its smell overwhelmed all other odours as it hung thickly in the air.

Smoke drifted past their eyes causing them to water and sting profusely. As the tears trickled down Jason's cheek he was forced to wipe them away with the sleeve of his coat.

Tom looked hard at the corpse laid on the floor, burned flesh that was once human charcoal-blackened like a waxworks figure. It was impossible to guess the sex or age of the body. The scorched remnants of what was once human, was now just strips of burnt tissue and bone; its contorted shape looked like something out of a horror story.

Tom controlled the urge to vomit, sweat dripping down the back of his neck making his shirt collar wet. There was movement deep down within his gut, he wanted to be sick but was afraid to show his emotions. Although he had witnessed this scene many times before, it still pulled on his emotions.

Jason sensed his mate's feelings and with a firm hand on Tom's shoulder he gently squeezed once to let him know that he understood.

The human shape under the now blanketed body bag was dead, burned alive in the stripping heat of the fire. There were no witnesses; by the time the fire was noticed it would have been too late, the smoke would have done the deed long before the flames of the fire reached his body.

Tom could still sense a faint smell of burning flesh; the lingering odour filled the air, a sweet sickly smell that stays in the nostrils for hours and seemed to cling to the fibres of their clothes forever.

Anyone that has experienced this pungent fragrance knows that you cannot disguise its presence. Sometimes crews find themselves in dangerous and uncertain situations, from light rescue to pub violence and this is an accepted part of their work. Nothing can ever prepare them for this sort of carnage, nothing for them to do except walk away and store it in some dark recess of the brain. The police and fire service would deal with the tasks that were needed to close the book on this sad case.

Tom and Jason climbed into the cab of their ambulance taking five minutes to prepare themselves for the next call to come in, watching the firemen roll up the tubing and stowing it on board the tenders ...

CHAPTER FIVE

The physical energy of the day had been too much; he found himself suddenly exhausted and near to collapse. He said his goodbyes to the night shift before easing into the driving seat of his car. Turning the key, he set off in the direction of home feeling like death, legs of jelly and his head buzzing still full of adrenaline.

After the hard days experience he arrived home that evening shattered. He partially ate dinner, sat and watched some TV for about an hour, although he had no idea what the hell was going on or what had been said. It was no good, he could not stay awake; kissing his wife, he said goodnight and crawled up the stairs to his bed; within minutes he fell into a deep sleep almost as soon as his head hit the pillows.

His subconscious mind flicked through the pictures of the calls of the day as he sank deeper into an exhausted sleep. Before long he was having another dream. This time he was pinned down under a truck unable to move an inch; he could not breathe as the heavy metal pushed down on his chest. He knew that it was a dream, but try as he may he could not escape; fighting his panic he willed himself to wake, but he found the struggle beyond his capabilities. The faces returned, pleading with him to relieve their pain, the sight of their torn flesh never leaving his tortured mind. Dead and distorted faces haunted his sleeping world, driving him to destruction as the guilt stung his soul as he remembered all those unfortunate people.

Finally he drifted back to reality, sat bolt upright, staring into the half-light; sweat was pouring out of his skin like a squeezed sponge. His heart was racing as it beat like the wings of a bird in flight. Trying hard to swallow, he found his throat was parched and dry, not even the smallest spit passed his lips.

The bed was damp from his lost moisture; his wife was always complaining about the heat that radiated from his body causing her to fling off the covers. He sat up through most of the morning knowing that it was pointless trying to sleep; his mind was far too active.

Olive woke and was surprised to find the bed empty beside her. But she guessed that Jason had gone through another night of bad dreams. Once again she worried; this was getting too frequent and she knew that it was gradually wearing her husband down. She cheered slightly as she remembered that tomorrow they would spend the day together and he could try to blot out the horrors of the job. For a few hours she would get him to forget and relax. Settling her composure she put on a false face and greeted Jason with a smile, giving the outward appearance that all was well ...

Jason's moods were so transparent that his wife knew the signs even before he was aware that they had changed. She had seen the anguish many times and if he had suffered a rough day, the best way to approach Jason was to let him alone to unwind in his own way, and to keep well away until he was ready to respond more favourably.

Because of her husband's stress Olive would lie awake in bed quietly waiting in the darkness, ears straining for Jason's footsteps on the drive outside. She would not close her eyes until she heard his key enter the lock of the front door; only then would she settle down and relax for the night.

Jason would never go directly to bed, he needed time to unwind from the stress or he would stay awake for hours trying to switch off his brain and the pent up tensions that he had been suppressing throughout the shift.

She would not dare to call out, informing Jason that she was still awake; that would trigger at least two hours of her husband's detailed exploits of work. Far better to pretend to be asleep and leave him to sort things out in his own way ...

He sensed her concern as he looked over at his wife, who seemed deeply disturbed even though she was aware of most of his problems.

"What has happened? I know when you have something on your mind," Olive asked, but there was no response.

Jason and his wife had talked for hours about the problems that drove him to restless nights; in fact the whole family were concerned about his health, which was rapidly declining.

The next morning he woke feeling tired and drawn, his body felt like it had been run over by a steam engine. He dragged his weary frame around the house like a reawakened zombie. Shifting himself into the kitchen, he made a large mug of coffee hoping it would revive him a little before going to work.

Jason's mind drifted back to the start of the changing season. The leaves of autumn with spectacular colours of gold and amber that filled the trees in their last blaze of glory before they fell to the ground covering it with a leafy blanket. He remembered the breeze as it picked up the golden layer, clutching it close and whipping it into a mini spiral before laying it back to earth once more. His heart leapt as his thoughts relived the walks with his wife on those lazy laid back days that took him briefly away from the pressured environment.

Some days he would arrived at work in a sombre mood and very cynical of everything that moved. Yet at the same time he held onto his dry humour and sharp wit. Perhaps it was the combination of his mood swings blowing hot and cold that made Tom more aware of his partner's deepening depressions. He would make remarks concerning Jason's behaviour trying to be tactful in his approach.

"Are you all right? You seem extremely tense today," he would enquire.

"No I'm fine, just had a really bad night, that's all." Jason would lie even if he felt like the crap had just been kicked out of him, his body drained and exhausted from a night of broken sleep. Why he thought that it was necessary to hold back on his feelings from everyone was beyond Tom.

He was a family man, not really a romantic but he would always try his best to say the right things. Jason remembered the first day he looked at his wife as a woman and not as a colleague from work. She was acting as a temporary station officer and he was the Health and Safety representative for the 'Ambulance Trade Union'. They had both been working on the same project to improve the lifting of incubators into the back of vehicles.

This was the day that he had looked at her in a different way. On this occasion they were drawn together, but neither one guessing that they would end up married a few months later. The trouble was he did not have very much in the way of confidence when it came to chat-up lines. It took almost three months before he had the courage to take her out on the first date.

From the first night in her company Jason had known that he had no doubts about his feelings, he could not have loved anyone more, her smile would give a warm glow and her personality made him feel totally at ease. Within a short period their love for each other blossomed. With this lady he had found the perfect soul mate, a partner for life he could share all of his joys and troubles with. As each day passed his love for her grew stronger, for she is his lover, best friend and partner. They had no secrets, life was shared equally, each trusting the other fully.

He had found contentment and lasting satisfaction at last, his future was secured; she made him feel wanted and had a way of totally relaxing him after a long day's work. He would reach the front door and give a sigh of relief as he entered; he was home again and could leave the day behind.

Because they both worked on the same job and mostly on opposite shifts they would spend most of the time leaving each other little notes. On most days they were like ships that passed in the night. If the shifts alllowed her to be at home she would rush forward to greet him with an excited smile and a string of questions about his day. Looking into her eyes he would give a grin then gently brush away her hair to reveal her perfect face.

No matter what the pressures had been or the stress that he felt, she had a way of reducing him to fits of laughter and within a short space of time he would be completely relaxed. Settling down to a hot meal and a friendly voice to lift up his spirits, he was indeed fortunate to have a wife like Olive ...

The drive into work only took nine minutes extra because of the weather conditions and considering the snow on the ground, that was not bad. On the way he had passed the night crew steaming up the road with all lights flashing on route to a late emergency call. He had mixed feelings as they passed: firstly, he felt sorry for the night crew for they would finish late, but he also felt relief, for it meant that he had a little extra time this morning before the mayhem started.

Pulling into the station yard he parked the car, opened the crew room door and made a beeline for the kettle. While he waited for it to boil he collected his equipment from his locker and placed it by the front door ready to board the vehicle on its return. Switching on the television set, he settled into the chair to watch the morning news before Tom walked into the station.

Making the most of the peace and quiet he began to relax; looking out of the station window, he observed the bright sparkle of the frosty snow capped on the rooftops; then he observed the shuffle of an old man walking his dog trying to keep the cold from penetrating his ageing bones, his dog happy to investigate every tree and lamp post that they passed. He walked over to the window to get a better view of the street outside.

Jason shivered, although it was not cold inside the station, as the heating system was working overtime because of the sudden unexpected drop in temperature outside. Tom would arrive any minute now, always preceded by the sound of his motor cycle engine and the double toot of the horn to alert Jason of his presence and the fact that the garage door needed to be opened. He had the journey timed to perfection, always arriving fifteen minutes before the start of the duty, leaving him just enough time to park the bike, change out of his protective clothing and collect his first aid bag from the locker.

He turned away from the window, fell into the easy chair and put his feet up on the small coffee table. The night crew would be some while yet before they got back from their late shout. He lifted his cup of coffee and took a long gulp but it had cooled. Just then he heard the familiar sound of Tom's motorbike out side the garage door, he glanced at his watch. "Spot on time," he said out loud.

Tom drove into the garage bay before the electric door had opened half way.

"Morning, you old bugger, how do you like the snow, then?" He greeted Jason this way every day the same.

"Cobblers," Jason replied ...

It was cold this winter's day, and there was snow in the wind. The air was crisp and fresh; it felt comfortable to be up and about in the light of the early morning. Moving down stairs towards the kitchen to make the first drink of the day, she caught her foot on the frayed stair carpet. Detaching her frail body from the steps, twisting and spinning out of control, she barely had time to scream out before she hit the stone floor at the bottom with a sickening thump. The small bundle lay at the foot of the stairs and was ominously stilled on the hard cold ground. Her scrawny legs stuck out of her skirt like twigs from a dead tree, a small pool of blood lay alongside her head while a trickle of urine ran between her legs, leaving a wet patch around her.

Her husband, hearing her cry, had ventured down to investigate and was curiously poking and prodding her gently trying to get some response, but there was none. He ran next door, banging on the door as if the devil himself was breathing down his neck.

"Quickly, can you call the Doctor? My wife has had an accident and she is breathing funny," he cried.

"Slow down, Joe, and tell me exactly what has happened and slowly."

The old man explained that he had heard his wife scream out and that he had found her lying at the bottom of the stairs. The neighbour phoned for an ambulance before going next door to help...

Trying to forge past the build up of slow moving traffic was a nightmare for Tom. A thick layer of snow hampered their progress as they eased forward the wheels crunching into its compressed layers. The gritting lorries had not been able to stop the conglomeration of snow from overwhelming the streets, creating havoc for the vehicles as they slid and slipped on their hazardous journeys. It was like scenery from the front of a 'Christmas Card' as the white-formed covering engulfed everything that it touched.

One of the two-tones had frozen making a ludicrous lament, but it gave them both a laugh. The progress was agonisingly slow; vehicles in front were concentrating on their own problems and were not aware of the approaching ambulance until it was emphasising its presence in their rear view mirror.

Once Tom located the main road he found conditions much improved and he managed to pick up a little speed. When they finally arrived at the house; Jason eased his body gingerly out of the cab and onto the hard packed ground. For a moment Jason hesitated before he touched the frail and broken bundle lying before him on the cold stone floor. He was stunned by what he saw, even though he had seen similar situations many times before.

61

He gently examined her body for injuries, and then with the help of Tom he eased her head a fraction away from the edge of the bottom step before bending forward to feel her frail arms for a pulse.

A negative voice from over his shoulder asked "Is she dead? Oh God, don't let her be dead."

Her pulse was weak, fluttering under Jason's fingers. "No, she is alive" he replied, 'but only just,' he thought to himself. Quickly he examined her body; blood stains matted her silver hair, and the bones were broken in both legs. Her eyes opened briefly before closing once more as she slipped back into unconsciousness.

Tom and Jason worked fast; she would not die if they could help it. Wounds were bandaged and the legs splinted. Jason slipped the needle into her arm, saw the flashback as the blood appeared suddenly into the porthole of the cannula; he advanced the hollow sheaf forward into the vein before securing it into position. A drip was set up to help with the fluid loss from the two leg fractures and to alleviate the shock. Her blood pressure would have to be closely monitored for her condition was poor.

She responded a little and opened her eyes she looked fearful, not sure of her location. Jason bent forward closer to the frail form that lay before him and took her hand in his. "You will be alright now my love, we will take good care of you," he said.

Looking around the small room he observed for the first time the surroundings; the old fashioned kitchen stove with its open grate and ovens, the cold stone floor that had worn away in places like the rush-mat that lay in front of a large oak dresser. He could see that it had been a well used kitchen, giving its owner many years of service.

This was her world, a place that held many memorable experiences; the signs of her regular physical activity showed in the cleanliness of the utensils and the working surfaces. He tried to imagine what she must have been feeling; was she in a strange land surrounded by weird people that were fussing about her? Why could she not move or stand up? What was happening and why did she feel this way? As Jason placed the oxygen mask over her face he said: "This will make you feel much better, then we will try and get you more comfortable."

She still had a puzzled expression on her face; still trying to recall the past events that led to these invasions that had suddenly entered her life. Her face twisted and contorted with onset of pain that started to bite into her skull, causing her stomach to heave as the nausea swept through her body in waves. Her head started spinning and the colour drained away from the surface of her extremities.

Jason felt a surge of pity for the woman as he watched her shaking body.

She reminded him of his own mother, weak and frail, trying to fix the pieces of the puzzle back together again. He gave a sigh as his thoughts turned to his mother, remembering some of her little ways and how vigorously she had struggled to raise her two sons.

How she fought to make the small amounts of money stretch through the week, while frugally shifting the bills to keep the debt collector away from the door.

She was the stanchion for the whole family and Jason's admiration for his mother would remain in tact forever, for her standards had long been an inspiration to him.

As a small child he did not comprehend the tribulations that his mother had to endure. It was only when he reached his teens that he realised the full extent of her unflinching sacrifices.

The thoughts of his mother did not last long; he quickly turned back to the task before him to give comfort to the old woman and to try easing her distress. He pushed aside everything else as he painstakingly concentrated on the task in hand. Blood was still seeping through the bandages and her Glasgow coma scale kept dropping away to dangerous levels. He was not happy with the old woman's condition, she had some very bad injuries and her chances of survival were looking grim.

With care and compassion they lifted the old lady onto the stretcher. She was still alive, at least for the moment anyway, and they would do their best to keep it that way. They were willing her to survive, while she had a spark of life there was always hope. The poor soul slipped into unconsciousness once more, her face ashen and wet with perspiration.

Jason looked at her colour, then quickly checked her pupils; the right pupil had blown and was fully dilated. The indications suggested that she had developed an intracranial bleed and the pressure was increasing within her skull. With no escape route for the flow of blood the pressure would continue to increase until her brain could stand it no more, causing death to follow soon after.

The need to get their patient to hospital was extremely urgent. Unless she could get help from a surgeon to release the mounting pressure caused by the blood clot growing inside her head, she would suffer brain stem death and nothing could save her from that point.

Jason moved his fist up and down signalling to Tom to speed up if he could.

"You had better try and give them some warning of what to expect," he yelled through to Tom. "Let them know that her GCS is only six, right pupil is fixed and dilated and I am now assisting with her breathing; she is not doing very well, we'll be lucky to make the hospital in time."

The casualty room was ready; lights were playing with the shadows and the equipment was casting weird shapes on the walls. Nurses in their predominant uniforms were making themselves busy before the onslaught that would soon rush through the entrance doors. Everything was to hand, ready to receive the casualty, not knowing what they would be presented with until the arrival. One of the Doctors and a nurse went outside to wait for the approaching ambulance, ready to assist the crew when they unloaded their precious cargo.

Sounds from the siren broke the silence, giving warning of the approaching vehicle.

Tom shot through the tunnel leading to the casualty unit, engine hot and racing, the smell of the heated brakes mixed with hot engine oil filled the tunnel as he came to a stop. Back doors were flung open with a rush. Jason was working with a fury on the old woman in the back. The sweat was pouring down his face with the effort that he had put into the journey; he was totally exhausted, trying to expand his lungs and stop the trembling he felt in his legs.

As they wheeled the stretcher through the doors of the casualty department, Jason gave a running commentary of their findings and the treatment they had given her since the first assessment.

She was almost at death's door, her Glasgow coma scale now down to five, blood pressure readings were not audible and her pulse was so weak that it could not be recorded.

They quickly wired her to the cardiac monitor and fitted the rest of the equipment into place. They did their best to monitor her pulse, blood pressure and oxygen saturation levels. The old woman was making discursive sounds and her body started convulsing, just two more signs suggesting she had suffered serious head injuries. Her twitching limbs thrashed out as her agitated brain sent strange messages to the nerves controlling her muscles. Genteel but firm hands restrained the limbs to stop them suffering damage from the metal cot sides.

The casualty Doctor started his examination, calling out found injuries so that one of the nurses could record the details onto paper. "Fractured base of skull; I understand the neurosurgeon

65

is on his way to us? Bruising behind the left ear; bruising and swelling to the eyes; right pupil has blown and is fully dilated. She has bilateral femur fractures; query the pelvis. This lady must have hit the ground with a lot of force. Keep an eye on the monitor her observations are so low she could arrest at any moment."

"Do you want x-rays and a CT scan Doctor?" asked a staff nurse.

"Yes, lets, have the full treatment; C-spine, pelvis and a CT scan, although I must confess I'm doubtful she will make the latter. Can you get a cross match on her blood as soon as possible?"

Some 20 to 30 per cent of trauma accident victims don't survive and this lady looked sure to become one of those statistics. Her life-threatening injuries were causing a rapid deterioration. If she did not get a burr-hole operation immediately to release the intracranial pressure caused by the blood clot, she would not recover.

Each member of the casualty team worked in unison, drawing drugs, removing clothes or assisting the doctors with their tasks.

Suddenly the atmosphere in the emergency room changed. "She is going off, cardiac arrest," warned the unit sister.

Two senior Doctors who specialised in casualty trauma started resuscitation immediately. They worked with quiet determination, each fully practised in their routine, checking drugs, monitor and equipment as they performed each task instantaneously.

Unfortunately all their efforts were in vain. Her injuries to the brain were traumatic, and the massive bleeding within the skull had caused the pressure to build to extreme degrees ...

Jason had moved away to complete the recorded log sheet; he felt exhausted from the physical effort that this call had taken to complete. As he worked his way through the paperwork he felt drained; the sweat still running down his back and neck, he felt his body shaking as the adrenaline rush subsided, blissfully unaware of the drama unfolding in the casualty room they had just left behind them.

"I need a drink before we do anything else," he whispered to Tom.

They made their way to the nurses staff room at the back of the casualty unit. Tom and Jason took a crafty drink; it was the only place that they could hide themselves away for a while without the fear of detection.

It was sad that they were made to take chances like this to obtain a small break to unwind. It had not been long since another crew had been disciplined for doing the same thing, but they knew that if they had not taken these steps they would go without refreshments altogether.

After their gratifying drink and short rest they made their way back to the casualty department to collect the stretcher and the rest of the equipment.

When they arrived back at the unit they saw Brenda, one of the nurses, wheeling the casualty trolley towards the small chapel at the far end. She gave them a benevolent smile; this told them that all of their efforts had been in vain and that the lady did not make it.

"What a shame, she seemed a nice old dear," said Tom.

"There are some you just can't win and we are not god," Jason replied feeling a little sad. They had put a lot of effort into trying to keep the old woman alive, but deep down Jason had known that she was not going to make it.

Back at the vehicle they stowed everything back in its rightful place ready for the next call. Settling themselves into the front seats Jason picked up the hand mike and called control. "Green after the last red call, what have you in mind for us?"

Stan Canon sat staring up at the large picture placed over the mantel: a painting that he had produced himself some twenty years earlier. From its taunt canvas it portrayed the magnificence of a mighty vessel. The scene setting was that of the Aircraft Carrier

USS Yorktown, displaying the Star Spangled Banner from the mast above the Command Island.

It sat proudly in the blue water as a Dauntless Dive-Bomber took off from its wooden flight deck. Just below this magnificent portrait was a silver-framed photo of a young sailor dressed in whites.

Now in the last dying stages of terminal cancer this once strong son of America looked hard at his beloved ship and remembered those days long gone when he served on board the *Yorktown* ...

"How about a nice hot cup of coffee?" asked his wife.

"Yes, please, that would be nice," he replied as his memories were interrupted.

It took only a few minutes to make but on her return she found him fast asleep again. He looked so weak, so tired it was like watching him drift away from her as each day passed. He had been distant for some time since they had increased his medication to its present dosage.

She leaned forward and clasped his hand; his skin was warm and dry but he would complain always of being cold. It had been a terrible shock to both of them when they had been told that the diagnosis was terminal cancer. This thing inside was eating away at his internal organs and sucking the life from his wasting body.

Stan had always been the fit one of the partnership; he was her rock that she would cling to when things were getting on top. They had met and married before the battle of 'Midway,' and when Stan went off to War Jane returned to England to be close to her own parents. When her husband returned home they had made the decision to stay in Britain.

He woke and grimaced as the pain swept through his body. It was time to for him to take his next dose of MST (morphine opiate), one of the medications that controlled his discomfort.

Stan had come to terms with the fact that he was dying, but he could not cope with the scathing pains that raked his body. He was on a 100mg now and this was causing him to hallucinate, dragging a mixture of fact and fiction into his dreams. The screaming faces of ex-buddies dying in front of him over and over again. Burning and exploding bodies. Guys that he had known as friends who had been torn into pieces of raw meat by canon shells or burnt to a charcoal crisp as exploding fires spread outwards. His dreams revealed all the horrors of war and would place him walking on the deck in a sea of flesh and crimson blood.

The prolonged pain periods between the MST opiate necessitated interim top up drugs to eliminate his discomfort. In the beginning Stan had made regular trips to the local hospital for Radiotherapy. Hyper accelerated radiotherapy prevented the cancer cells from multiplying between treatments. But this was not only traumatic; it was short-lived in its relief. It had caused him hair loss, vomiting and painful burns; all of this was not the way that he wanted to end his final days. His choice was to decline further treatment and live whatever time he had left with dignity. The treatment had made him feel worse and he decided that while he was still mobile he would use this period to enjoy life.

These early days had little impact. From outward appearance no one would suspect that there was anything wrong. But with increasing pains and the introduction of drugs to combat his condition things took a steady decline.

As the weeks passed he began to have continuous hallucinations followed by confusion and unnatural aggression, as he became more and more frustrated with his condition. Jane found that coping with her husband's demands was becoming unbearable and the stress was making her ill. She was tormented by her sense of misguided guilt, although she had nursed him and faithfully taken care of his every need; there was this overwhelming feeling of betrayal. This man had been her lover, partner and best friend and she was no longer able to care for him in the way that she wished. On the rare occasions that he was able to get out of his bed he would follow her all around the house like a puppy dog. Each time that she left the room he would think of a reason or excuse to call her back.

The doctor had called this morning and had decided to make arrangements for Stan to be accepted by the local Hospice. He had observed that Jane was no longer coping and it was apparent that there was nothing more that could be done for him except to make his last hours more comfortable. The medication could only do so much; it was now so strong that Stan was not fully aware of his surroundings. He would sit looking at the picture on the wall, eyes staring ahead and transfixed on the image before him. Stan's body was in the room but his thoughts were far off in another time as he tried to focus on the images that flooded his mind. Closing his eyes he searched the darkest corners of his memory until those memories transferred him back onto the deck of that vessel ...

The *USS Yorktown* had been sunk during the 'Battle of Midway'. This proud Aircraft Carrier that had launched fighters and bombers from its wooden flight deck against the Japanese was sunk despite the ferocious struggle to save her.

On the 4th of June 1942 it was hit by three bombs and two torpedoes but remained afloat. The guns sent up a hail of bullets and canon shells from the mighty structure of the *Yorktown* as they tried to knock the Japanese aircraft out of the sky. One after another they flew in to attack its giant construction; some flew so low that the men on board could almost reach up and touch the enemy pilots.

Those on the deck of the carrier watched in dismay as the first of the torpedoes dropped into sea. They watched as the silver missiles streaked through the blue water towards them leaving a white trail of wash in their wake. Two of the torpedoes struck on the portside making a jagged hole in its hull amidships.

Explosions tore and ripped into the armour plating before rupturing fuel tanks. The moment of impact had rocked the vessel, sending up a mushrooming geyser of water high above the Command Island of the ship. Although badly damaged, the *Yorktown* continued the fight, even the burning from the bomb damage did not deter the seamen from their tasks.

The American fleet had left Pearl Harbour in two waves; the carriers Enterprise and Hornet were the first to leave on May the 28th, followed two days later by the *Yorktown* and support ships. The rendezvous was under four hundred miles off Midway Island on June the 2nd. Their plan was to seek and destroy the Japanese fleet lead by Admiral Yamamoto, commander in chief of the attacking force heading for Midway. He was the same commander responsible for the attack on Pearl Harbour.

The Japanese hoped to spring a second surprise on the American Navy, but this time they were ready and waiting for them to arrive. Although the plan originally was to seek out the enemy and surprise them before they had the chance to attack, they were not sure that they could successfully locate the Japanese.

Lady luck was to favour the Americans, for at nine o'clock on June the 3rd a Catalina flying boat on a search mission spotted the Japanese fleet and reported their position in a radio coded message back to base. Three carriers backed by their destroyers and cruisers prepared battle plans. Alerted by the discovery, they waited to pounce on the Japanese fleet.

On the morning of the 4th of June as the early dawn rose upwards the Japanese launched a mass air attack from their carriers. The strike force attacking the Midway Islands and the American fleet were surprised to be met with fierce resistance from the ground and air. But the Japanese 'Zero's' were outclassing the Americans and the consequent result in many conflicts turned into a massacre for the pilots from the Island; many of them had never flown assault missions before. They had launched one hundred and eight warplanes on the US base at Midway before turning their attention on the American fleet. It was a victorious battle for the Americans, although they did not command supremacy in the air; their bombers had managed to sneak in unnoticed and sink four of the Japanese carriers at the end of the battle. The Americans had lost one hundred and forty three aircraft and one badly damaged carrier against the Japanese loss of four carriers and two hundred and forty seven aircraft.

On board the *Yorktown* the crewmen had doused fires to keep in the fight.

Even after the end of the battle they struggled to save the ship and tow her back to the safety of Pearl Harbour.

The *Yorktown* finally lost its lucky streak after being spotted by a lone Japanese submarine, as it lay dead in the water on the 6th of June. Submerged beneath the surface the submarine was manoeuvred into position before firing a spread of four torpedoes at its chosen target.

One of the torpedoes hit the *USS Hammann,* tearing her in half. As she sank beneath the waves, her depth charges started to explode killing many of the poor souls in the water. She recorded eighty-one confirmed dead. Two of the remaining torpedoes hit the already damaged *Yorktown* signing her death warrant. She finally slipped deep into the Pacific Ocean the following morning on the 7th, her battle flags still flying proudly from above. The Japanese submarine had made a successful strike and had escaped unnoticed but the Japanese cruiser *Mikuma* was not as lucky, sunk by US carrier aircraft while trying to withdraw from the battle area.

The United States could claim a magnificent victory and the history books would record that it was to be the turning point to the Pacific conflict. Its cost in human life was 362 Americans and 3,057 Japanese ...

Now close to death Stan senses were heightened to the memories of those dark days back in June of 1942. Almost as if he was regaining his experiences from the scenes that he was once reluctant to discuss. He recognised the atrocity that he had witnessed and the faces of the dead that were left behind ...

Control had instructed them to transfer a terminal cancer patient from his home address to the local hospice. This was not an emergency call, but would need special care and attention.

Most calls of this nature were on a one-way journey, although the odd occasional patient would go for respite care.

Tom drove along the pea-shingled driveway, the tyres crunching on the hard stone surface before halting outside the front entrance. His partner decamped from the vehicle and walked up to the front door, while Tom prepared the equipment inside the saloon.

The sharp ringing tone of the doorbell wrenched Stan back from his dreams, the inferno of war disappearing. His transformation from a state of deep sleep to suddenly being wide-awake startled him. He stared at the picture on the opposite wall, trying to gather his senses. The fearful circumstances of his memories and the endless faces of old comrades that had flooded into his mind slowly faded away.

Jason walked into the room and introduced himself to the patient. "How are things with you today, Stan?" he inquired, trying to break the ice between strangers.

"Not bad considering, but thanks for asking," he replied weakly, the American accent still broadly prominent as he spoke.

"Have you been to this hospice before?" still trying to break down the barriers and put the man at ease.

"A couple of weeks ago when the wife had to go into hospital for an operation," he replied, warming a little to the paramedics questions.

Jason noted that Stan was having problems clearing his airway and that his breathing was becoming laboured. His attempt to breathe was a pitiful sight as he struggled to force air past his lips, his uncoordinated chest heaved under the physical effort of tired and laboured lungs. The build up of phlegm caused a throaty cough as he tried in vain to shift the thick sticky bolus clogging his windpipe.

Things like breathing are taken for granted by us all; we never think about the way the body keeps its mechanisms working twenty-four hours a day until it malfunctions.

Tom returned to the vehicle to collect the portable suction unit so that the offending bolus could be aspirated. The cancer had taken rapid control and it allowed just a modicum of relief between the spasms of pain. Even the oxygen seemed to work against him.

Once the sticky mass was removed Stan was a lot easier and the panic in his eyes dispersed.

Jason pulled the carrying chair over to the bedside and began to prepare the blankets ready for the removal.

"Where are my spectacles, babe?" he asked his wife.

"Here they are, all nice and clean, try not to get them dirty again." She placed them into his pyjama jacket pocket after wiping them one last time with a cloth.

Tears started to trickle down his cheeks as he looked out of the window at his beloved garden for the last time. Even as he watched, a robin settled onto the snow-covered lawn, its spruce red breast spectacular against the white of winter. He observed its unsuccessful beak digging at the frozen ground, foraging for food. It was this time of day when the birds would swoop down for their evening feed that Stan had grown to enjoy; their clever antics had kept him amused for many bedridden hours.

Pain sat heavy on his chest as they wheeled him out of the front door; it was a sort of bereavement pain for he knew that once he was taken from this house he would never set eyes on it again. He looked at his wife with numbed senses; her sadness showed visibly on all her facial expressions even though she tried hard not to display her grief.

Tom climbed into the driving seat and set off towards the hospice. It was only a short journey normally but on learning something about Stan's history Tom decided to go the long way along the coast road.

Even though he could not see out of the darkened windows Stan knew that they were close to the sea. For someone that had spent his young years around ships like Stan his sixth sense told him that they were close to water.

Thick layers of snow and ice melted as the slight warming of rain began to wash the road surface. A slight breeze helped the falling rain to disperse slush and snow into the drains, making the journey easy.

The effect of the morphine and his weakened state made Stan suddenly very sleepy. He tried to fight off the tiredness that swept over him as he lay on the stretcher looking up at the changing lights shining through the glass roof of the vehicle. Stan closed his eyes; the heavy dose of drugs caused him to hallucinate as a wispy white smoke filled his mind. This apparition turned into a white clad figure dressed in a sailor's uniform. He could not recognise the face but the band on the cloth cap clearly read *USS Yorktown*. The sailor's hand seemed to beckon him to follow as it moved in slow motion.

A sharp pain spread across his chest, burning like molten lead before radiating down his left arm. Everything turned black; then, as the minutes passed, the pain eased off and he realised the apparition was back, its hand encouraging him to follow as it beckoned again...

Jason quickly leaned forward into the cab space to speak to his partner.

"Step up the pace a few notches, I don't think he is long for this world."

75

Tom understood and picked up the speed. If the patient was about die it would be much kinder if it happened in the hospice. If they lost him before the transfer was complete they would be forced to re-route to the local hospital. This would cause all sorts of legal complications for the relatives, apart from the fact that the casualty department did not have the time or facilities that there were at the hospice.

On their arrival they made the transfer swift and without too much discomfort to Stan. The nursing staff were fantastic as always; not only did they make Stan's last moments peaceful they also took extra care of his wife's needs. Although she had prepared herself over the months for this moment, it was still hard to accept that this was the final end.

Before the crew had finished collecting their equipment the patient had slipped away. No more pain, fear or grief, he was off on a journey to join friends that had been lost in time.

Jason's experience of death was that most, when the time arrives, seem to have a sign of relief on their face. The exceptions are to those that have meet death by unexpected violence. He had a strong personal belief that there was something else other than this life to move onto.

Making a discreet withdrawal, they made themselves scarce and returned to the vehicle. The two paramedics sat in the cab reflecting the last call before announcing their availability to the control operator ...

CHAPTER SIX

Marge Wilson put down the telephone receiver, she seemed irritated and there was a look of concern embedded on her face. Something was wrong she could sense it. After phoning her son for most of the week and getting no reply, she could not put it off any longer. A chill ran down her spine before spreading to the rest of her body causing her to shiver. Slipping on her coat she made for the front door. 'Why did he behave this way? I wish he'd let me have a key to his place, but then we have not been close for some time now.'

The drive to Mark's house took her twenty minutes, time for her imagination to increase her anxieties. It had been three years since he had taken to drink and drugs. He had spent many nights in jail because of excessive alcohol and then, when he had turned to drugs, it had almost cost him his life. After two drug overdoses she had endeavoured to get him to stop and seek professional help, but all Marge got for her trouble was verbal abuse. To pay for his habits, he had stolen money and sold off her property to indulge in his costly pastime. The need to comply with his craving had encouraged him to become a crafty and wayward liar.

The last time that she had been allowed into his house it was like a rubbish tip. There were chip wrappings; cigarette packets and empty bottles scattered everywhere. He had degraded and embarrassed himself as he lay in his own stench of stale urine and other bodily odours. Flinging his arms about in a rage he had cursed and almost pushed her out of the house when she tried to tidy the mess, but she was sure the truth was that she had refused to give him money.

When she arrived at Mark's front door there was a close resemblance to the local tip. Discarded newspapers, an old mattress, bits of an old bicycle and many cardboard boxes lay where they had fallen. She picked her way slowly through the rubbish baring the door and after several attempts on the knocker, she lifted the letterbox. The unmistakable smell of decomposing flesh oozed out of the small gap in the door; the outrageous aroma stole her breath away. Fear struck with a quivering hand as the realisation of her worst nightmare perforated her struggling heart. Somehow she managed to compose herself and run to the phone box at the corner of the street. She fought back the tears that blurred her eyes, making it hard to see the numbers on the dialling pad.

"Hello. Yes, could I have an ambulance, please, I think its too late."

She had no idea how she had managed to make the triple nine call and get back to the house. Marge shook her head as if reassuring herself; she had known that this day was possible; after all, she had lived through this twice before almost as a trail run. Perhaps sensing her son's pain she had made the effort to make contact with him again. But she knew that it was far too late. A moan escaped her mouth, as she could not contain her grief any longer ...

They had been instructed to return to base. There were some days that made it impossible to get back to station for a break because of the sheer demand of calls. So when the control operator gave them the directive, they took the opportunity as a welcome chance for a quick cup of tea.

Tom stretched the speed limits as they raced back along the coastal road. They had a need to put distance between the hospital and the ambulance station; the further they could get away from the hospital the better the chances of making it back.

On arrival at the station Tom reversed the vehicle into the garage bay and switched off the engine. He did not get the chance to alight from the cab before the radio bleeped. Scrambling frantically for his pen, Jason hurriedly wrote down the details passed to him on a scrap of paper. Then depressing the mike button on the side, he repeated the details back to controller, finishing with the usual 'Roger' before jamming the mike down onto its securing mount. It missed and fell to the floor of the cab. 'Sod it,' he did not have time for any distractions.

Tom had rolled out of the garage and was headed towards the direction given. Road traffic was light as they sped towards the other end of town, but the rain was picking up pace and this did not help. Details of the call were vague except that the police were also on route, 'believed collapsed behind locked doors.' This normally meant that it would have to be a forced entry, plus if they could not get to the front door then the prognosis was normally grim.

It did not take them long to get there; a police car had just pulled up in front of them and the officers were being spoken to by an ageing woman screaming and pointing towards the front of the house.

By the time Jason had heaved his para-bag out of the cab, one of the police officers had smashed a small window in the door and was reaching through the glass to slip the catch.

Jason and the police officer went through the door in unison. The inside of the house was worse than the outside, a complete and utter mess. And that smell! They picked their way over the debris checking rooms running off the hallway as they progressed.

It was fifteen forty-five when Jason entered the room, there was nowhere to move about freely, for it was filled from ceiling to floor with strange objects. Dark corners where the sunlight never touched making it hard to breathe; ornaments, books and sculptures were everywhere gathering dust where they stood. The walls and mantels were covered with cobwebs where spiders had been busy establishing their territory.

How many years had passed since the room was last attended was hard to imagine. Furniture that had once sat proud and

79

expensive now looked tired and drab faded by the wear and neglect.

Jason heard a creak of a loose floorboard and quickly spun around. Tom stood looking in amazement at the museum appearance of the room.

The overwhelming stench that seemed to ooze out of the very brickwork of the walls stopped him dead in his tracks. It was not a dank dampness or rising mould, but stench of human decomposition and bodily fluids. They gasped because the putrefaction was strong and it choked them all as it hit the back of their throats.

A large blanket-covered mound lay the full length of an old worn sofa on the far side of the room. It was soon realised that it concealed a body as an arm was visibly seen dangling over the edge.

Stepping forward Jason removed the blanket for a closer look. "Oh Christ, poor sod," exclaimed Tom.

It was impossible to guess the age of the corpse; it was blown up with rotting gases and the flesh was blackened by dead tissue. The telltale sign of the syringe lay on the floor and the needle tracks were clearly visible on the arm of the cadaverous form.

Jason explained to the police officer that it looked like a drug overdose had been responsible for death, but that would be up to the coroner's office to determine the cause after an autopsy examination of the body. Out of compassion Jason laid the blanket back over the corpse and looked about for any other evidence that would throw light on the probable cause.

The paramedics left the police to make their arrangements with the coroners officer and made a swift exit out into the cool fresh air. Outside they both sucked deep, filling their lungs to disperse the smell of decomposing flesh.

Tom's first reaction was to light up a cancer stick and draw in the nicotine fairy's elixir. It was then that Jason caught sight of Mrs. Wilson sitting on the low front wall.

She was shivering as he approached; her eyes were bloodshot from crying and the tears were streaming down her cheeks. The thought of her son's death filled her with an emptiness that was incomprehensible. He had been her whole life, a part of her body and to have one of your offspring die before you was not exceptable.

When he was born and the midwife laid him down upon her belly for the first time, she could not describe the joy of that moment; her life had been fulfilled and she could not believe her good fortune to be blessed with a son. Many nights after his birth she used to climb the stairs and creep silently into his nursery. So tiny, he lay sleeping, this small bundle that was her creation.

She could not resist the urge to pick him up and feel his soft face pressed against her cheek. Now he was gone forever!

Mrs. Wilson looked a pathetic figure as the tears flowed from her eyes.

She explained that her boy had not always been bad: he had been at the top of his class when attending school and was a loving, attentive child.

His drinking had started with small amounts but after a break up with a girl friend he had hit the bottle big time. From this point on he was to change his life style completely. Drugs were the natural progression and he turned into a stranger. She had tried hard to get him to seek help but he would not have anything to do with counselling. Slowly he turned away from her seeking solace in his habits, shutting himself away in the house for days on end.

Jason placed his hand gently on her shoulder and did not say a word until she had finished. He tried to get her to come to the hospital for she was clearly shocked and distraught by what had happened to her son. But she refused, insisting that it was not necessary. Her son had been only thirty-nine, a wasted life because of his addiction to alcohol and drugs.

The paramedics were finished; there was nothing more they could do to change the sad outcome. As they climbed into the cab of the vehicle and prepared for the next call, Jason thought of his own parents. His mind drifted and he remembered his mother, her mop of jet black hair that did not lose its colour until just before she died aged eighty-two. One of the lasting memories was her bursting her sides laughing at some silly joke, how her eyes would sparkle and the tears rolled down her cheeks. After her stroke, considerably weakened with her loss of mobility and greying hair, she still managed to keep the sparkle almost to the end.

She had started her working life caring for an ageing lady of financial means who used to put the fear of God into her. This persuaded her very quickly to seek employment elsewhere, the first chance she got: she went to work in a paint factory in Stratford.

Jason's mother soon became friendly with one of his future aunts and they would often go ice skating together. On one of these occasions Jason's father, who was home on sick leave from the army having suffered a broken leg, met his mother at one of the local skating rinks. During those dark days of war romances almost sprang up over night, for they never counted on there being a tomorrow.

From photos that Jason had seen of his mother in her twenties, she was a beguiling creature with deep, large brown eyes matching her gentle face, a face that he remembered as beautifully exquisite.

A smile spread across Jason's own face as he reflected his mother's first visions of his father on crutches. What was it about him that first attracted her? Was it pity or physical?

He remembered his childhood, the harshness of those days with little money and very few comforts. His mother would send him to Mr. Cornball's grocery store to purchase half a dozen eggs from which she would try and produce a meal. With sixpence clasped tightly in his small hand he would buy the six eggs and a single stick of Spanish – wood for his trouble and still take home some change.

Jason's mother earned her money working on an assembly line at the 'Bryant and May' matchbox factory, while his father and granddad had a lot to do with the rebuilding work around the Bow area. The heavy bombardment of the London East End had reduced many of the old houses into heaps of rubble.

All building work had been halted at the advent of the war, but was soon resumed when peace returned.

The post war building program saw intense construction take place all over the country. Experimental, prefabricated Orbit houses made of pre-cast concrete sprang up wherever there was a need to rebuild. The demands for sort-after living accommodation to replace the bombed structures were paramount to house the survivors and their men returning from the fighting.

Bath nights, he recalled, were always on a Friday, they began by the lifting of the metal bathtub from its hook on the back of the coal house door; then the labouring task of filling the big copper heating pot and then bringing the water to boiling point. This allowed his mother to add more water and fill the tub placed in front of the warming fire.

When Jason's brother was born they had to share the water; normally his brother first, because he was the younger and deemed to be less dirty.

Life for his mother was hard, no modern appliances in those days. To do the ironing, the iron was heated on the cooking range; two were needed: one heating on the stove while the other was in use. There were no toasters, washing machines, microwaves, vacuum cleaners or television sets to make life easier.

But those were good years: there was a different atmosphere then; no need to lock doors and windows and everyone knew the name of the families in their street who would pop in and out without a care. Children could play and roam in the streets without any fear of being abducted.

Jason thought of life now and a sadness swept over him? What had his grandchildren got to look forward to. He was sure that his generation had experienced the best era where ethics of morals and principles had been drummed into them from an early age. No one would dream of beating a little old lady to within an inch of her life for the sake of a few shillings then ...

Control instructed them to proceed to one of the local stand-by points for accident cover. This was a part of the job that Jason hated above all else; sitting waiting for some poor sod to have an accident or to collapse with some sudden illness made him feel like a vulture waiting for its prey to arrive. Apart from that, he always felt like he was in a goldfish bowl on view to all that passed by. So boring was this kind of cover that they would sadly sit and count bricks on a wall to pass away the time.

A few years previous they had ignored the order to go to stand-by and had decided to cruise around, but fate worked against them as they came across a road traffic accident miles away from their supposed location. It had not been taken any further because they had been able to deal with the crash directly. They had been given a severe reprimand and a warning never to disobey an instruction again.

Most crews felt that the service was down graded because the public would see an ambulance sat around like this and they would form the impression that it was all they did for a whole shift. To make matters worse Tom spent the whole time sleeping with his head lent up against the cab window. Jason felt embarrassed as the cars slowed at the roundabout and stared into the cab at his partner. He reflected that for a guy that spent so much of his time telling everyone how fit he was, sleep seemed to be his all-conquering master.

Tom stirred and woke himself up again, looked at his wristwatch and sighed. It had been a bloody cold winter so far this year and both were feeling the strain. They started to discuss their individual families to fight off the sleep. Both men knew everything about each other's kin and would often share their problems. With seven children between them they had a constant topic of conversation. It would normally be money or boyfriend problems and both agreed that they got more grief from their offspring as adults than they ever did when they were children.

After putting their families through the microscope they sat working out their next social event. Tom was extremely good at arranging coach trips or nights at the local curry house. This was how they passed the time for nothing stirred, in fact, it was very quiet. There was no continuity in this job, it was either an exhausting assortment of work or deathly silent, no happy medium. Unfortunately the silence never lasts long and both knew that it would only be a short respite before they were called upon again. Jason shifted his knee into a more favourable position; he just could not sit still in one place for any length of time without the nagging pain returning to his ageing joint ...

CHAPTER SEVEN

Jason had suffered the 'Ambulanceman's' worst nightmare. That is, to be called to a house that you know to be that of a close friend or to a member of your own family. This had happened to Jason three times in his career with the service. Being called twice to his mother then once to his eldest daughter. His daughter had almost bled to death after a fall down the stairs and landing legs apart across the baby's stair gate. Her crotch had taken the full force of the impact. As luck would have it her sister, who was a Staff Nurse, was visiting at the time of the accident and knew what to do.

Unfortunately Jason was in the vehicle that was called. Everyone in the service had a fear of being sent to one of his or her own family or to close friends. He knew that his daughter had a bad haemorrhage, but he was not aware just how bad until they arrived at the hospital. He was told, that the chances of this type of injury happening from a accident like this was one in a thousand.

Jason had studied the situation carefully, giving it serious thought before making a move. Taking a long gasp of air before advancing the cannula he seemed almost on auto - pilot as his skilled fingers worked with amazing speed. All those years of practice made the movements slick and sure. His mouth felt dry and bland as it always did when the adrenaline started to flow. You could almost smell the excitement, not of joy but that of fear. He had been trained to be and act professionally; this part of him would now take control.

The nervous dry taste and the panic within his head now subsided.

Every move now went with clockwork precision. Protocols that had been learnt at the training school flowed down to his skilled fingers. The drip was in place putting back vital fluids that had been lost. His heart rate was like a drum beat, as it pounded within his chest.

Her blood pressure and pulse rate started to come back to a more stable condition. It had been a pulse of 120 and the BP was below a 100 when he had started. The breathing rate and skin tone had also improved slightly. It was at this point that his thoughts turned to inward panic. 'What if she had been on her own with just the baby?' His body gave a little shudder ....

On arrival at the hospital they had pushed their way along the corridor. "Stand aside! Coming through!" Tom yelled in his best authoritarian voice. He might just as well have saved his breath, for not many took any notice. The plastic doors of the trauma room burst open as they wheeled the trolley inside.

Doctors and nurses were swarming around another stretcher where they were shocking the patient's heart. 'Stand clear' sounded a voice, then the body on the trolley arched as 360j of electricity shot through it.

"Still flat lined," exclaimed the voice again.

The charge nurse looked up from his task of chest compressions and spied the new arrivals. "Oh shit, that's all we need, another bloody catastrophe patient."

Jason grabbed the first nurse who did not seem to be up to her neck in anything important. He gave her a quick history and made her aware that it was his own daughter before being directed to place her on the second trauma trolley.

He had given the charge of his daughter over to the Doctors. Knowing that they would do everything that needed to be done. One of the Nurses took his arm and showed him into a small room. "Don't you worry I promise to come back soon when we have some news," she whispered.

Jason could not remember much about his time spent in the room, except for Tom popping back and forth, asking him if there was any news.

After what seemed like hours the Nurse finally returned. The news was good. She had been very lucky indeed. His daughter had ruptured an external Vein and although she had to spend a short time in hospital, would soon mend.

His tear-stained face showed in the light and the shock of what he had just encountered came bearing down on him. For this was after all 'KIM' his first-born child...

Unlike Kim, Jason's mother was not so lucky; she had succumbed to two strokes, the first happening while he was on night duty. He had worked all through the night and then gone to visit his mother before going home to bed. On arriving at her house the next morning he sensed that something was not right from the moment he opened the door. He found his mother lying on the floor of her bedroom confused and bleeding from where her skin had rubbed away as she struggled, trying to get herself up.

A quick check had told him that she had suffered a stroke. Her speech was slurred and her eyes were bulging. She was covered in her own excrement from head to toe, from where she had rolled and wriggled to get up from off the floor. There was no muscle tone to her right arm and leg. This was to remain like that for the rest of her days.

He had left her for a while to make a phone call, requesting an ambulance.

Then, as quick as he could, he tried to clean her up in the short time left before his colleagues arrived to take her to casualty. reflecting on how clean and meticulous she had always been, being self conscious at the slightest mark or body smell.

At the time of her death he had wanted to be with her through it all. But because of the twelve-hour shifts at work and the sleep needed at home, he did not spend as much time with her as he had wished. He had made it widely known with the control management that his mother was not expected to last long, requesting that they give him some time in between calls to visit her on the hospital ward. This did not happen, they kept his vehicle fully mobile for the two days before her death and he had to rely on phone calls for updates on her condition.

It was not until he finished the last early shift before a rest day that he was able to get to the ward. That night she died. It was almost as if she had held on waiting for her son to arrive before she slipped away. Jason never forgave his superiors for not letting him have the time with his mother.

The last seconds of her life would stay with him forever. He remembered holding her hand for almost an hour before he called the nurse to let her know that his mother had gone. He prayed that he would never lose the memory that he held so close to his heart. She had remained semiconscious for three days before her death and could not speak to anyone.

He would give anything now to be able to spend a few hours just talking to her. To gaze upon her face once more and see those wrinkled facial expressions and looks of amazement before they developed into a wide broadening smile, a kind of mischievous smile that he loved so much about her. He remembered as a child she would lay him down for the night into his warm cosy bed and the feel of the clean crisp sheets around him that she had so carefully washed and ironed. She would sit with him until sleep over came his will to stay awake. Then he would wiggle down under the warm covers feeling safe from the black of night, for there were no harrowing dreams then.

There were a thousand memories like this of his mother's love. She was always on hand to protect and comfort him. Her life had been hard, but she always looked after her sons. She was a good mother, one that he would miss dearly forever.

One of the conversations that Jason remembered was his mother telling him how she felt after her second stroke. She felt trapped within the four walls that surrounded her life. This had become her destiny since the stroke took away her freedom: forced now against her will to sit and stare at the walls of her small world. She became desperate for the love and the company of her family and friends. She was fully aware that Jason did his best to get in to see her at least once every day. But she knew that he had a job and his own family to manage.

Until two years previous she had been shackled in what seemed an eternity to a loveless marriage, unable to break away from it because she had no financial support of her own. She longed for her freedom and to be able to take control of her life once again; somehow she never seemed to have the strength or courage to seek what she craved for. Her suffering had been long and hard over the years and she had often thought that her life was not worth living.

When her husband had died her release was short-lived. The 'stroke' had her trapped in a body that no longer functioned to any degree worth the mention.

Her brain had returned to its full capacity, sharp as ever but now aware of the prison-like surroundings that lay around it. Restricted in her movements she was totally dependent on her Zima frame for her mobility. She wished that someone would free her from this wasting life, for it was no longer her will or desire to live like this, dreaming of a quick release from what she considered to be a living hell.

But it took another four long years before the end finally gave her the peace that life owed her.

Jason would sit and listen to her talking like this, feeling that it was daft to even think that way. It was not until the last few days of her life, as she lay dying in hospital, that he realised that this wonderful lady had truly taken all that she possibly could. Her will to continue life had now totally diminished. She had no more fight left, desiring a long peaceful rest.

After she died, Jason looked long and hard at the shiny surfaces of the old photos taken over the past few years. It was at this point that it dawned on him just how much she had deteriorated. He wanted to spend a few more minutes in her presence just to be able to tell her that he loved her so much, but then she already knew that.

His elder daughter had taken her death really hard, wishing that she had made more visits to the home; outwardly her grief was much stronger than Jason's. He did not show his emotions, they were private, but he had understood his mother's feelings and her desire for release at the last giving him the strength to continue ...

Mother

Why do you look at me with your pitying eyes, what do you think you see?
For I have had the best life, full and fancy free.
We did not know of toxic gas or the need of being green;
There were no fears of ozone holes for life was fresh and clean.
We had the freedom to roam the fields full of sun ripe corn;
To listen to the meadow lark on a warm misty morn.
I could hear the many bird sounds as I began to wake,
The scrapping of the horseshoe as the milkman reached the gate.
So if your eyes see pity and that is all they see,
Then my friend, you're the one to pity, so much more than me!

They had been called to a Doctor's urgent case with a pick-up time within the hour. These calls are one step down from emergencies, mostly seen by the Doctor just before the call comes in or the Doctor has full knowledge of the patient's condition at that time. Despite the term 'urgent', most of these calls are bread and butter work for the crews. Although they require qualified ambulance personnel, these calls are normally just straightforward pick up and transfer to hospital jobs, mainly providing only 'tender loving care' or minor treatments. No one could have predicted the mountain of errors that were about to take place ...

Tom had driven the vehicle along the edge of the footpath by the side of the village green, to enable him to position the ambulance directly adjacent to the patient's house. He should have departed the same way, but for some reason he had decided to drive out across the grass. The ground looked firm enough until the full weight of the vehicle fell upon the soaked surface; within seconds they were bogged down to the level of the rear axles. Wheels were spinning and the mud was flying off in all directions, all the while the tyres dug deeper into the marshy surface.

Neighbours came out of their homes to investigate the commotion, curious at first, then anxious to help shift the bogged vehicle; but it was an impossible task. the harder they tried, the deeper the road wheels sank into the soft earth.

One neighbour went off to fetch his four-wheeled drive jeep, the idea being to push from behind while he towed from the front. He was sure that his plan would work, convinced that it was the answer to the problem as they set about the task of resurrecting the ambulance from the sucking mud; only to fail minutes later, leaving the 4x4 driver cursing as the clutch burnt out under the strain, leaving two vehicles stranded on the village green. Tom could not believe his bad luck; what he thought would be a simple task had turned into mayhem. This was going to be the talk of the village for years to come; he could hear the comments now.

"Did you hear about the stupid ambulance driver that got stuck on the green? What a job it was to get them free!" Oh yes, he could almost feel the laughter behind his back ...

Meanwhile in the back of the ambulance things were not going well with Jason. He had just finished suggesting that they move the patient back to the warmth of her own house, when suddenly without any warning she deteriorated rapidly and slipped into

92

respiratory arrest. 'This cannot be happening, it was just a normal Doctor's call and it was going pear-shaped in front of his eyes,' he thought to himself.

Jason almost leapt across the aisle between the two stretchers, quickly selecting and inserting an airway into position before using the bag and mask to assist her breathing.

Things were not going right; the situation was becoming awkward as Jason found himself in an unfavourable position. He needed Tom inside the ambulance, but he could not hear Jason as he cried out for help. Tom was engrossed in the task of trying to free the vehicle from the sodden ground outside.

Acquiring the help of the woman's husband, Jason continued to assist with her breathing. Intermittently she started to breathe unaided, only to keep slipping back into an arrest state.

"Can you reach into the cab and fetch the radio mike, it should stretch this far," Jason asked the husband. He instructed the husband to hold the hand mike and to press the transmission switch on his command; this kept his efforts from being interrupted while he continued the resuscitation attempt.

Quickly he gave the control operator an update on their plight, requesting that a second ambulance should be dispatched without delay.

Jason observed that the lady was displaying signs of Anaphylaxis (reactive shock). "Did the Doctor give your wife any medication?" Jason asked.

"Well, she started a course of antibiotics yesterday," replied the husband.

Quickly Jason showed the woman's husband how to hold and squeeze the resuscitation Bag, then he drew up 1mg of adrenaline and eased 5mg into the deltoid muscle.

Taking control of the bag and mask once more he continued with the resuscitation and within minutes his patient showed slight signs of recovery.

"Has your wife ever had problems with antibiotics before?" Jason asked.

"No never, she has always got on well with them before," replied the husband.

Suddenly there came a roar from a large engine as the local farmer drove his tractor towards them. The farmer and Tom walked around the crippled motor, weighing up the options, before attaching a heavy metal tow chain onto the front supports of the ambulance.

With the help of many hands pushing from behind and the tractor unit pulling from the front end, the vehicle very slowly heaved itself from the sucking pull of the thick, clinging mud. Two minutes later they were free, back on the firm Tarmac surface of the road, with the embarrassed Tom trying to explain to the control operator that they no longer needed the second ambulance and that they were mobile to the hospital.

"Try and keep on firm ground on the return journey," laughed the controller.

Thankfully the lady's condition improved on route to hospital and by the time they arrived it was hard to believe that she had suffered an arrest. When the receiving nurse was told of the respiratory arrest she would not except the story Jason had given her, until the woman's husband confirmed everything and thanked Tom and Jason for all their efforts.

"I pray that you two, or I, never experience the like again," he said.

CHAPTER EIGHT

The shrill Wow – Wow – Wow of the sirens sounded outside as the ambulances rushed backwards and forwards. They had been constantly increasing their input into Southsea Hospital for the past two hours. As fast as they unloaded one stretcher the door would be burst open by yet another crew. Patients were lined up alongside the casualty unit, trolleys carrying all forms of emergencies, slivered torsos, fractured arms and legs, asthmatics fighting for breath, abdominal pains or illnesses of all descriptions lay waiting in turn to be seen by the casualty doctor.

Tom and Jason sat in the nurse's station talking to Julie one of the 'Triage nurses'. She had worked in the casualty department for many years and was friendly with the two paramedics. Tom had a strong fancy for Julie and had spent more time than Jason would have liked flirting with the dark skinned beauty. She positively radiated her sexuality and Jason had to admit that she was the kind of woman that men would undress with their eyes, slowly! He was sure that Julie also had a soft spot for Tom. If ever there were a coach trip or a night out for a meal that his partner had arranged, Julie would move heaven and earth to be there.

Jason finished writing the patient report form, tore off the top copy and slipped it into the casualty folder before heaving himself out of his seat.

He stood tall in his uniform and black shining shoes that were polished and brushed until they were like glass mirrors. At first glance you would think them to be black patent leather. But they had taken hours of buffing and loving care to achieve the effect of perfection. The creases in his trousers were razor sharp, in fact everything about him was clean-cut and presentable.

The rain had stopped by the time they had left the casualty

unit and made their way back to the vehicle. Jason eased into his appropriate seat while Tom decided he needed a smoke. He lit the cigarette and inhaled deeply. Jason's knee felt a little better as the pain eased to a dull ache, it had been throbbing for almost an hour keeping his mind off the work in hand.

Tom stretched himself, as he looked skywards at the blackening clouds building above. He raised the cigarette to his mouth, took another long drag before flicking the ash towards the ground. Then, making a sound just loud enough to get Jason attention, indicated to the direction of a cute little nurse walking towards them. "Get a load of that," he hissed in a low whisper. But his partner's attention was on the sky as the clouds were gathering pace; within minutes the rapid cloud movement was joined by an increasing breeze that preceded the first rain drops. Large droplets cascaded from the sky, soaking everything in its wet deluge and forming vast puddles on the ground. Jason sat and listened to the steady patter as the fat drops were driven against the roof of his vehicle.

Tom was forced to finish the cigarette that he had been holding, threw away the wet butt and forced himself back into the driver's seat. "Hell fire, I did not expect that lot!" exclaimed Tom. "You fit?"

Jason nodded his head and moved his hand towards the radio mike.

"Let's see what they have in store for us now ...

Herbert Smith was feeling anxious as he drove along the dual carriageway heading towards the airport. He had to meet the 17.20 flight from Glasgow whence his wife was returning home after a two-week holiday. The rain was fine drizzle, taking just the occasional sweep of the wiper blade to clear the windscreen, but the sky ahead was dark and foreboding. His car was cruising at a steady sixty miles an hour. Then suddenly without warning he ran into a grey wall of torrential rain. It fell so heavy that it completely obliterated his forward vision. The wiper blades were useless to cope with total haemorrhage from above.

Sitting in the centre lane, he eased his foot slightly off the accelerator pedal. If he eased off too much, the risk would be a rear end shunt from the traffic behind, and if there were another vehicle in front he would have little chance of seeing it in time. He leaned forwards to change radio stations; a little music to soothe the nerves.

It was then that he caught sight of a large dark shape moving in from his near side. His foot shot towards the foot brake, pushing down hard onto the pedal, at the same time the sound of heavy rubber wheels trying to gain a grip on the wet road surface screamed as they skidded on the Tarmac.

The lorry jack-knifed, scooping the tiny car in its claw-like grip. A devastating impact swung his car sideways; the metal structure of the lorry seemed to wrap itself tightly around the smaller vehicle. He felt the front wing and door panel crunch and grind; metal to metal filled the previous silence.

His upper body lurched forward when the car stopped abruptly; the seat belt bit deep into his chest as the impact forced him backwards. Sharp pains shot up his back like a bolt of lightning and the taught webbing closed tightly around his chest restricting breathing.

He sat still in the strange quietness for some minutes before he tried to release the buckle holding the seat belt, but found that his fingers were numb and lacked the power to release the red clip. Sitting still once again, he tried to regain his strength; he heard the rain lashing down against the metal roof, tapping out a steady drumming rhythm. He tried to move again but a fresh wave of pain engulfed his body making him cry out loudly just before he blissfully succumbed to a loss of consciousness.

By the time the ambulance had arrived on scene, many other road users attracted to the crash site were busy climbing into the wreckage and had started to remove debris to gain access. The lorry driver was hauling his body out of the cab shouting at the top of his voice.

"Oh my God, it was the tyre! It just blew without warning."

The situation looked appalling, from first glance it looked like the lorry had completely crushed the smaller car under its enormous load. Jason could see someone looking into the wreckage and calling to the driver trapped inside the car. Picking his way carefully through the carnage he made for the car door, or rather what was left of it.

The driver was unconscious when he first arrived but he slowly responded to the sounds around him. On examination the paramedics found that a piece of metal had entered the flesh on his right arm and dug a huge groove along the muscle. Blood had poured out when the stretched vein had been severed like cut string. The driver complained of a deep-seated pain in his lower back, and, although there were no obvious signs of injury, Jason took the precaution of placing a cervical collar around the driver's neck to be on the safe side. His pulse rate was 120 - with respiration's thirty and shallow breathing. On inhalation he winced with pain and this became more acute when he tried to take a deep breath.

The paramedics suspected a small pneumothorax. Jason picked up the stethoscope from his first aid box, put it into position and auscultated both sides of the chest. There were no breath sounds on the right side, suggesting the right lung to be probably in a collapsed state. He was getting short of breath and the pain seemed to be increasing.

Tom had placed an oxygen mask onto the driver's face, while Jason inserted an intravenous line and gave 'Nubain' for the pain. He explained his concerns to Tom. "I think he may have a small pneumothorax building up," (that's when a tiny leak appears somewhere from a hole in the lung and traps the air between the lung and its lining). The air pressure would build with each breath and without treatment the internal organs would be squeezed, the lungs would collapse and the heart would no longer be able to pump blood. They had to work fast or the driver could die very quickly if he did not get treatment.

The driver was struggling to remain conscious, but was now gasping for air. Meanwhile the Fire Brigade had been working like mad men to free the trapped driver, cutting and forcing the twisted metal away from the injured man, then carefully taking the car panels away a little at a time.

Rain continued to fall making conditions awkward and the use of equipment such as the defibrillator had to be carefully managed. The two paramedics were so engrossed in their task that the rescue was almost unnoticed even though the total time taken for the extraction took twenty-five minutes. Once the roof of the car was removed it made the extraction so much easier; all were thankful that the rain had stopped as suddenly as it began.

Then, lifting out the driver with back slab fitted for immobilisation, intravenous drips and oxygen leads were secured into place and wired to the monitor of the defibrillator.

"How are you doing?" Jason asked.

"Bloody awful." Herbert answered through clenched teeth. He looked like shit; he was turning a distinctive grey and was very clammy.

Jason decided that he could not wait to get him to a hospital doctor. He had to act now!

The condition of Herbert's skin was a sign of shock; its surface was wet and cold to the touch. He lay listlessly on the stretcher, his glazed eyes searching from out of their sockets at the unfamiliar surroundings. He was aware of his situation and the difficulty of his shortness of breath.

Very gently the paramedic placed his hand on the driver's chest and felt the broken bones rubbing together under his fingers; he did not need the stethoscope for he could feel the crackling crepitating of air pooling under the surface. Sweat ran down his neck and made his shirt collar wet, he felt the clammy coldness on his back as the perspiration soaked into the cotton material; his adrenaline was working overtime. Jason knew that he had to insert a brown cannula with syringe attached into the second intercostal space and aspirate the air that had caused the lung to collapse down. But he had only practised on a dummy in the training school classroom and the thought of doing it for real was something he hoped would never happen. This was not exactly a sterile environment and the prospect of putting a needle blindly into some one's lung did not sit well. He explained what he needed to do to the patient, increased the Nubain being the only anaesthesia he could use. He was unable to give pain-relieving gas as it would make the condition worse by increasing the pneumothorax. He wiped the area with antiseptic and instructed the driver to remain still.

With the adrenaline pumping he with drew the plastic sheath, revealing the stainless – steel needle. Jason was surprised to find himself calm and controlled; the shaking had stopped and his hand was steady. He paused for a second, then advanced the needle one hand's breadth from the mid – line until he felt it pop as it entered the air – filled pleural cavity.

There was an immediate burst of air as it escaped through the syringe. It was questionable who got the most relief, the patient or the paramedic. The later was ecstatic at the prospect of completing his first tension pneumothorax without killing the guy. He attached a makeshift one – way flutter valve made out of oxygen tubing with a small hole cut in its side to prevent air from re – entering the chest cavity.

Herbert's skin changed from grey to pink as he started to breathe more easily. The pneumothorax was stable for the present, but it was a dangerous condition that could quickly turn to a complete collapse of both lungs.

There was still the need to keep watching for signs of deterioration, as the situation remained critical.

"I don't want you to hang about, Tom. Go like hell: this guy could go off any minute," Jason whispered.

The crew needed to get Herbert to hospital urgently because Jason had fired off his big guns and if the condition worsened, he would be fighting an up hill battle.

Tom hammered the ambulance towards the casualty as fast as he dared with out putting his passenger in distress.

It had snowed on and off for most of the week, but luck had deemed it to rain, washing away all traces of white. If there were to be a sharp frost tonight it would turn the ground under foot into a skating rink. They had started the week with two tons of rock salt on station, now they were down to just one last fire bucket full.

Jason knelt down beside his patient, praying that he would not notice the tremble in his voice caused by his own fear. Reaching out, he took Herbert's hand into his own, trying to act calm; he spoke with a cool, slow manner. Picking his words carefully, he explained what was needed to be done. The soft tones of his voice were saying, "Don't be scared – trust me."

Herbert's eyes were damp and tears rolled down either cheek, the fear clearly taking its toll. For the first time he questioned his survival and the thought crossed his mind 'Am I going to make it?'

His Glasgow coma scale was constantly monitored on route to hospital and the changes were noted. Thankfully the release of air trapped in the pleural cavity and the one – way flutter valve were enough to get him safely to the casualty unit where his injuries were treated in depth ...

Jason put away his equipment and signed himself off on the station log sheet, said his goodbyes to the night crew and headed for his car. He slid himself behind the wheel, turned the key in the ignition and the motor burst into life first time. Putting the gears into drive he set off towards home, all the while his mind was focused on the days work that he had just completed. Halfway home on a quiet stretch of road he could contain his frustrations no longer. He let out a scream that filled the inside of the car and punched the air. It was at this moment that he made the decision to think about early retirement. He did not know exactly when but vowed to at least think about it.

On arriving home his mood was transparent. Jason's wife had seen the signs many times before and knew that he must have had another bad day.

She also knew that the best way to handle the situation was to let him alone to unwind slowly and to keep well out of his way for a while until he overcame the depression that had gripped him. He would come round after he had filled his belly and calmed himself down; he always did given time. But today she sensed that something was different; he could hardly talk to her and his eyes were full with tears. "What has happened? I know when you have something on your mind."

Jason and his wife had talked for hours about his changing moods. The whole family knew that things were not as they should be. The stress was starting to get to him causing him, to bring his work home in the form of endless nightmares. Faceless shadows disturbed his sleep; pitiful cries filled his ears as they beckoned to him: dead staring eyes that seemed to be boring into his brain like surgeon's drills reaching into his very soul. They filled his head with whispered muttering's and the phenomenon of spectre shapes refused to leave him alone.

Waking in the middle of the night screaming with eyes bulging as if being chased by demons was normal for Jason. His body thrashed as if fighting some unseen creature, while water would be running off the surface of his skin like oozing juices from a peach, soaking the sheets of the bed with its wetness. This self-torture had been a way of life for some time and he knew that these obnoxious apprehensive spectres were of his own making. But he felt unable to exorcise their existence. His pent up feelings, which had been suppressed to hide the stress and inadequacies were fighting to get to the surface via his dreams. So far these haunting nightmares had not penetrated his performances while working out on the road, somehow he had managed to keep the lid on. But for how long? Olive wondered ...

CHAPTER NINE

Yesterday Jason and his wife had returned home from the local cemetery, after placing flowers on his mother's grave. It was the first time in months that he found himself thinking about his dear mother. He remembered his father, the hard man that never came home before the pubs shut. He recalled the many nights the drunken cursing of his father awakened the house as he crashed and staggered around. Remembering also the many nights that he lay awake listening to his parents argue, and never understanding why his mother had put up with this constant abuse. Most of all he remembered his father's thick leather belt and the way he cowered when he saw him release the buckle; then his screams as it was laid across his backside.

His father was a good man deep down, strong in body and mind.

Unfortunately when he took to the bottle, drinking heavy his personality changed. When sober he was a loving husband and dad, but with the drinking came episodes of violent aggression. Jason's father had in the past beaten his mother within an inch of her life whilst in a drunken rage. On one occasion he had physically beaten Jason for the loss of a ten-shilling note. His mother had tried controlling the situation and had received a beating for her trouble.

It was not so much the whipping, but the unjust punishment given. He had not lost the money deliberately and had walked around for over an hour trying to find it again. Jason could remember vowing never to treat his own wife and children in the same way when he grew up. He truly believed that the drink was solely responsible for the loss of most of his childhood without his father. When the drinking stopped and he was in a sober state, he would constantly promise to quit the booze and cure his tempers. But these promises wore thin when it was soon realised that these periods between drinking were soon forgotten. In fact, the episodes got steadily worse, until Jason's mother decided that she could not put up with the abuse any longer and soon after filed for a divorce. The sad thing was that they both still loved each other, but neither could cope with the demon drink that had taken control of their lives.

It was not long after that his father had suffered a bad stroke, leaving him paralysed down his right side; with speech and mobility now handicapped he was a sad sight to see.

Who was it that came to his rescue to look after him through his last years before he died, 'Mother'. She nursed him, cared for him and almost destroyed herself in the devoted way that she looked after the man that was no longer her husband.

Two days before Jason's father died his mother was verging on the edge of a nervous breakdown. In fact Jason had already set the wheels in motion with the doctor to have his father taken into hospital. Looking back, he felt that deep down his father knew that he had become a tremendous burden on his ex-wife ...

He had arrived early to start another duty; the station was still and the quiet peace was just what he needed. It had been his practice for some time to arrive ahead of time with the view to unwind and prepare himself for what the shift could bring. For twenty odd years he had faced the total despair of his patients, their families and the general public at large. He had faced death, carnage, sickness and just plain old stupidity. The price he had paid for this had taken its toll, affecting his health and state of mind. In his younger days Jason could have coped with anything that was handed to him, but now it was becoming an effort to force himself to get up and be ready for work.

The strain of all those years of pain from others had started to take over his body and soul. For as he slept at night all of the memories would come flooding into his dreams for him to relive over and over again, until it turned into a large shadow that he carried everywhere he went. On three occasions he had lost confidence in his ability to cope with his line of work almost to the edge of quitting. He was still good at his work, but the battle that was going on within himself caused him to become moody and short tempered with his own family.

Officers in charge of the day to day running of the service did not accept that there were such things as stress within the job. This made the staff afraid to admit that they had a problem; they just kept it bottled up inside and forced themselves to get on with it. But Jason knew that he had been to the edge of a breakdown three times now. Each of these periods he had reached down to the very depths of his self-control and struggled to pull himself back into the driving seat and fight on. Jason was much older now and he knew that the time was fast coming for him to give up the career that he had once loved. It was down to a stark choice: take early retirement or wait until he lost control with one of the Saturday night drunks and got suspended for his trouble.

People close to him would never guess that all these thoughts were bouncing around inside of his brain, for on the outside he forced himself to act like the rest of his colleagues. It was only his close family that any idea of the problems that he faced; he had to unload his frustrations onto someone or slip over the edge and be lost forever. His family was extremely worried about his stressful state of mind and they had been encouraging him to leave the service and seek early retirement. Even though he had felt like this for over four years, he could not afford to leave just yet, as the pension payments would not cover his expenses.

No, Jason would have to struggle on for a while longer. Just then the door opened and in walked Tom ...

Tom had known Jason for almost thirty years; they had worked together on the same Transport Company before joining the ambulance service. Both families had grown alongside each other

106

for the length of that time and they were friends as well as work mates. The difference between them was the social aspect. They would go out together for the odd meal or for a night down at the local pub or for week's abroad on arranged trips. But there the interest stopped; Tom being into sport and Jason was into computers or books.

The love of sports kept Tom lean and slender and he would dedicate most of his spare time down at the local sports centre. The fact was that he became almost fanatical about fitness. He would think nothing of working all night, then going down to the club for the odd hour's work-out followed by a long swim before going home to bed. He would often come into work boasting about how many laps of the pool he had achieved that day.

Jason was the complete opposite; he thrived on games that kept his mind alert. Games like chess, which required a board and pieces to sort out in his mind's eye. Or he would sit in front of the computer and the hours would slip past unnoticed. He was never the athletic type; in fact, to play a game of football would exhaust him. No Jason found most active sports bored him. In all probability that stemmed from the fact that he was not good at anything like athletic.

He was always the kid at school that dropped the ball or drew back from even the weakest tackle. He found joy in books and anything that challenged his mind. But his main love, apart from his family, was motor cars. Jason had a thing about cars; he just had to have that shining lump of metal no matter what the cost. And cost it did: he must have spent thousands of pounds over the years to justify his craze; at one time he changed his car four times in one year. But age and common sense now prevailed: he could turn away from the car showrooms without a backward glance.

The two partners worked well together, each knowing almost what the other was thinking without a word being spoken. They both knew that if there was any trouble the other would be on hand to back him up. Good partners were hard to come by; it took time to build up the trust and respect that made a good team. Being long-term friends made it easy for Tom and Jason; they were like brothers...

The first call of the day was a regular patient that they took to the hospital outpatients department. Arthur Doyle was a frail diabetic who had suffered years of rheumatoid arthritis and could no longer make his own way to hospital. Jason loved to convey this old boy, for each time that he travelled a new story would emerge. Most would not give him a second glance but this frail old man, if anyone took the time to look beyond those tired eyes and listened to his stories, would find that Arthur Doyle was a man of extreme courage.

He became involved with his first love while at Durham University: she was a human dynamo and her vigorous activities were boundless, as was her love for Arthur. The two undergraduates lived life simply, studying by day and enjoying each other's closeness at night.

Alicia started to receive worrying news from home. Spain was not a secure place to be at this time; the letters she received from her family were full of upsetting stories of suffering and bloody attempts to suppress the peasant population. The regular troops, led by an insensitive, Socialistic government, were killing and torturing hundreds of Spain's young men and women, who had received years of repression before rebelling against the unjust authority.

Alicia could not stand to sit back and do nothing about the problem back in her own country. Arthur and Alicia were soon bound for the shores of Spain along with many others who, caught up in the tide of passion, wanted to help. They had both joined the freedom fighters like many other volunteers to help take on the Socialist government. In those dark days French, British and

Americans fought bloody battles along side the peasant population of Spain. Men and women struggled side by side; the only requirements were a belief in the cause and the survival of the group. Dozens of innocent people were wantonly murdered; madmen on a single impulse would gloat as they performed mass assassinations of men, women and children all in the name Communism.

The stories that Arthur told of many slaughtered victims of that so-called legitimate government and the ruthless methods used against Spain's innocent people had given Jason a history lesson that he could never have learnt at school. The partisan army acted like swarms of bees, stinging the tail of the government troops. Their weapons were old and in poor condition; many rifles would explode as they were fired; captured arms were a prize to take.

Their lives had been hard during those vicious times when many families would simply vanish overnight never to be seen again. They were indeed dark depressing times that were hard for any civilised nation to comprehend, but for those that lived through the darkness came a new bright light of hope. The reports of these terrible atrocities that were taking place slowly leaked out of a country that had tried to hide the horrors from the outside world.

Pressures would soon be brought to this shameless administration, for the power of the media was stacked against its politicians. Arthur fought with Alicia by his side and loved her until the day she died, not in battle, or a death of glory, but walking with friends along a quite road. There had been a dog-fight in the air and no one knows if it was an enemy or friendly aircraft, but Alicia and two of her close friends were killed in a hail of bullets fired at the other craft.

When he heard the news of her death Arthur was beside himself with grief; his mind refused to take on board the truth and after they buried her in a makeshift grave, he went off to grieve alone. Arthur could not stay in Spain after that and within weeks he had crossed to the coast and returned to England. The ideals were gone; with the death of his lover there would be no more fighting for him. He would put aside the ideals that had driven him to fight on a foreign soil, until the Hitler invasion. But that was another story ...

When they had arrived at Arthur's house they were meet at the door by his sister. She had politely asked the crew to step inside, as Arthur was not quite ready. "I just have to finish getting him dressed and he will be right with you." This was not like some of the homes that Tom and Jason were used to walking into, this house was well decorated and there was well cared for furniture placed around the rooms; personal objects were all around, displayed with pride by their owners. These were strangely familiar objects that Jason had not seen for many years, since his younger days living with his parents. Yes, these were the perks of the job: to be privileged by being allowed into other people's homes and to share the pleasures that had taken many years to collect. This was like taking a trip down memory lane into a world of antiques. Many of these older patients were sitting on little gold mines with some of the items that they had collected over the years. Most would not part with their heirlooms, anyway, but the odd one or two could live in luxury for the rest of their lives by cashing in on the old article sitting quietly in a dark corner of a room gathering dust.

Arthur and his sister entered the room. "Morning lads, where are we off to this time? Brighton?" he asked jokingly.

"Anywhere you like. We could do with run out of town," exclaimed Tom, knowing full well that they were tied down taking him only to the local clinic. But it was their usual banter to try and raise a smile or two and take the patient's mind off their problems for a short while.

Although Arthur was in good spirits this morning the crew knew that he must be worried about the outcome of today's clinic appointment. For today's results would reveal if he were to keep one of his legs or not. A common problem with some long-term diabetics, damaged arteries suggested that he might have to undergo surgery to amputate at least part of a leg. Because of the loss of elasticity and thickening of the arteries caused by the diabetes, his legs lacked full circulation. Arthur's toes had shown signs of gangrene turning black through the loss of blood supply reaching the flesh around the toes. They were basically rotting away.

Jason looked across to Arthur's sister; she swayed perilously for a moment as if about to faint and he realised that she was close to tears. Putting his arm around her shoulders he attempted to comfort her. She tilted her head upwards and signalled her approval briefly with her eyes, so as not to alarm her brother. She frowned as her anxiety deepened; she was worried about the hospital results and the effects that they might have on her brother's mobility. She had been under pressure for sometime but had managed to hide it from Arthur until now.

As previously mentioned Arthur Doyle was a man of extreme courage and even something as realistic as this horrifying prospect he managed to turn it into a trivial matter. He would face what ever despondent situation came his way and handle it as he always did with any crisis.

"Let's go then, lads, we need to find out if I am going to be legless by the end of the week, and you can take that anyway you like," he said with a laugh. He continued like that the whole journey to the hospital, but they all knew that he was terrified at the prospect of losing part of his body to a surgeon's knife.

On arrival at the hospital they dropped Arthur and his sister off at the clinic and booked him in at the reception desk for the appointment.

"See you later on, mate, we both wish you the best of luck," said Tom. Jason squeezed the sister's hand and told her to try and relax a little. They all said their goodbyes and the two paramedics walked away to get ready for the next call.

"He really is a nice bloke. What a way to end up after all that he has gone through," said Jason as he mounted the vehicle. He radioed through to the controller. "We are green and available, what are your wishes, Oh wise one?" he said jokingly. They were indeed fortunate for they were given a transfer journey to London with a wait and return option. This would take up the rest of the day, a dream ticket to most crews for it meant the pressure was off and they could relax for the remainder of the shift.

Their call was to take one of their regular children to Great Ormond Street Hospital for treatment. Young Jamie Wilson was a familiar patient with most of the crews; he had suffered from Hydrocephalus or 'water on the brain,' caused in his case by inflammation on the meninges during his infancy. He was also susceptible to fits and was a chronic asthmatic hence the need for a qualified ambulance crew. Many nights his mother had been forced to call for an emergency ambulance to rush her son to the local hospital to control the fits or yet another asthma attack.

These trips to London were enjoyable for Jamie was an angelic child who could melt the coldest heart. His one treat was that on the return journey the crews would make an unauthorised stop at the drive-in burger bar for a special reward. It was sheer joy to see that little lad's face light up when they pulled into the car park. That fifteen-minute stop made the trauma that his treatment caused worth while.

The day had gone well without any mishaps and after dropping Jamie and his mother off, they made their way back to the station for a prompt finish and a couple of days rest before the Christmas season began in earnest ...

CHAPTER TEN

Jason was in agony knowing that he would be working over the Christmas period. He would miss his Christmas dinner and he would not get the chance to see his grandchildren open their presents for yet another year. The worst thing of all was he would not be spending the day with his wife. He had worked like this for the past twenty of the twenty-two years of service, often wishing that he had the courage to make excuses for not showing up for work.

Flicking the switch of the bedside light he settled down for the night, hoping that sleep would come quickly. So many nights he had drifted into a dream that put him back at work and in the middle of some major incident; It would seem so real that when he woke the memories were astoundingly vivid. The faces haunting him in every dream always, there to remind him of some previous tragedy, mirrored visions that were reflected in his mind, pestering his sleep as they whispered to him. These strange sensations were almost overwhelming, driving him on through out the night; desperation pierced his emotions until the relief of his waking moment gave way to reality ...

Christmas morning arrived and the house was silent as he eased himself quietly out of the bed, trying hard not to disturb his sleeping wife lying alongside. He felt drained, as if he had been awake all night; his head was thumping the pain causing him to grit his teeth.

Moving towards the drug cupboard he opened the door and found something to ease the pounding headache. Outside in the dawn of morning the first birds were waking and their soft song filled the air. There was a snow on the rooftops, sparkling crisp and white, but at least the snow had eased away to a gentle flurry.

After his morning wash and shave he moved to the kitchen, placing two slices of bread in the toaster; he then flicked the

113

switch of the kettle. He stopped and glanced at his reflection in the mirror: he looked haggard and drawn, but he knew that things would improve after the first cup of coffee touched his lips.

Thirty minutes later, after his normal routine was almost completed, he put the final touches to his uniform and crept into the bedroom to kiss his wife goodbye. He reached down and lightly kissed his wife on the forehead. "Sorry to invade your sleep but I'm off to work now, merry Christmas," he whispered.

His wife gave a little sigh before turning over once again into the warmth of the bed covers. Making his way towards the front door; he turned briefly, looking back at the bedroom before stepping out into the cold morning air ...

Charlie Walton became conscious of his own breathing; the pain in his chest was outrageous, cutting deep like a sharp knife. He clutched at his breastbone as if to try and pull out the object that caused the crushing discomfort; this was the worst pain he had ever felt.

Born in 1915 he had lived through two world wars, a time when fifty-shillings would purchase a smart suit of clothes, a long-playing record would cost sixpence (that's about two and a half pence at today's value). His wages were paid in pounds shillings and pence; thirty old pennies were then called half a crown and went a long way.

Like many other young men of that time he joined the army to help their country fight against Hitler's hordes. He spent his time with the Royal Engineers, first in a bomb disposal unit; then on to building bailey bridges after his nerves got the better of him. For many more times than he deserved he had been busted back to the ranks, being de-mobbed as a lance-jack. This was not to say that he remained innocent, most of the charges brought against him were well founded.

In his own way, he made the best of his time in the services.

You could say he enjoyed his war, but that was his character and no one could change him.

On leaving the army he went to live in a small cottage, which he shared it with his senile grandmother on the far side of the town. She was his only living relative and although she spent most of her remaining days drunk as a skunk, he still held full respect for her, even though she always wore a strong smell of whisky on her breath. Her tormented life ended abruptly when she slipped and cracked her head on the hard stone floor, the look of surprise still held firmly on her dying features. Charlie had never married; he spent his life quietly living in the cottage, keeping himself private and reserved.

Like his grandmother before him, he liked a stiff drink now and then and spent many nights at the 'White Swan' public house on the other side of town. Most nights he could be observed his body swaying slightly as he made his way unsteadily home. He would hear the whispers of the locals asking 'how many drinks did he have?'

Charlie had spent hours at the local casualty department getting patched up after falling over a wall or tripping up a kerbstone on his way home from one of these binges. Now his tired creaky old bones objected to every movement they made, he could not get about like he used to. In his aged years Charlie's bladder made him go to the toilet with frequency. It had caused him the anxiety of many sleepless nights and the embarrassment of waking to find his crumpled bed-soaking wet with a large yellowing stain that had settled through to the mattress.

On this night he awoke with an urgent need to empty his bowels and bladder at the same time. He eased his creaky frame out of the bed and made his way towards the bathroom at the end of the narrow hallway. His hand gripped between his crutch, trying desperately to hold back the inevitable flow. The hall was in darkness and he had to slide his spare hand along the wall until he located the light switch. With one quick flick the hallway was illuminated. 'That's better' – he could see his way forward to the toilet door. He cursed as he realised he was too late: a large yellow stain started to spread across and down the front of his pyjamas. He had pissed himself.

It was at this time when sitting on the toilet seat that the shearing pain returned to attack his chest. Cold wet sweats drenched his shaking body and he found that breathing had become hard and laboured. His eyes closed with the pain and the knuckles of his right hand turned white as he clenched the side rail for support. The squeezing around his chest was becoming unbearable and he knew that he had to get help urgently. Easing himself off the toilet, he crawled out of the bathroom towards the telephone table in his bedroom, stopping only when the chest pains became too much for him to bear. Those few feet from the bathroom to the bedroom seemed to take forever, but in fact only minutes ...

The two paramedics sat watching the television trying to relax while they had the chance. Jason felt a bit peckish and decided to have a chocolate binge. He reached out towards his uniform jacket that was lying over the back of a spare chair and sinking his hand into one of the pockets, pulled out a fist-full of change. He had a quick count, took what he needed and replaced the rest back into the coat.

"I am just going to the corner shop, I think he is still open. Is there anything you need while I'm there?" he asked.

"No. I'm ok, if a call comes in I'll give a couple of blasts on the two-tones," replied his partner.

Jason did not even reach the front door before the station alarm went of with a deafening pitch. They had been given a 'Cardiac arrest', the most fearful of all emergency calls, mainly because it required the most intense amount of skill and work plus the fact that someone's life was at stake.

Tom set the vehicle into racetrack mode, driving like the devil himself was on their tails. He pushed the gearbox to its limits as he snaked his way through the traffic in front of them, cursing out loud when a car in front did not respond quickly enough or caused them to slow down. The sirens and blue lights normally work well and most drivers respond quick but there is always the odd one or two that either panic or are driving in a dream world and just don't know you are there. Worst offenders are those with their radio sets turned up so loud that they cannot hear anything outside the vehicle they are driving.

The smell of the hot engine oil and brakes filled the cab as they sped their way towards the location given. By now the adrenaline was coursing through Jason's body as he went through the protocols visualised in his mind, not that he needed to, for when the chips were down he went into automatic pilot mode ...

Charlie reached for the phone and dialled 999, then, struggling to get the words out, he managed just – ambulance – pain – quickly - and the address as the sharp, crushing pains intensified. His chest felt like it was going to explode at any moment; heavy perspiration oozed onto the surface of his body and he sensed the chill of death sweep over him. He tried to call out, but the sounds stuck tight in his throat; his vocal cords were paralysed, allowing just a gasp of air to escape.

The room around him seemed blurred. He swayed, then, reaching out, tried to steady himself. Flux hit the back of his throat and the burning acid caused him to get a sudden urge to vomit. This was when the stark reality told his ageing brain that it was about to die. Fear spread across his face, the kind of fear that comes only once, when you realise that you are alone and that you are about to kick the bucket. A single tear rolled slowly down the side of his left cheek. Then the pressure started to build; a terrible pain tore into him and continued to intensify until his heart could stand the pain no longer. His lips, ears and nose

117

turned purple, perspiration poured out of every exit in his skin and he felt the cold chill of fear. Boom – dit – Boom – dit – Boom –d – Boo— then his heart stopped and he was still ...

By the time the ambulance had arrived, Charlie was no longer in a position to open the door to let in the crew. Tom and Jason searched frantically for an open window for them to gain an entry point. There was none to be found they had to make a quick decision; did they call for police presents or break a window and force an entry themselves?

Fortunately the control operator had decided to contact the police when the call was dispatched and they arrived just as Tom went to look for a large object to chuck at the window by the front door. The police were experienced in this sort of forced entry and had the door opened in seconds. Jason soon located Charlie slumped by the phone where he had uttered his dying words.

His skin was a blue – purple, suggesting that his heart had stopped some time ago, but the flesh was still warm to touch. Tom set up the defibrillator and attached the leads to the victim's chest. The monitor showed just a straight line on the tiny screen.

"He's in Asystole," shouted Tom, who had started cardiopulmonary resuscitation while Jason sorted the drugs and intubation equipment needed to carry out the procedures necessary. Tom eased off as Jason moved the Laryngoscope forwards into Charlie's mouth gently easing the tip past familiar landmarks until he caught sight of the white strands of the vocal cords. He gripped the laryngoscope firmly with his left hand and skilfully slid the endotracheal tube down alongside the blade, giving a sigh of relief when he saw the tube pass through the vocal cords and into the trachea. He quickly secured the tube and inflated the cuff to hold it into position.

Then, connecting the ventilating bag, gave two squeezes to inflate the lungs while checking with a stethoscope to see if the endotracheal tube was correctly sighted by listening to both sides of the upper chest. This procedure sounds simple but there are many pitfalls that can happen while the operation take place: damage to teeth, tissue and vocal cords to name but a few. Satisfied that the procedure had been a success, he opened two adrenaline syringes and shot them both down the tube before commencing CPR once more.

Tom broke off for a few minutes to insert a wide bore intravenous sheaf into a suitable vein to allow better drug access. Both men knew that they were on a losing streak before they started but protocols insisted on resuscitation being attempted no matter what.

Jason and Tom, like many other crews, wished that they, like their counterparts in the hospitals, had the power just to let them give the dignity of death and let the patient go peacefully.

But because they were not in the position to judge the overall prognosis, they had to attempt resuscitation even if they knew it was pointless.

In some cases it was a good procedure, for it helped the relatives to think that the paramedics had at least tried to win them back. Jason had often talked about having a tattoo placed on his chest with the words. "Piss off paramedics," or "Do not resuscitate or else."

They went through the full Asystole protocol, driven on by the fact that it was Christmas day, a time of joy for most of the world. They tried everything but the outcome remained that poor Charlie had departed this mortal coil on the 25th of December alone and fearful. His peace and goodwill were lost in the crushing pains that erupted within his chest. His tormented life was finally at an end and yet he wore a smile on his face that almost described relief.

Jason informed the police that they had done all that was possible and asked if they could try and trace any relatives that he may have had. Next thing was to contact the hospital and notify them that they were coming into casualty with a dead on arrival.

"What a crap thing to happen on today of all days," remarked Jason.

Tom looked around the room; a room that was sparse with just a few personal belongings scattered around; not one single decoration adorned this house.

Sadly Charlie had been one of the many neglected old people living alone, either by relatives or social workers who had gone to the door and for some reason had not entered. Maybe they had not got an answer when they knocked or they had witnessed the queasy aroma oozing out from under the door. Whatever the reason, this old man had died alone like many of this nations elderly population. This was not a lot to show for someone's life, but how were they to determine that?

Outside both men stood forcing themselves to take deep breaths, sucking in the cold fresh air as if their lives depended on it ...

Chapter Eleven

They were instructed to make their way to the hospital for emergency cover. This was the chance they had been waiting for; it was Christmas and the food was in plentiful supply. Control was well aware of this factor, using the stand-by as a way of saying thank you for the effort throughout the year.

The good thing about working on the ambulance service is that you get to know all the doctors and nurses on a personal basis. You get to know how good they are with patients and the scope of their medical skills. Although most of the staff was extremely qualified and skilled medically, the odd one or two lacked tact when discussing patients conditions with the crews: forgetting they can hear most of what is being said about them and forgetting their fears.

Another good side of working alongside casualty staff on a regular basis is that when you need care for yourself or a loved one, they bend the waiting times in your favour a little. The down side is you have to have a good sense of humour to cope with the continuous wise cracks that are slung at you. There is also the social aspect; all emergency services have an interactive affinity towards each other. The party life is not quite as strong now as it used to be because of the working environment but there are still lots that have inter - service involvement.

Tom and Jason got on really well with most of the casualty team and were made extremely welcome in the staff room where they had set up enough food and drink to last through to next Christmas. They stayed as long as they dared, not wanting to push control over the edge.

Tom gave his favourite nurse a big hug and kiss before they departed. Saying their farewells, they made their way to the waiting ambulance and the inevitable next call. Jason thanked the controller for their indulgence and they headed back to the comfort of the station.

They had not gone far when Jason had this overwhelming need to pass water. So much coffee had caused his bladder to feel heavy and overloaded. He shifted his position, trying to take his mind off the powerful urge to urinate. Turning to face Tom he almost pleaded with him to put his foot down and make all haste towards the ambulance station.

"I'm bursting for a pee and if you don't hurry I am not going to make it back."

Tom thought for a moment about making some wisecrack, but the look on his colleague's face described the discomfort that he felt. He did as he was asked and put his foot down heavy on the throttle.

No sooner had they arrived into the station yard, than the radio alarm sounded. "Oh shit. Take the details for me, Tom, I can't make another job without a trip to the loo." The ache in his crotch was too much; for his throbbing bladder was now at bursting point and overshadowed everything else. He ran to the station door and opened it faster than he had ever done before; he rushed to the toilet, unzipped his fly and with a great sigh of relief he let go of his pressure pot.

Tom smiled as he watched his partner race back to the vehicle, climb aboard and sink flagged into the seat. He handed the job details to Jason and asked, "Are you feeling better now!"

"If only you knew how close I was to peeing my pants back then." Lifting the slip of paper he read the job details, ' attempted suicide in car.'

Most attempted suicides fail but the hose in the car jobs normally make the full trip to another place. No one just grabs a hose on the spur of the moment and decides to end it all; they normally spend a lot of time and effort carefully planning every move.

Locations are picked miles from populated areas where they are sure that the chances of being detected are slim. To complete this act you either have to be extremely brave or so depressed that there are no alternatives. The normal cry for help is done with an overdose with just enough taken to guarantee survival ...

Jan Van-Hinsbergh sat by the lake on his six acre small-holding, watching the trout swim and play with the brief sparkle on the watery surface. Life had been kind: his business gave him a good half – million pound turn over each year, and he did very little work himself, being quite content to let others slave away while he sat back and collected the profits. He had once told one of his children that. "One should never do the work while you have money to pay for others to do the work for you." Jan had never known what it was to worry about finances as he had come from one of the rich families in Holland. It was taken for granted that whatever he needed his parents would always provide, until the day came when he upset the head of this proud family and he was cast out with just enough to start again from scratch. He had decided to try his luck in England where he still had one or two business friends who would give much needed contacts.

It was not long after his arrival in Britain, when on one very special day he had walked into a public house and there sitting at the bar was one of the most radiant ladies he had ever seen. Her sparkling eyes and fiery red hair made her stand out from the crowd. After a short courtship Ann agreed to marry him, and from that moment his world changed for the better. They started a small nursery, growing flowers for special occasions and selling the excess bulbs back to his contacts in Holland.

After a few years had passed and his bank balance had grown, they sold the nursery and purchased the six acre spread, It consisted of three acres of under – glass growing area, beautiful gardens and grounds, a well stocked lake, ample paddocks and a very large car park. There was a large five bedroom, Dutch design house with an open planned ground floor and small auxiliary rooms. The lake had been well stocked with good size trout and a small rowboat to enable him to reach the tiny island in its centre.

They had almost everything, except for one missing factor. Ann could not have children and this had put a large blot on their contentment. When they finally considered adoption they had not gone with the intention of coming back with three children. But that was the number that they settled for. Ann had been unable to make up her mind and to save the heart rendering decision of which child to choose, they adopted two sweet little girls and a cute blue eyed-baby boy,

For nineteen years they had all lived and worked on the estate and enjoyed their lives to the full. Jan and his wife had been good to the children over the years and they were loved as if they were their birth children. Life had been sweet for this family and even the past rifts with the relatives in Holland had been resolved.

Not satisfied with the flower and bulb business, Jan started to play the stock markets. Concentrating on the commodity shares like gold, silver, oil and coffee. He did extremely well. At first it was easy money, he could make a quick ten thousand in a few short minutes just by making a phone call, and of course pre - guessing the correct way that the shares were to go. It got so that he did not have to get up from his chair; his luck was holding extremely well and with the knack of forecasting the changing values of stocks, was soon able to make a name for himself amongst the brokers.

For almost two years Jan found a new source of income, but it made him neglect the small-holding business. This was easy money and he intended to milk it for all its worth. But nothing stays the same forever and pretty soon things started to go wrong. Making a bad prediction time after time made the slow depreciation tend to nibble gradually away at his assets until the inevitable

124

happened. He started to chase lost money without the funds to pay the brokers. The more he tried to recoup his losses, the deeper the spiral became until he could no longer get anyone to give credit. The banks closed ranks; the brokers chased him for money he no longer had and even the Inland Revenue wanted a slice of his empty purse.

He could see no way out – he could not pay – he could not run and he had nothing left to sell. As a last resort he turned to his Dutch family for help: tail between his legs he pleaded for their support. But they shunned him completely, having no time for anyone who could lose everything the way Jan had.

As the depression set ever deeper he could see no way to improve the problems that he had created. He cursed his foolish behaviour. Never having to work for anyone or being able to turn his hand to manual labour made the situation worse. He was too proud to beg. The solution was easy, but did he have the bottle to do it?

Jan sat and contemplated his options. His first choice was to take an overdose of drugs: he knocked back a whole bottle along with a half litre of Scotch whisky. He had expected that the contents of the drug bottle would send him off to sleep and that would be an end to his misery, but it did not work out that way. He was discovered and dispatched to hospital for a washout. The Doctor gave him a lecture on the stupidity of taking an overdose, as they don't act as a quick fix, believing that Jan had taken them as some grand gesture to draw a sympathetic reaction from his loved ones.

"Paracetamol the drug taken, when consumed in large doses, attacks the liver and kidneys. What many don't realise is that, if treatment is not dealt with quickly, it can result in a terrible death, taking days not hours to work," explained the doctor.

It was up to the casualty doctor as to what treatment would be required. This would range from Naloxone intravenously.

Activated Charcoal Emetic or Stomach Lavage washes. If they were trying to put the patient off repeating an overdose, the washout would be used, not a pleasant experience for anyone. Some repeat offenders are prone to violence, normally with nursing staff rather than ambulance crews. The 'Crack' overdoses are not at all happy after a big shit of a paramedic has shot them full of 'Naloxone' and blown away their expensive fix. The problem with naloxone is that, although fast reacting, it is a short-lived treatment and the overdose can slip back into respiratory distress very quickly. Junkies had told Jason to 'Foxtrot Oscar' more times than he could remember, after many occasions of arriving to find the patient in respiratory arrest and looking like a good candidate for an 'Al Jolson' movie, face blue – black through the lack of oxygen.

By managing the airway and giving a bolus of naloxone, amazing results were achieved; it was like waving a medic magic wand. But do they get thanks for saving a life? Do they hell! As like, all they get is a mouthful of foul abuse and insults. You would think that once their partners had explained to them how close to death they had come, they would never go near drugs again. 'Wrong, wrong, wrong'. As soon as they could raise enough money to buy 'crack' they would be at it all over again without a second's hesitation.

It would have been totally unprofessional to say what went through Jason's mind; these people made him so furious at times through sheer frustration. He had to fight hard to hang onto the thought that he had done what was expected, anything above that was out of his hands ...

Ann knew that Jan was determined to produce his own suicide and he had talked over his plans in great detail, explaining why he needed to complete this task. It takes a really brave or desperate person to be that serious about his or her own death, and Jan was both brave and serious.

Ann had sat with her husband all through the day and most of the night discussing the way to end their troubled minds; Ann wanted to end the marriage the way it had started, 'together,' for she could not imagine life without her husband by her side. They invited the family to an early Christmas dinner the day before Christmas Eve, with the pretext that they were going to spend the holiday away in a hotel. The children suspected nothing, as Jan and his wife had done this many times before.

With the exchange of presents, plenty of food and drink, they sat down and said their goodbyes, the children blissfully unaware that it would be the final Christmas that they would spend together.

On the Christmas Eve Ann and her husband spent the day putting their personal papers and lives' possessions in order, then sat and wrote a letter to each member of the family in turn, trying to explain why they had made this drastic choice. That night they drank, made love, and fell asleep in each other's arms just like young lovers. They woke early and around four-thirty drove off into the country. They had decided to end their lives in the family car, and that was how they were to be found the next morning...

The two paramedics had arrived at a quiet spot frequented by courting couples; the car had been parked slightly off the road and nosed into some trees. They had not had any trouble finding its location as it was surrounded by police cars on their arrival; two police officers were attempting resuscitation on the vehicle occupants. "They are still warm," yelled one of the officers.

Tom and Jason both hurriedly peeled themselves out of the ambulance and rushed to either side of the car. The police were right: they were both still warm, but the heater was fixed to full and the officers confirmed that the engine was still running when they had arrived on scene.

Jason examined the driver. Searching around his lower extremities confirmed his suspicions. There he found the tell tale pooling, (where, after a long period of non-circulating blood, it lays at the lowest level.) Closer examination revealed signs of rigor mortis.

"I'm afraid they have been dead for some time The reason they still feel warm is the heater," explained Jason.

A vacuum cleaner hose had been attached to the tail pipe of the car and the other end taped to the window. It was hard to say how long they had sat in each other's arms, quietly drinking brandy and inhaling the exhaust fumes until their lungs could no longer make exchanges of air. The carbon monoxide had given them both a cherry red appearance.

At first glance they looked as if they had just both slept in the car overnight and that they would wake at any minute. It was hard to believe they were dead.

'Sorry, lads, there is nothing we can do for them. It's all down to your police surgeon now. Time of death 11.45 Hrs. Merry Christmas, I don't think ..."

Jason picked up the radio handset and called Ambulance control. "We are now green after the last red call."

"Roger. You can return to station for accident cover," replied the control operator.

The roads were much clearer, although the snow still retained a firm hold on the grass verges and footpaths. Watching the people outside struggling to make headway gave them comfort, for they had the warmth of the cab heaters to give them some solace.

Tom made good time on the journey back to base spurred on by the prospect of liquid refreshments. He reversed the vehicle into the garage bay, for he dare not leave it outside in this weather. The last thing they wanted was a call and the vehicle would not start.

On station they sat down with a much-needed drink to await the next job, knowing that it would not be long before they were called out again. Jason asked Tom about his son, who was also trying to get into the service.

"Has he received a letter from personnel yet? In all probability he should pass the entrance exam this time," said Jason.

"He will know next week. Hopefully, the news will be good this time around," replied Tom.

The entrance exams were getting much harder to accomplish now. Since the early 1990's, from the time of the longest industrial dispute known to the ambulance service, changes had occurred with a swift determination,

There is little doubt that the dispute advanced the emergency ambulance service out of the depths and into the modern mode of today. It was well recorded that previous Governments had looked upon the ambulance man as just another driver to pick up the sick and injured and convey them to the nearest place of care, even within the health profession, most only had a basic understanding of what the purpose of the ambulance-man was. In truth they were a highly skilled and very well trained professional organisation. It was soon acknowledged that it would not take much effort or cost to advance these skills and the paramedic as we know it today was born.

The telephone rang. Jason picked up the receiver and answered; it was the control operator.

"Could you please make your way to the local Railway Station for emergency cover, all our vehicles in the area are on calls and you are the only ambulance for a twenty mile radius."

"Well that was short-lived. No peace for the wicked!" exclaimed Jason.

Within minutes they had reluctantly mounted the vehicle and Tom set off towards the stand-by point. They had not travelled two miles when the radio inside the cab burst into life. Jason picked up the hand mike and responded. The controller immediately started to pass her message. "Take details of red call three six zero, location is given as 58, Broad Street, Weston - believed to be a burst 'Varicose Vein' - control out." Jason read back the details to confirm that he had received the entire message correctly.

Tom flicked the switches to activate the blues and twos and gunned the ambulance towards the address given. The location was well known to them, as it was a large block of old people's residential flats. It took just a couple of minutes to reach their destination. Speed was essential, for a simple call such as this could end up as a fatality.

They were met at the front door by the warden, who told them "that the flat they wanted was at the top of the stairs to the right."

On arrival at the correct flat they found the front door slightly ajar. "Hello! is anyone about?" shouted Tom, but he was greeted with silence. Not being completely sure that this was indeed the right flat, they opened the door with caution and went inside. Tom looked into the bedroom and Jason went into the lounge, but no signs of life were found. They kept on calling out but still no answer then. They opened the bathroom door and were greeted with a horrific sight. There on the floor was amassed a large pool of blood at the feet of an old lady sitting in a chair. She was so pallid that she almost looked transparent, white hair hanging limply on her shoulders Her breathing was very laboured and she made no response to touch or sound.

Jason had seen this before and he knew that they needed to act quickly if they were going to have a chance of saving this lady. Tom moved rapidly to put a large dressing on her ankle, at the same time Jason gave the woman oxygen from a portable unit.

"She is almost bled out, we must get some fluids into her. I need to get a drip set up, if she is going to have any chance at all," said Jason.

"What equipment do you need?" Tom asked.

Jason's mind was already racing, for he was remembering a similar situation a couple of years previous when they had found a man that had bled to death from the same type of injury. "Right, you had better get me a green. I do not think that I can get anything larger into her, she has almost shut down completely," Jason replied.

With a great deal of luck Jason managed to find an obliging vein and with one slick movement he slid the needle forward and secured the plastic sheaf into place. Quickly he set up a fast running drip with a bag of "Crystalloid Solution"; this was a good treatment for replacing fluids for blood loss cases.

"I can't find a readable blood pressure, it must be in her boots," said Tom.

"Well, I am not surprised, we had better get moving or we are going to lose this lady," Jason responded. The urgency sounded in his voice. This had been one of the worst cases that he had seen. Alive, that is!

Jason was left to care for the old lady while Tom went back to the Ambulance to collect the equipment required to get the woman down the stairs and into the vehicle. Once the patient was loaded, Jason asked Tom to contact control and give them an update on the lady's condition, also a rough estimated time of arrival at the hospital.

As soon as Tom returned with the equipment they hurriedly scooped her into the carry chair and carried her down to the waiting motor. They loaded her into the back and set off fast towards the casualty unit. What ever they had done so far was only a stabilising action, and she needed urgent hospital treatment to get her out of the woods. On route to the hospital the fluids that were given started to take effect: along with the high concentration of oxygen the lady started to show signs of slight improvement.

131

Looking down at her Jason gave a sigh as once again he interrupted his thoughts to remember the frailty of his own mother just before her passing. She had looked so tired, then distant, as if she was engrossed in some deep thought or dark problem. The dehydration caused total confusion and at times her eyes would be staring straight ahead as if transfixed. It was almost as if her body was in the room but her mind was elsewhere. By the time they arrived at the hospital the patient was trying to remove the mask from her face, her bewilderment causing an agitated state ...

They quickly unloaded the stretcher; the woman now struggling to free herself from the restraint straps, her confused mind unaware that they were only trying to help. Tom and Jason wheeled the patient directly into the resuscitation unit, where they were greeted by the stand-by team that had been waiting for them to arrive.

Jason gave the staff of the casualty department a brief history, giving the facts of what their treatment and findings had been to date.

"Sounds like she is very lucky. Thank you, lads, well done," said the Consultant ...

Tom and Jason booked the lady in at the reception desk, finished up the paper work and made their way to the nurses' rest room for a cup of Christmas cheer and a few mince pies.

So far it had been a pig of a Christmas day and Jason wished that he was at home with his family, a drink in one hand and the TV control box in the other. Two of the nurses came into the rest room and after moaning about the amount of work that Jason and his mate had caused them, they wished them both a merry Christmas. (Not that there was much of it left.)

Outside, they took in a full breath of air; the job had been a real close call. If they had been a few minutes later, it was most probable that the lady would not have made it. It was a nice feeling to win one back, especially after the last couple of calls.

The rest of the duty was made up of mostly Doctors' calls and transfers between hospitals, that was, until the last job came in. Working twelve hourly shifts made it a very long day. It could be a nightmare if things were going badly. This last call was going to finish their Christmas with a bang ...

They were just about to get ready for the changeover with the night shift, when the last call came in over the radio. Tom picked up the hand mike and started to take down the details given him by the controller. "We are sorry about this but there are no other vehicles to send at the moment. There has been a serious road traffic accident involving a child and a car. We have no other details for you as yet but we will try and update you on route. Control out."

"Just our flaming luck I was looking forward to finishing," said Jason.

The two paramedics jumped into the cab and they set off down the road like bats out of hell, lights and music going full blast. For when children are involved every ambulance person senses a special need for urgency; above all else they had to get there as quickly as they could and that required taking a few chances.

They were lucky that the roads were clear of snow but they still needed to be cautious, as they were very wet from the melting snow running off the banks on either side. Tom negotiated the vehicle through the traffic like a snake going through the grass; his foot pushed down hard onto the accelerator pedal as they raced to the accident, their minds were working overtime. They both had a good indication of what was going to greet them, for they had witnessed the same many times before.

The ambulance turned the corner and they saw a large crowd congregated to the right hand side of the road. Tom was out of the vehicle like a shot and made his way quickly towards the crowd that had gathered around a small child of about ten years old. Alongside him lay a bicycle that was totally wrecked, its wheels were twisted and the front forks were bent backwards.

"Can you all give us some room to work in, please," Jason boomed at the crowd of people that were all trying to get a close look at the child. It always amazed him why people crowded round any form of tragedy. What pleasure did they get from other folk's misfortune or was it just plain morbid interest?

"Is there anyone with this child or anyone who knows where he lives?" he asked. They were told that the lad lived locally but his mother was out at present and was not expected back for a while yet.

Jason and Tom set to work with cool determination as they both assessed the scene and appraised the child's injuries, all the while asking questions of the bystanders, "Has he been moved at all since the accident? Or did anyone see it happen?"

Both minds of the crew were racing as they took in all that the voices coming from the crowd were telling them, at the same time they were making observations on the condition of the child that lay in front of them. Visual observations told them that the child had three long sliced wounds, one to his head, one about four inches deep on his right leg and a large open wound to the right arm.

It was unlikely that the child had been knocked out, as the witnesses had all agreed that he started screaming almost immediately. But to be safe, Jason slipped a neck collar onto the child just in case. He had checked the back of the boy's head and down the neck, looking for any deformities, but he had found nothing that gave cause for concern. The ears, nose and mouth had been checked for fluid loss; he had also checked the eyes for pupil reaction and to make sure they were equal, this being a early indication of any trouble inside the skull.

At this moment Tom asked Jason if he was happy to start to dress the wounds. "Just lay dressings over the leg and arm at this stage, it is likely that he has fractures at all of these sites and I will lay a pad over the head wound," Jason replied.

The child was screaming throughout. Very gently and with quite determination Jason leaned forward and asked the child his name.

The child replied "Richard" almost at a whisper now.

"My name is Jason," he said to the boy with a smile, "we have come to help make it all better for you and take some of that nasty pain away. Try and keep still as much as you can, just for a little while; if you move around it will make things worse."

They proceeded to do a full body scan from top to toe, looking for any malformed limbs. Then they dressed the wounds fully to stop the bleeding and splinted the legs and arm, for they had found that the lad had fractures to both of his legs and to his right arm; he also had a large discoloration to his abdomen which they were not very happy about.

The child was given oxygen to help with blood loss and also to help reduce any swelling that could take place within the skull due to the head injury. Just at this point the 'Traffic Police' arrived and started to take details from the driver of the car involved, who had not received any injuries she was just shaken up by the fact it had been her car that hit the child.

As there was no problems with the traffic flow the crew had requested the help of the other policeman to assist Tom while Jason set up an intravenous drip also to help combat the blood loss and maintain the blood pressure.

Everything was going along smoothly. The call seemed to have taken hours but in fact it was only a few minutes. Jason continued to make his observations on the child, but as he started to take the boy's blood pressure things took a turn for the worse. The child's condition was not looking good; he became very clammy and grey and his blood pressure started to fall rapidly. Jason increased the flow on the giving set to allow the fluids to run fully open and turned the oxygen up to 100%.

Then Jason remembered the abdominal bruising. "How far have we got? he asked Tom.

"Almost finished now," came the reply.

"Right, we need to move. I think he may have a ruptured spleen or torn liver, his abdomen is distended and he needs an urgent gastric- lavage and bloods. Finish what ever you are doing now and lets get going," he whispered in Tom's ear. Enlisting the help of the police officers they loaded the child into the ambulance. Jason quickly set about getting a second intravenous line, running it wide open. "The faster you can get us to the hospital the better I'll like it."

Tom by this time was busy putting in a 'Stand-by Call' over the radio, to give the accident unit some warning. The police could see that urgency was needed and had offered to give them an escorted journey into hospital, which they accepted without hesitation. On route to the hospital the child's condition deteriorated: within seconds he had lost consciousness and then went into respiratory arrest; his limp body allowed an arm to drop over the side of the stretcher. Jason could see the life draining away from the child. Fighting against his own emotion, he hesitated for just a moment before his long experience took control. Swiftly and with certainty he moved to intubate the boy; with bag and mask he assisted the child's breathing.

As Jason used the equipment to help with the child's breathing, he found himself getting increasingly worried about the exacerbated condition, for the next stage could be a full cardiac arrest. He looked at his wristwatch, before poking his head through the cab window trying to get his bearings; he knew that it would only be a few more minutes before they would see the hospital.

"There must be better ways to earn a living than this," he thought

136

to himself. His throat was dry and the sweat was pouring from everywhere. The tension in his belly eased as he saw signs of improvement in the boy. Lady luck seemed to be smiling on the child for his condition very slowly responded: little by little the colour of this limp and vulnerable child started to return back to normal and the whole picture started to improve. But he was not going to be out of the woods for a long while. The bleeding inside the child's abdomen needed investigating and surgery would still be required to ensure a full recovery.

"We are arriving at the hospital. How is he doing?" Tom yelled back to Jason.

"Thank God for that, things were getting more than a bit hairy back here."

At the hospital the trauma team were waiting for them to arrive. As the child was wheeled into the resuscitation room, Jason called out the observations and treatments that they had given. They approached the awaiting doctors and nurses; their many pairs of skilled hands took over from the two paramedics.

Mr. McKee, the surgical consultant, took control with his usual precise skilled ability, giving orders to the support staff whilst listening to every word that Jason told him. Anyone that did not know him would expect to see a man in white coat, sporting a stethoscope in one pocket and a copy of the BNF in the other. Not this man: he stood upright wearing an open neck shirt, jumper and baggy corduroy trousers.

The paramedic gave him a full account of all that had happened before their arrival at the casualty department. Mr. McKee was taking in every last drop of detailed information while his skilled fingers worked with a frenzied determination. He made a small incision into the child's abdomen and entered the lavage set between the newly sliced muscles. There was an immediate show of bright red blood running up the clear plastic tubing, confirming the presents of an internal bleed.

By the time the two very tired paramedics had booked the child in at the reception desk, they found out Jason's fears had been well founded: the child had a confirmed ruptured spleen; also two fractures on the right leg and one on the left, and a fracture to his right arm. If the operation went well the child would spend a long time in hospital but hopefully would go on to to make a full recovery.

Unlike doctors and nurses, the paramedics never get attached to patients that they bring into hospital. Normally they would never see a patient for more than an hour unless the call left its mark, then possibly an interest could be shown by a phone call to the ward to seek a progress report. Many times the news was not good, causing the crews to go away deflated ...

The two paramedics climbed up into the cab and set off down the road back to their base to finish off the day. They were already one hour over time and it had been a pig of a day; the money had been well earned and they just wanted to go home to unwind.

They had made about two miles back to station when the radio in the cab burst into life again. Jason could not believe it; he could feel a lump swell up in his throat and at this point he was close to tears as he picked up the hand set to reply. Tom muttered some four letter word that Jason did not quite catch.

"Where are you now"? asked the control assistant.

"Eastern Avenue, approximately one mile before The Ship public house." replied Jason.

"We are very sorry about this but we have just had a report of a male lying in the road about half a mile in front of your location. He's believed to be unconscious," explained the control assistant.

Jason felt sick to his stomach; after all that they had done that day he could not face the thought of more of the same, yet here was yet another job to make his stress more acute. He needed to

138

have finished hours ago but now it seemed that they could be fighting to get back to station all night. Tom must have been feeling the same way judging by the comments that were floating around the cab. Make no mistake, ambulance crews are not saintly and when upset they react the same as anyone else; they just learn to curb their temperament in public.

They arrived at the location given but there was no sign of any body lying in the road. In fact the road was empty except for the steady stream of traffic coming up behind them. They looked to both sides of the road and saw nothing at all. Starting to doubt the location that had been given, they drove further down the road. Still no sign of anything unusual. Five more minutes were spent looking for a body that never was before they gave up and got back to control. The usual questions were asked, but in the end they had to put it down thankfully to a hoax call.

The feeling of relief they both felt was fantastic. Just to know that they did not have to perform on yet another road accident victim or cardiac patient settled them slightly from the rush of adrenaline that had been built up within them. Tom drove like hell to get them the last mile back to the ambulance station, just making it with seconds to spare before the radio went off again. But now they no longer cared, they had made it back to base and it was down to the night crew to take over.

Jason could not hide the feeling of relief. Inside himself he was shaking with the emotional stress that today had placed upon him. All he wanted to do now was get home to his wife, put his feet up and try to dismiss the events that had taken place. It would be hours before the adrenaline stopped coursing through his veins and his mind settled back to normal ...

He dreamed of the day when he could put all the pain behind him and let someone else take over. This was not a fantasy; this was what he truly yearned for. No he needed this to happen. He was tired of all those nights that he would see other people going out to enjoy themselves while he had to work. Jason's ageing body could no longer keep pace with the demands that this job now required of him. He had shared the suffering of others so many times, cried when they cried and felt their deep sadness.

All he wanted now was to quit while he was still able to walk, not spend his retirement years locked into a wheelchair to stagnate for the rest of his days.

Jason had entered into medicine by chance twenty-two years ago. He had been a successful company sales rep. But one day he had witnessed a competitor almost begging for a sales order.

He had worked long and hard all of his life. Never, being unemployed for more than a couple of days since leaving school at the age of fifteen and always managing to move from one job to another without signing on at the dole office. Always trying to improve himself with every chance that came his way, he would spend hours reading about a subject that would enable him to reach his goal. He wanted to spend as much time with his wife as he possibly could, to walk amongst the flowers, the winding rivers and to look at the many trees through the four seasons of the year. He dreamed of snow-capped hills in the winter, cold, stark black and white, then the blaze of colours bright and warming in the fullness of summer. These were the wonders that nature brings, his needs were simple just the beauty of life itself instead of the dull grey of despair. What was needed was a well-earned rest, to shift the responsibilities away from the work place and to establish closer communication with his family. Each day that passed he wished that this could be soon, for he wondered just how much longer he could continue before he finally cracked under the strain ...

Chapter Twelve

He took a deep breath, then held it for a second before letting it out with a sigh. Jason felt a profound sense of relief as he eased into the seat of his car. Whilst setting the wipers into motion he wiped a cloth over the inside of the glass screen to clear the condensation. 'I have escaped from that hell hole again,' he thought to himself, a faint smile crossing his face as he drove out of the station yard. This had been a bad week, far too many hairy moments had taken a hard toll on him. His back ached, his knee was throbbing and his feet felt like they had been trapped in two dark little boxes all day. He had managed to grab the odd half-hour of broken sleep whilst on station but that had made things worse. Christmas day had come and gone and while others had been knocking back the booze and the turkey, Tom and himself had made do with the odd mince pie and coffee. But his heart was lifted for he had a day off work tomorrow, a whole day to rekindle the soul and his aching bones.

The journey home was uneventful. He parked the car and went inside the house. Jason had arrived home out of that cold winter's evening, the events of the day were over and he needed to relax. He shook his coat before hanging it up on the hook behind the door, made his way towards the living room to find the door open and the welcoming heat from the fire radiating outwards.

"How was your day?" Olive asked from the kitchen behind him.

He just shrugged his shoulders before replying. "Ok. Not too bad I suppose! Turning to face her he bent forward and gave her a kiss. "What have you been up to?" he asked.

She looked up as she replied. sure at that moment she had seen tears in his eyes, but she could have been wrong about that.

If she was right, it meant that he was holding back from her again. That would not have been good for he could not continue to keep bottling his emotions up inside.

He wished his wife a merry Christmas, exchange carefully hidden presents and then settle down to eat his late dinner. Normally he spoke very little about work; but today he had discussed some of the calls that they had dealt with. It had been a traumatic day for Jason and his partner: what was a day of joy for most had been a nightmare shift for them. Lucky for him he had a wife that understood the kind of horrors that he and his colleagues had to face up to. Before her retirement she had also spent eighteen years on front line motors and she knew what her husband had to cope with.

Very little was achieved that evening: he spent it lazing about. Christmas Day was almost at an end and he was not in the mood to rekindle the festive spirit. Tomorrow was Boxing Day and his girls would be round for a family get – together; there would be time tomorrow to enjoy quality time and relax. Feeling shattered, he was drifting and the images of the day flooded into his mind. His experiences of the past hours turned to apparitions. Images that forced him to relive and examine his actions, dissecting each call in order and asking the same question of each; 'Had the results produced been correct?' Surely he was not the only ambulance paramedic that felt this way? The stresses of the profession made him question his ability at times, leaving him with a sense of insecurity. His outward appearance would seem cool, calm and collected. But inwardly it was a different story; the constant misery and death of others tore deep into his soul ...

Jason woke with a start; he felt that he had only just closed his eyes moments earlier before his wife shook him.

"Come on you, get yourself off to bed."

It took him a while to clear his head; he felt worse after his short nap than he did when he first came home.

The ticking of the clock drew his attention, it was ten twenty and he realised that he had been asleep for almost three hours. He felt cold and shivered slightly, but then he always reacted this way after an exhausting week or if he got over tired. He dragged his weary body towards the bedroom and crashed down with an almighty thump; it was as if he had been on the tiles all night and had come home drunk. Pulling of his clothes and literally leaving them where they fell, he flopped into the bed and within minutes his tiredness took hold and he was out of this world ...

The next morning he woke early, eased himself out of bed and slipped into his dressing gown. It must have been five o'clock: he looked out of the window; a heavy frost lay thick on the ground and the sky was grey and foreboding.

Looking back towards the bed, he noticed it was badly crumpled where he had tossed and turned in his sleep during the night. He caught sight of himself in the mirror; his reflection had a haunted look about it. Puffy eyes stared back at him; the calls of yesterday had exhausted him more than he realised. Too much grief, too much pain was ageing him with rapid progress. 'How much longer could he function like this?'

He dressed and went downstairs to await the arrival of the rest of the family.

No matter how badly he felt he could not spoil their day, and he was sure that the smiling faces of the grandchildren would soon lift his spirits ...

Boxing Day had arrived with a vengeance; it came in as a snowstorm that lasted all morning. A thousand swirling pellets bounced off the ground before settling, then being picked up by the wind that blew it into drifting banks of white-blanketed mounds.

His grandchildren had found it thrilling; playing and throwing snowballs until each of them was soaked to the skin. The young enjoyed the crisp white mass, building first a snowman and then an igloo with its cold moulding material as they would use sand to build castles on the beach.

They sat circling the fire, exhausted by their new - found playground, drying out their soaking clothes and wet skins. Their laughter echoed around the house, filling it with that special kind of sparkling electricity that puts a lump in the back of the throat. Eager young mouths consumed sweets and fruit as they enjoyed the warming of the fire, each individual happy with the prospect of a second day of opening presents; in fact, a second day of Christmas all over again. To sit and watch their facial expressions and their little eyes light up with each new gift was what made this a very exceptional day. Today this was a happy house, filled with the love that only children and families can bring to each other.

Late Christmas presents were handed to each member of the family. With the most joy gained from watching the younger children open up parcels with feverish hands. There was a frenzy of ripping open wrapping paper, tearing away with enthusiastic interest. Faces lit up when they reached the inner container, then the shriek of pleasure when they found its hidden prize.

This was Jason's dream, not the nightmares that he suffered night after night, but the relaxing dream of being in the comfort of his own home and surrounded by his own family.

Apart from work, most days passed unnoticed, but days like this were special.

He was content to watch his grandchildren energetically shifting with excited anticipation. Except for Charlie. He was different from the others and it was obvious that the effects from his Ritalin medication were wearing thin and needed topping up. He was struggling to cope with an invisible disability for Charlie had a battle royal going on inside. It was a battle, that without the help of his medication, there was no way of controlling his behaviour.

144

He was one of the many unfortunate children that suffered from Attention Deficit Hyperactivity Disorder. The symptoms ranged from bad behaviour to attention manipulation. Actions can be like a climbing scale on a graph, from mild misbehaviour to aggressive anger with moods swinging uncontrollably. Charlie had been known to wreck his bedroom in a temper storm, and then be so apologetic and sorry for his actions once the medication had kicked in and he was calm.

His loving ways when not gripped by the ADHD were worth all the knocks it gave to the family members around him. When controlled by his medication he would sit with perfect behaviour, concentrating on some small object that would tempt his creative mind and produce all manner of magical inventions. For a few hours he would be a normal happy child, either playing or quietly watching the television with a brother or sister. Then very slowly the changes in his behaviour would start to appear as the medication wore off. A slight twitching in his face and limbs, a raised voice, deliberate aggravation against whoever was close at the time, followed by the demanding of things that normally he knew he could not have. When told 'No' he would storm off into an angry rage.

Once he had reached this stage, medication was overdue and behaviour would be erratic until the effect of the drugs kicked in. His attacking behaviour would swing back and forth as he crashed about the house screaming out hurtful words or striking out at the people that cared for him the most, as he desperately sought their help and understanding.

When he calmed down and the tempers cease, he was full of apologies, very conscious of what he had done and how distressing it was for those that care about him. His mother is worried about Charlie, for he will soon be going to senior school. This will bring back the problems that she thought were long laid to rest. What will happen to him when he starts his new school is a daunting prospect. How will he cope with a classroom of boys that don't understand why Charlie is sometimes different from the rest of them? What will he do if led into criminal ways whilst in a state of non-medication control? All of Charlie's family share these fears.

Recently, on a bus, he had gone into one of his fits of anger over something minor and screamed like a two-year-old the whole journey. He drew attention from all the other passengers, whose eyes only saw a badly behaved child or spoilt child that was out of control. Their accusing looks directed at his mother were typical. "Why don't you keep your child under control?" "You're not a fit mother if you can't bring them up properly." They make judgements without knowing the facts, all the time thinking that Charlie is a defiant little brat who is causing a disturbance in their space.

Once the demon within had been laid to rest, Charlie was a loving, bright and happy child. With his medication controlling the condition, his talents were able to come forward and show that he was a truly gifted child. Take away the Ritalin and he was like hell on wheels. Hyperactive was an understatement: he suffered deep depressions, learning disabilities and anxiety. His mother summed up his distress in a poem, for she took the full force of her son's frustrations.

MISUNDERSTOOD'

The fridge lock is broken; there's milk on the floor.
Yoghurt, egg yolk, I can't take much more!
I've paints and play dough, so much to do.
So why has my child got his hands down the loo?
We've locks on the windows and bolts on the doors.
Our house is escape proof our captive is four.
He's up at five-thirty, ready to play.
And just doesn't stop for the rest of the day.

He is loving and open, feels misunderstood.
I really believe that he tries to be good.
I'm told he's not hyperactive because he sleeps at night.
But I am his Mum; I know something's not right.

Poor Charlie was almost expelled from school until he was diagnosed as being one of the many children who suffer in silence in their own confused world. Once the school was made aware that it was a medical problem and not just an out of control, disruptive child they changed their strategies and became supportive, making adaptations in his classroom education. From this point onwards his life took a complete turn around. He surprised everyone with his newly found abilities and showing talents that no one knew he possessed. With his mother's full support he managed to build his self-confidence and self-esteem. She did what ever it took, and more to help her child succeed...

Later that afternoon the weather set icy: the soft snow had turned into a congealed frozen block echoing the crunching footsteps as the last of his family departed from the house and headed home. Jason sank into the contours of his armchair and relaxed with a long drink letting the contentment engulf him. This was so different from the tortured work environment that kept him so tightly wound like a clock spring.

He had enjoyed the day more than he could ever describe. It had been a good day, one without stress, even Charlie had been well behaved and had experienced, like his cousins, a day to remember for a long time to come. He closed his eyes and remembered a letter written by Charlie's grandmother, a letter that would make sense to those that had one or more of these children as a family member. Reaching into the cupboard draw he pulled out the well-thumbed sheet of paper and started to read ...

147

'FROM A GRANDMOTHER'

Years ago when I was young and naïve, I thought I knew it all, as so many of us do when we are twenty and just starting out as parents. I would see other parents in shops, in the park or on buses with a child who refused to comply, or a child running miles ahead of its screaming mother, heading for a busy road, taking no notice of the frantic adult behind. And in my uninitiated pre AD/HD days I would stand and watch saying to myself. "I'll never spoil my child to that extent, I will bring mine up to behave when they are out with me, my children will never show me up in public like that!"

Twenty years later and a proud mother of three daughters that were brought up to walk by my side, sit still on buses and in doctors' waiting rooms and only screamed in shops or parks when they had fallen and hurt themselves. I was so smug with my "see!" I knew, "it could be done, its how you bring them up that makes the difference" attitude. HOW WRONG CAN YOU BE!

My first daughter, the one that sat still on buses and did not show me up in public because I had taught her not to, has given me four beautiful grandchildren, two boys and two girls. They are being brought up with the same do's and don'ts that I brought her up with, the same 'this is right, this is wrong,' guidelines that I instilled in her. So why, when she takes her children out to the park or the shops, is she the frantic adult yelling at the fast disappearing, apparently deaf child heading for the busy road? Why? Are the, 'know it all mums' staring at her with the " Can't you control that child? You shouldn't have had them if you can't bring them up properly," looks on their faces.

I know why, (Attention Deficit Hyperactivity Disorder) That's why. I have six grandchildren, four of them walk by my side, sit still on buses and do not show me up in public, the other two would love to be the same, but they have AD/HD. They do not know how to be the perfect little person we would like them to be, their behaviour is sometimes beyond their control, let alone their parents.

So please! All you 'SMUGGIES' out there, (I used to be one, remember!) do not be too quick to judge. The child causing the disturbance may not be brought up out of control, awkward, defiant horrible little demon. He or she may be someone's much loved and much wanted, desperate to be understood, AD/HD grandchild ...

Jason carefully folded the well-read piece of paper, neatly tucked it back into its storage box and closed the cupboard draw. Olive stood by his side and placed her hand on his shoulder, squeezing it slightly. He lifted his head and smiled, "had enough? Then let's away to bed."

The day had left him still on a high note; unable to close his eyes, he sat and read a few chapters of a book. Olive on the other hand was more than ready for sleep and within minutes she had drifted off. Her day had been busy with the cooking and making sure that there was always a drink to hand whenever anyone wanted one. He put aside the book and looked across at his wife, who was sleeping soundly beside him, unaware that he was still awake. Pushing the covers off, he eased himself carefully out of the bed and went to the window. Looking out, he stood watching the snow fall and observing the spectacular shapes of the trees materialising from out of the darkness disrupted by the shadows of the streetlights. Sleet mixed with the snow was whipped up by the wind and driven against the window glass like dried rice. The sight of all that whiteness made him feel cold, causing goose bumps to rise up on his skin surface. Turning away, he went back to bed feeling thankful that he was not at work. 'I feel sorry for all the poor beggars that are out on a night like this,' he thought to himself. His wife was sleeping soundly, her back turned towards him. Gently lifting the covers he climbed in and snuggled up close behind her feeling her, warmth before closing his eyes for blissful sleep ...

It was still dark when he woke from yet another dream, one of those nightmares where he wanted to cry out but found himself void of voice. The faceless shapes had returned, floating towards him as they whispered their demands.

"Why do they drive me on night after night? "What is it they seek from this tormented sleeper?" He found himself asking these silly questions, knowing that they were silly because he had been asleep; it was a dream and these phantoms were not real. These were the constant catalogues of dreams that kept his eyes mobile under closed lids. All he wanted was to sleep undisturbed; not this constant troubled sleep that left him totally drained the following day. Olive had sensed that something was wrong and woke to find him sitting up staring at the opposite wall. "Was it a bad dream again?" she asked.

He could hear her anxiety as she spoke, knowing that she had been put under stress worrying about him. She was scared of these constant disturbing dreams, scared of what they were doing to his personality. Most of all she was fearful for his health.

He bent forward, kissed her forehead and squeezed her hand before swinging his legs over the side of the bed. Being aware of her anxiety he tried to give the appearance that all was well; he did not want her to share the torment that came from his dreams.

He was aware of his own heart thumping, like an animal trying to escape from a cage. Standing upright, he moved to the window and drew back the curtains. Looking up, he stared at the thin chink of light in the sky. Darkness was giving way to the pale of the morning; a new day was about to be born.

Dawn broke with a film of white over everything in sight; sleet that was picked up by the wind sent a flurry of frozen particles against the bedroom window, that sounded like tiny grains of sand dropping into a metal tray. 'It's not very good outside this morning,' he thought to himself as he crept back to the warmth of the bed.

Olive snuggled up to him; she was determined to get to the bottom of her husband's deep-seated problems. Once again she raised the subject of a visit to the doctor's, only to be turned down with a flat 'No'. Her loyalty to Jason kept her still, but knew she would have to bring up the subject again, 'soon! The warmth of the bed and tiredness soon took hold and they both succumbed to sleep once more ...

December the 27th looked like something from a North Alaskan movie, nothing but white as far as the eye could see. He plunged the spade deep into the snowdrift; little banks of hard packed, white frozen snow covered the driveway blocking access between the house and the road. Flexing his muscles, he started to clear a pathway and wondered how he was going to get to work tomorrow if this snow did not clear. The distant outline as far as maximum vision would allow was just a blanket of white, unbroken save for the odd silhouettes of houses and trees. A warm feeling came over him as he thought of his colleagues struggling to reach calls in these conditions. Having these couple of days away from work had been well selected; this weather was not good for someone of his age, to be fighting with a spade, digging a vehicle out of snowdrifts or cutting out a path through the hard snowy ground. He remembered doing just that some five years ago and how it had taken its toll on his aching back. That year like today had been hell on earth to work in. Each job had taken so long to reach that they had only managed five calls in ten hours. They had to struggle to get to each location, fought to carry each patient into the vehicle and then put up with the slow nightmare journey to the hospital. After the effects of those few days he swore that he would not lift a spade to snow again.

Yet here he was clearing snow from his own front yard; but then, there was no urgency, no pressure or any time limits to get the task completed. "Once this was done he could take the day to relax a few glasses of brandy and worry about tomorrow when it came."...

CHAPTER THIRTEEN

He had arrived early on this last day of December and while waiting for the shift to begin he tried to prepare himself for what was ahead. Tonight would produce an abundance of crazy festive dipsomaniacs, who could not escape trouble if their lives depended on it. This would be a night to take extra care both on the roads, in the pubs and clubs alike. With bellies full of booze their hostilities would become unstoppable, devastating anything that lay in their paths.

The temperature outside had dropped; the nip in the air was a sure sign that they were in for a frosty night. Inclement weather was just an added extra to the turmoil that he was already expecting. Looking out of the window and beyond the road into the fields, he watched the locals that were out exercising their pets before settling into the warmth of their homes for the night. The deciduous trees stood with their leafy carpets at the base making grotesque shapes in the half-light as their arms reached upwards towards the night sky.

He remembered when he first started all those years ago standing in almost the same spot. In those days he was full of enthusiasm and dedication, wanting to be the one that could make a difference. Although at that time he was employed on the emergency side of the service, most of the workload dealt with out – patients. This was easy work: just taking them to hospital clinics and collecting them after their treatments to return them home again. Unlike the fast pace of the emergency work, the 'Gerry – Ferry' runs as they were fondly known were taken at a far more sedate pace. These runs had allowed him to get to know the characters of his patients in depth.

The stories that the older folks used to tell were not only interesting but they gave a short history lesson, giving an insight into times shared and lived by his own parents. As a child Jason had often heard his mother tell the stories of her life during the war and the years before that time. This was his source of information, apart from his constant readings of many books that fed his vivid imagination. The stories of his mother's past life gave him a closer look at his own family history.

When he first joined the ambulance service the elderly patients gave credence with their own stories to what had been shared with him as a child. Jason's natural curiosities fed on the individual tales that were passed to him by many of the people as they made the journeys to and from the local hospital.

His thoughts were interrupted by the sound of Tom's motorbike outside in the yard. It was time to start work ...

Alice Brown was fifty-six, and married to Bob for over thirty years. She looked very tired and walked with discomfort caused by severe Osteo-arthritis. The pain was not confined to her lower limbs; her hands and shoulders were also giving her hell! To look at her hands you would believe that they belonged to someone more senior in years. Her twisted and gnarled fingers pushed out of shape by swollen joints, made everything she did seem like hard work. Hard work was no stranger to Alice and over the years she looked the part of a woman that had lived through many hard knocks.

Her life was kept busy with the grind of keeping her house clean and tidy, but slowed down by aching joints, making each day an up hill struggle. Today, the pains in those limbs caused her to gasp as the fire passed through her inflamed hands and hips.

The pains were monstrous, even painkillers were not doing anything to alleviate the agony that she felt. She was obliged to take the pressure off her legs and sit down. Perhaps if she sat a while and took a few more pills, the pains would ease. Flicking the switch of the television set, she eased herself into the chair.

The midday news finished and was followed by the afternoon 'soap opera.'

After watching the first ten minutes her eyes started to feel heavy and she fought to keep them open. Dreams of her youth flooded her mind as she drifted into a deep sleep ...

She woke to the sound of the theme music; the soap was just finishing. Slowly she glanced over to the clock on the table, five – fifty- nine.

"That can't be right?" Sitting bolt upright, she grabbed the clock and made sure that it was still ticking. Her realisation was suddenly enlightened when she heard the announcement of the 'six o'clock news.' For a few seconds she sat frozen like the 'Tin Man' from the *Wizard of Oz*, stuck fast for the lack of oil.

Alice was angry with herself for not keeping an eye on the passing time; angry for allowing herself to drop off to sleep in the middle of the day like that was inexcusable. Bob would be home within half an hour and she had not started to prepare the evening meal. Filling the large pot with water, she set it upon the gas ring to heat while she prepared the vegetables. How could she have let the time slip by unnoticed? He would not be in a good mood and the meal not being on the table when he walked through the door could send him into a rage. She was flushed and in a panic, not because she feared Bob, because he would never harm her. She loved him so much and needed everything to be perfect. He was a humble man really and his rages were short lived, but their life style was such that there were to be no misplacements.

So engrossed with the chores the water on the stove boiled over spilling onto the cooker top. Without thinking of the consequence, she turned and seized the handle of the heating pot. The minute she gripped the metal handle a sickening pain shot up her arm and her reflexes made her let go. She had released her grip spilling the scalding contents down her front. She staggered backwards, screaming as the hot water soaked into her clothes and then ran down the front of her legs.

The intense pain was caused by her lifting skin, which produced large watery blisters, swelling up and hanging like sacks from the surface of her flesh. Alice swayed perilously feeling the waves of nausea sweep over her. Blissfully the shock and the pain were so intense her brain switched off and she sank to the floor unconscious.

She was found some ten minutes later by her husband, who had returned home expecting to be greeted at the front door. He knew immediately that something was wrong.

Alice lay twisted on her right side, almost in a foetal position curled up and still. Her breathing was shallow and she looked almost transparent.

Bob knelt beside her and touched her face; her eyes flickered in response to his hand. "Are you able to move at all?"

"No. I can't. The pain hurts so much just the slightest movement makes it unbearable. I am not able to move my legs or even wiggle my toes without the pain increasing."

Her husband was frantic; his mind was racing as he tried to collect his thoughts. "I'll get some help, try and remain still, I won't be long."

He raced into the next room, grabbed the phone and dialled triple nine. "I need an ambulance. My wife has some terrible burns, please come quickly."

The woman on the other end of the line got him to calm down long enough to give the correct address and number that he was calling from. "We will get someone out to you soon. Go back and stay with your wife until they arrive." ...

The 'phone' in the crew room rang; it was the start of the New Year's Eve night shift.

Both paramedics had just finished their checks of the ambulance equipment. They wanted to be prepared for whatever dramas the night had in store for them.

Unfortunately they could not always trust all the crews that

156

handed the vehicle over to them; some did not keep the drugs and equipment up to scratch. Sometimes it was a case of overwork, but there were crews that did not give a thought to others or they were just too lazy to care.

The call passed was a collapsed unconscious female, cause due to burns.

"Don't sound good, she could be in deep shock," said Tom.

"Well. At least its not a drunk or road accident. Let's hope that its not as bad as it sounds."

A sharp smell of diesel and engine oil hung heavy in the garage as they boarded the ambulance. Tom sent the vehicle off into the rush hour traffic, steaming towards its location, lights flashing, giving off a blue tinge that lit the darkening sky.

They made the trip across town without any mishaps and Jason started to prepare the burns kit ready to bail out as soon as they arrived. Tom cursed as he suddenly hit the brakes, causing Jason to jerk forwards, the seatbelt tightening around his middle giving slight discomfort.

"Sorry about that, think we just overshot a little." He stuck the gear lever into reverse and backed up to negotiate the turning.

Both men strained their eyes to pick out the correct address from the line of houses.

Once it was located the two men were quickly out of the vehicle and moving up the path towards the front door. Jason gave the knocker two quick taps and waited for a response ...

Bob opened the door, a sigh of relief passing his lips before he directed them into the kitchen. Jason was pleased to find a clear passage from the front door to the kitchen at the rear. Normally they had to squeeze past furniture, books or even a bicycle stacked in the hallway. There was plenty of room to negotiate the carry chair should the patient need to go to hospital.

Jason squatted down to examine the extent of the burns; he dropped to one knee and started to work his way through her injuries.

157

Alice screamed, then screamed again as the paramedic's fingers tended to the damaged tissues.

He spoke to her softly trying to calm her down; his voice was steady and had a soothing effect. Jason estimated that she had approximately twenty-five per cent 'partial thickness burns.' He knew the importance of assessing the damage carefully; if he got everything right he should be able to anticipate any complications. The associating problems would be interference with the circulation supply to the limbs caused by swelling of the tissues. They would need to keep the blistering clean to prevent infections later.

Both paramedic's worked together covering the scalded area with sterile burn dressings, not only to stop infections but also to keep the draughts away from the burns. Unlike full thickness burns, which are pain free due to nerve damage, partial thickness burns can be extremely painful.

Jason rigged up a wide bore intravenous drip with 500mls of a crystalloid solution. He did not open it up fully, for over infusion is worse than under infusion, but handy to have ready just in case of emergencies. Tom was administering oxygen via the portable unit, while Jason gave her 10mg of 'Nubain' to try and take away some of the pain.

By this time Alice was past caring what they were doing to her. The pain was increasing and her legs felt as though a large steel band was slowly squeezing them tighter and tighter.

They had done all that was possible; there was nothing else except to get her quickly to hospital before the risk of shock caused by the loss of plasma increased. Gently they popped her onto the carrying chair and out to the waiting ambulance. The paramedics would have preferred to lift her out of the house on the stretcher, but it would not negotiate the awkward corners of the hallway.

Once safely on board the vehicle Tom radioed ahead to warn

the hospital of her symptoms and arrange for a team to be put on stand-by.

The 'Nubain' had started to take effect, her pain was almost gone and it did not hurt so much. In fact it felt really comfortable. Jason used his full vocabulary of banter to keep her mind away from the swelling flesh on route to hospital. She was good in spirits considering what had happened to her and they made good time to Southsea without any more complications.

The handover went smoothly, but the consultant requested that they remained while he inspected the degree of burns.

"We will probably transfer this lady to the 'Burns Unit.' If you can square it with your control, we should be in a position to make a decision very quickly."

Ambulance control sanctioned the stand-by and they started to prepare for the sixteen mile rush to the burns hospital while they awaited the emergency consultant to say 'Yes! Or No!'

Twenty minutes later the decision was a 'Yes'; her condition required that she be moved to the Specialist hospital. Alice, now full of 'Pethidine' to keep the pain down to a minimum, was ready to be transferred into the back of the ambulance. It was nineteen thirty hours, an hour and a half since she picked up the boiling pot of scalding water. But she was stable and the pain relief made her feel more comfortable and able to cope.

The journey took just under twenty minutes, without any mishaps along the way. Jason had used everything to keep the conversation light: silly things, just to keep her from thinking too much about what lay in front of her.

If Tom braked hard or did anything to give Jason the opportunity, it was "Excuse my partner, his wooden leg is playing him up today," or "Sorry about that, he only passed his test last week." It was good to see her smile; even after all that had happened over the last couple of hours she still had a sparkle in her eyes.

159

At the burns unit they handed Alice over to the ward staff, said their goodbyes and wished her luck. Every working day they had to deal with desperate situations like Alice. People who think that it will never happen to them are suddenly stuck down and brought in sick or injured.

They did their work to the best of their ability; some calls would stick in the mind: often upsetting calls that got under their skin would require self-control; that's when the professional training takes over, to stop them showing their emotions.

Most ambulance personnel will admit that they have been close to tears more than once in their careers. In fact, Jason had seen macho men built like barn doors reduced to jelly over calls. Nature has a particular cruelty about it. There is no compromise for old age, no compassion for human suffering and no second chances for the dead. All too often they walked amongst the dead and sick; it was their memories that were slowly destroying Jason. Like their colleagues, this crew had to rely on the few joyful moments that uplifted their spirits. To save a life, do a job particularly well, achieving good result or be present and take part at the birth of new life were the only rewards ...

Emphysema had withered and slowly eaten away at the alveoli tissue of his lungs, leaving them beyond repair. His daily routine of coughing up white frothy sputum from the damaged lungs had left him in a pitiful state. It was as if he was drowning in his own fluids. These last few months had seen a marked deterioration in his health and a decreased ability to take care of himself. Because of his lack of mobility he had abandoned the top half of the house and moved his bed into the lounge.

The chill in his bones made him shiver and created pains to his joints. 'Temperatures dropped I think its time for another blanket.'Placing the cover around his shoulders, he sat and examined the old photos that were scattered around the table. These images of a time lost and forgotten.

Smiling faces of men in uniform reflected the captured moments of the camera lens. He stroked his old gnarled and twisted thumb across the pictures in front of him, seeking out each of the faces in turn. His thoughts remembered the men that had died, taking those small stretches of beach in Normandy.

A faint smile crossed his face as he recalled the laughter from the lads that week before they were shipped over to that bloody awful stretch of sand. Six faces stared out of the tiny photo. Five of those faces never advanced more than twenty yards up the beach. Their young lives were snuffed out like a candle flame. One only survived that morning, only one was left to tell the tale and live to old age, to remember the others ...

They sat silently watching the traffic pass as the vehicle sat on the emergency stand-by point. The coldness outside was kept at bay by the internal heaters inside the cab. Tom was fighting off the heavy eyes that were causing him to nod off as the heat and the boredom slowly closed down on his body.

The radio alarm shot them both back to their senses as the control operator started to transmit details of a doctor's urgent case.

As soon as the name and address was passed they knew straight away it was one of their regular patients. Jock Bird was a regular outpatient of the chest clinic. His visits were two or three times a week that had been spread over the last two years and he was well known by most of the ambulance crews. He was an emphysema patient who had a long-term airway problem caused by excessive smoking. This was no ordinary man. Old Jock was a first class war hero and the stories that he passed onto anyone that took time to listen were fascinating.

When Tom and Jason arrived at the house the first thing that greeted them was the smell, the putrid smell of unwashed flesh and stale urine. The stark contrast since their last visit was incredible, for he had neglected himself completely. The place was a mess; his once prized furniture was covered with old books, bric-a-bracs and general rubbish. All this surrounded a large double bed that had not had the sheets changed for weeks. Worst of all Jock had a little dog that had obviously not been let out for quite a while because there was doggy-do everywhere. The whole house stank to high heaven.

He looked terrible; sweat was seeping out of his skin like a rotting water pipe.

Jock was breathing though his teeth as the difficulty of every gasp was laboured. They had to feel sorry for the poor old soul. This once proud man, who had served his country to the limit, was now old and dejected, fighting an enemy that he could not see.

Tom slipped the oxygen mask over his face and he immediately went into a panic attack. "I can't breathe, can't breathe." Jock thrashed his arms about in cold panic sure that he was not breathing.

Jason stood in front of him and calmly reassured him, convincing him to slow his breathing rate down. The paramedics both felt for Jock as he fought to breathe; his lungs were in such a poor condition that they only worked on one third of their capacity ...

Jock had been one of the surviving members of his battalion who had taken part in the Normandy Invasion on the 6th of June 1944. He served with the 1st Battalion South Lancashires during the Second World War as a machine gunner. He had spoken often of his beloved Bren-machinegun. Although a formidable weapon it was not in the same class as the German MG42, referred by the allied troops as the 'Spandau.' This was a far superior weapon to the British machinegun. The Bren was capable of firing off five hundred rounds per minute. It could not compare with the German MG42 with its staggering twelve hundred rounds per minute, plus its barrel could be changed in five seconds, preventing a jammed gun. The American forces attacking on 'Omaha' beach faced this weapon head on, causing demoralising casualties. It was reported that the Yanks were able to see from the amphibious landing-craft the fountains of sand as the spitting bullets hit the beach. Wave after wave of these young men were cut to ribbons as they stormed the shore. These men meet the full horror of the German gun, turning the blue-green of the sea crimson red with their blood.

After the terrible defeat on the Russian front, where the German army lost over two million of its seasoned troops, they were left with a weakened force, a lack of supplies and diminished armour to fight off the allied invasion on the Normandy beaches. Yet the Germans still managed to fight one of the bloodiest battles of the Second World War.

The D-Day Landings were the largest amphibious invasion recorded in history. The American First Army, led by General Bradley and British Second Army by General Dempsey, launched their battle groups on Normandy June 6th 1944. Normandy beachheads were stretched from Cabourg to Quineville. The allies attacked at five key points, which they named 'Utah, Omaha, Gold, Juno and Sword beaches. American forces hit Utah and Omaha while the British troops landed on Sword and Gold. Juno beach was a joint British and Canadian assault.

In terms of the appalling cost of human life for those that spearheaded the assault on Omaha, losses were far greater than anyone had imagined. Battles fought at Normandy cost the allies over two hundred thousand casualties; thirty seven thousand of these were killed. German troops also suffered two hundred and forty thousand casualties. Code named operation 'Overlord,' commanded by Eisenhower, it was to be a complete and absolute victory for the allies, but the cost was horrific.

Many of the landing craft were swamped as they tried to reach the beach, drowning most of the infantrymen on board. Most of the amphibious Tanks that were supposed to back up the infantry sank to the bottom of the sea. For some reason they had been launched hundreds of yards short of the beach and came off their landing ramps like lead weights straight to the bottom. Without the support of any armour the troops were left to fight their way ashore unaided. Loaded down with heavy equipment, many of them did not make it to dry land.

At the end of that first day more than two thousand casualties were on the Omaha beach. Hundreds were dead or dying, either from drowning, shellfire or the German machineguns. The devastation lay in the sea, awash with floating corpses in its crimson water.

Jock and his mates from the South Lancashires dropped their ramps on Sword beach. He lost many of his friends that morning, cut down by the hail of bullets from the MG42 or shellfire from the German 150mm guns. His best mate, Fred, had been just sixty yards in front of him when the shell landed. Jock was looking at the back of his mate's head one minute; seconds later it was blown clean off his shoulders in a mass of exploding flesh.

He remembered those days as if they were only yesterday. Jock would tell of the deeds of all those men. His stories would unfold to anyone that cared to listen. So vivid were his descriptions that Jason had almost believed that he had been with him on that beach. Every time they conveyed this man to hospital he would share some part of his history with them ...

With care and compassion they wheeled old Jock out of his house and out to the waiting vehicle. Just as they were about to load him into the back of the ambulance he turned his head back towards the house, almost as if he knew that it would be the last time he would see it again.

Jock sat in silence on the journey into hospital, not one story or smile until they reached the casualty unit. He had given up the fight, his tired old lungs were letting him down and he knew that there was no cure this time.

As they lifted him from off the stretcher and transferred him onto the bed, he reached out and grabbed Jason's arm. "God bless you, son, thanks to you and your mate for all that you have done for me over the last few years." He fought to get the words out between struggling breaths.

"That's alright, Jock. It was a pleasure and there will be many more yet," said Jason trying to reassure him.

This patient had the look of death about him and the paramedics had to work hard not to let it show in their faces.

He looked up at Jason and said. "Not this time. You and I know I'm done for. I'm going to find all of my mates that I left in Normandy waiting for me to join them!"

There was a little sadness as they made their way back to the vehicle. Both men knew that they would never see him again, and that was a pity. You don't get to meet many men like him ...

The air had grown colder, close to a frost as the windows on the parked cars were near to freezing. A New Year had just begun and they were heading home after the office party that he had felt obliged to attend: the party where boring business associates had spent the entire evening telling their boring jokes and trying to impress him with their narrow minded office sales talk. Still, the whiskey had been free and had taken the dullness off the non-interesting conversation.

Twelve years had passed the same way, twelve years of the same office parties, the same people, same old everything. If he had his way they would have gone off to a lively club or some other swinging venue. But his wife had insisted; she had pushed him for the last twelve years hoping that he would make the important impact on the management.

He had a good position with the company that he worked for, but no matter how hard he tried he was constantly passed over when the promotions were being handed around.

165

"What did they expect from him?" It hurt when he thought of all the effort and extra hours he had put in over the years. He had 'busted his balls,' for them.

His wife looked across from the passenger seat. "Just keep your eye on the road, you should not even be driving with the amount of whisky you've knocked back."

"Fuck 'em. I don't see why I should worry about them any more," he said out loud. He did not register what his wife had just said.

His gear changes started to get a bit messy, and the car was wandering from side to side a little to often for his wife's liking.

"I wish you would start thinking about what you are doing, or better ..." That was the last word she managed to utter. Her piercing screams filled her mouth as the car left the road and hurtled down the wrong side of the flyover, flipped over and came to a sickening halt on the road below. It was two – forty on New Year's morning, cold, dark and silent. The road was void of traffic. Had this not been the case, the consequences could have been overwhelming, for the wreckage was covering both lanes of the dual carriageway ...

They had joined one of the many that frequently caused the bulk of road accidents each year. Speeding is widely acknowledged but few think of sleep-related causes. Falling asleep while driving is a highly significant cause of many crashes. This can be caused by fatigue that creeps slowly into your brain, if you drive on long stretches of open roads, and before you known it you are asleep at the wheel. Then there is the drowsiness of drinking, where you are not aware of any warning signs because you're out of your brain after one or more drinks too many. If you add the strain of driving in the darkness to any of the aforementioned you have a lethal cocktail that can leave you driving on auto – pilot ...

Thick undergrowth and trees lined either side of the country road, their greenery capped by the frozen snow held in position like glue. The twisted branches of the trees formed a tunnel-like archway over the road before opening out into the clear stretch leading onto the dual carriageway. Blue lights from the top of the ambulance gave a soft blue tinge to the snowy surface as they passed.

Four miles on they knew that once they cleared the next bend the traffic accident would be in front of them. The headlights picked up the wreckage in their beams; they lay spread across the road in undistinguished pieces of twisted metal where they had landed after the explosion of the impact. Its bulk was still in one piece but the engine compartment was just a mass of crumpled metal.

Both paramedics decamped from the vehicle and hastily made for the upturned wreck. Fluids that had run out of the car, oil, water, petrol and antifreeze all made up a cocktail of pungent aromas.

They picked their way through the sharp shards of metal. Jason to the driver and Tom went to the other side. He saw her sprawled across the back seat lying face upwards; her neck and face were ripped wide open. The gaping wound looked like it had been torn apart by an animal. Blood had gushed out like a small dam and had showered everything in sight with its wet sticky redness. With blood everywhere Tom had no doubt that she was dead; he was sure of that before he moved forward to examine her more closely. He felt for a pulse but there was none, both of her pupils were widely dilated and her chest had been crushed in the centre. 'Yes, she was dead! He had no doubt about it.

He was aware of the pounding in his ears caused by his quickening heartbeat. The rush of adrenaline and increased heart rate was making him breathe more deeply, sucking up the oxygen to feed the muscular pump.

He kicked the car door, forcing it to stay in the open position to give more room to move about. Moving forward to help Jason with the driver he asked what his condition was.

Jason looked up, covered in crimson goo; there was a large patch of broken glass and gory red blood around the driver's seat that had come from his head and arm. "This guy is still with us at the moment; nasty head injury, though, and he stinks of booze. How is the passenger?"

"Nothing we can do for her, poor cow, she's dead in a big way," he whispered.

At that moment a young police officer poked his head into the cab space. "What have you got?" he asked.

"Driver's not looking to bright and his companion in the back has been pronounced 'moribund'."

The police officer glanced to the rear seat where the deceased woman lay. "Oh Christ, is all that blood hers?" He did not get an answer for Jason was busy checking the focal signs of the remaining patient.

The focal signs he was looking for were neurological signs of problems with the brain. (Example: a dilated or constricted pupil on one or other side; drooping eyelids, dropped lip or weakness of one or more limbs, all help to confirm a diagnosis.) Jason was concerned because the driver's pulse was down and his blood pressure was elevating. Other warning signs showed in his limbs that had become rigid and twitching.

Meanwhile the police officer bent forward, grabbing the rear side of the car for support as the nausea swept upwards. He was doubled up as the vomit left his mouth and hit the floor. The bile burnt the back of his throat as he convulsed.

"This looks like we have a serious head injury on our hands," Jason whispered to Tom.

The driver had suffered a severe blow to his head, causing the brain to bounce around inside the skull; injuries would occur on the opposite side or at a distance from the site of the main blow.

168

These injuries can damage veins on the 'Dura Mater', causing bleeding within the enclosed capsule, a fracture to the skull or damage the tissue to the jelly-like brain.

Jason checked the pupils, looking for tell tale signs of a bleed, blown or dilated pupils reaction would give an indication that he was on the right track. If there were a haematoma, it would start putting increased pressure on the brain. A falling pulse follows the effects; blood pressure starts to rise, paralysis and then death. The haemorrhage would put pressure on the brain and with no where to escape, it finally pushes down onto the brain stem. Once it has reached this stage, the Medulla that governs the respiration and the circulation will shut down.

Breathing will stop and the hearts actions will cease to function ...

The young officer had regained his composure and returned to the front of the wreck. There was a sound of ripping Velcro as Tom prepared the cervical collar. Velcro makes an unnerving noise, as the tabs are prised apart. The patient's pulse had dropped again and the blood pressure still continued to rise.

Jason checked for 'battle signs', a blush discoloration over the tip of the mastoid bone, signifying a skull fracture. They were looking at a closed head injury and the ticking clock was now running. The Fire Brigade had almost finished taking the last of the roof off the car and soon would prepare to extract him out of the wreck and into the safety of the ambulance. All they could do for this chap was to increase the oxygen to maximum flow, keep a careful watch on the observations and get him to hospital as quickly as they could. Both paramedics knew that if they failed to get this patient to a treatment centre, he was going to die. What this guy really needed was a neurosurgeon, like now!

They were ready to move him from out of the wreck; the stretcher was put into position alongside the crashed car to receive its patient. There was a deliberate purpose in the actions from the rescuers as they gently eased him out. Jason moved around them like a mother hen constantly monitoring vital signs for deterioration and making sure they lifted him without causing further damage.

Once he was loaded into the back of the ambulance, Jason crossed the small space between the saloon and cab and picked up the hand set and transmitted his findings to the control operator on the other end. He explained the situation and requested that a neurosurgeon and back up team be put on stand-by at Southsea Hospital. He knew that if his patient were to have any chance of survival he would need the skills of the well-equipped medical staff that should be awaiting their arrival. The high – tech. Cat – scan equipment would locate the exact position of the bleed and the neurosurgeon could perform burr hole surgery to his skull. This technique would release the building pressure that was slowly squeezing his brain.

The patient was intubated in the back of the vehicle before they moved off. Jason assisted the respiration with a bag and mask continuing the observations between two squeezes of the bag. The fitting, returned his limbs were shaking and his right pupil was now blown. Jason drew up 10mg of Diazepam, then looked through the hatch of the front cab trying to get a location and work out a rough ETA. Realising they were less than a minute away from the hospital he steadied his nerves and decided to hold off the sedative and keep it capped for the hospital staff to use. The blood pressure was up, 177 over 110 and his pulse was Bradycardic.

Tom swung the motor into the hospital entrance, gave a short burst on the two tones to give warning of their approach and pulled up under the archway outside casualty. The smell from the raced engine was a mixture of hot oil, metal and burning rubber. With a flurry of motion they unloaded the stretcher and wheeled it into the emergency room at the trot. Still assisting with the

170

breathing, Jason explained the situation, cause, history and findings. "Head injury, battle signs, blown pupil, bradycardia, high blood pressure and Babinski reflex," he yelled as they worked.

The neurosurgeon listened carefully to each word, then asked a couple of questions as he examined the patient. He ordered the transfer from stretcher to gurney before the patient was taken away to the Cat - Scan unit, leaving the paramedics to clear up the blood soaked stretcher, collect equipment and produce the required paperwork ...

They had played their part; galvanised into action they had done what they had to do. But they would not know how the crash victim had fared for they made it a policy not to follow up their patient's progress, past calls had taught them not to become involved. Both paramedics were happy to except that they had made an accurate diagnosis and treated the injuries correctly. The real work would start now: if the surgeons could locate the clot, drill a hole in the skull to release the pressure from the bleed, get the pulse rate and blood pressure stable and follow up with huge amounts of antibiotics to protect against infections. Then and only then would he have a chance of making some sort of recovery. Even with luck, he would need weeks of rehabilitation.

Tom could not understand why people took such risks; it's not the case that all ambulance men are not partial to the occasional tipple, but after working for the service for any length of time and seeing the aftermath that drinking causes, they would be mad to take the same risks.

The police had found the identity of the car's occupants from the details in the driver's wallet and the dead woman's handbag. They had contacted their next of kin, who were on their way to the hospital unaware of their mother's demise. Sadly, if their father survived the proposed surgery it was almost certain that the police would arrest him for drink – driving. Under the circumstances, being charged by the police was the least of his worries. He will live with the thought that he was responsible for his wife's death because of the stupid act of drinking and driving ...

Tom was busy talking to a nurse that Jason had not seen before, looking as if she had just stepped out of the training school for nursing with her unmarked uniform, pressed creases that were almost sewn into position and her blonde hair neatly pinned up out of the way. Her identity badge above her left breast told him that her name was Carol Ready. "That's going to raise a few smiles in this place," he thought to himself.

She left Tom and walked towards the main unit: the soft squeak of her shoes made him look back at her long slender legs and shapely body. Jason knew that it was his partner's failing when confronted by a pretty face and a shapely pair of legs. He could guess what Tom was thinking about, he was unable to resist making a fool of himself even with someone half his age.

They walked slowly out of the emergency room and into the freshness of the morning. Rock salt had been laid down and was washing away the last of the snow on the hospital Tarmac, leaving behind large puddles of water.

Tom lit a cigarette, inhaled deeply and held the smoke, not realising how long he was holding his breath until the need to exhale forced him to let it out with rush. Jason laughed as Tom coughed and spluttered, the smoke choking him as it attacked the back of his throat. They climbed up into the cab and settled themselves before letting control know they were available for the next job.

So far it had been a typical New Year's Eve, but there would be a lot more of the same before the morning was finished. Tom had stopped choking and once again he was making resolutions to quit smoking. Jason had heard it all before and was sure he would be listening to the same promise next year. Jason thought about the last call. He contemplated what a few drinks had done

172

to the occupants of the fatal car. One dead and the other would have a fifty – fifty chance of survival. At best he would most likely spend the rest of his days in a wheelchair.

He remembered something that his father had once told him: "Death is between the eye and the lid: blink once and it can snatch away a family or a friend."

It was three – thirty five, the morning had almost come to an end and they only had three and half hours left. Still they were getting double time and sixteen pounds an hour was not bad money. Jason pushed the send button on the radio and gave the details of their last call.

"I have not got anything for you at this time, return to station: and try and get a drink. Control out."

Tom gunned the vehicle in the direction of the station, with the prospect of a well-earned drink he found renewed energy. But this was not to be. Within two minutes of leaving the hospital grounds the radio bleeped yet again. The controller apologised before passing details of another 'Road Traffic Accident.' Its location was just yards away from their station but they had only just left the hospital and that would put an extra seven minutes running time on the response.

A fine rain started to fall as the weather warmed slightly, causing the wipers problems clearing the screen. Picking the fastest route Tom headed for the coast road, surprised by the amount of traffic that was still on the road at this time in the morning.

The radio bleeped again with an update on the situation at the crash site. "There are at least four casualties and they are trapped in the vehicle, the police and fire service's are also on way. Control out."

Two road crashes in a row was not unusual, but two reported trapped was. Jason turned towards his mate. "I don't like the sound of this one: it's that little cottage on the bend again." This was considered to be a local black spot and they had attended many smashes on this location. Somehow, Tom managed to shave minutes off the journey and they arrived before the other two services ...

Frosty windows were distorted by hazy lights illuminating from the interior of the quaint white painted cottage, which was shaded from the front by a large oak tree adorned with Christmas fairy lights hanging from its bared branches.

The front doorway was enhanced by its picturesque rose-covered arches that looked as if they been plucked out of some book of dreams. From the road this seemed to be the ideal dwelling of peace and tranquillity, but there was just one thing that spoilt this pleasant abode. It sat right next to the Oak Public house.

Most nights brought the usual vociferous sounds from the public bar as harden drinkers screamed at each other across the tables trying to conquer the noise. But on this night the sounds spread out to fill the countryside as people celebrated the end of the old year and the possibilities of the new. Tonight the reunions of old associates continued well into the early hours of the morning. The drinking, singing and merriment reached its crescendo at midnight. But it was another hour before the sounds eased down to soft whispers, as the last of the persistent drinkers left one by one to stagger their swaying bodies home to waiting wive's and mothers. Occasional sounds filled the crisp night air as old friends shouted their farewells across the car park. Then the muffled cries fell silent as the doors of the Oak were locked up for the night and the Pub finally closed. Lights from the cottage still shone brightly from the upstairs windows before a flick of the switch plunged everything into darkness ...

At three-twenty the silence was broken by the sound of screeching tyres skidding on black Tarmac surfaces, followed a few seconds later by the sickening crunch as metal struck wood.

Time seemed to hang frozen for what seemed like hours; its slow motion effect made the scene seem unnatural before the senses of those in the respective buildings were alerted enough to investigate the noise. They stirred from the warmth of their beds, sleep still filling their eyes as they struggled to the window and looked down at the carnage below. A speeding car had lost control, left the road and ploughed through the brick wall before striking the old oak tree full on. The front of the wreck had been lifted up by the impact and one of its front wheels was still spinning slowly without traction. Jets of steam rose from its shattered bonnet surrounding the car in a misty fog.

Paul Austin, the owner of Oak Tree cottage, looked beyond the wreckage to the road where a man was staggering around seemingly lost and dazed. He appeared to have no sense of direction or idea why he was standing in the middle of a country road in pitch darkness.

The landlord of the public house had also heard the crash of metal. "Some poor bugger's in a mess of trouble by the sound of that." He rushed to pour himself into a pair of trousers before racing out of the building.

It was too black to see at first but as he drew closer to his neighbour's garden he could pick out the distinctive shape of the car. The crash had taken out the street light and there was a power cut inside the buildings.

Paul had been the first to reach the vehicle. He shone his torch through the front windscreen: both the seats were empty. Moving to the rear, he aimed the torch at the back seats and was greeted by the sight of a mass of female bodies all tangled up together, arms and legs entwining to such a degree that it was hard to make out what belonged to who. He did not notice the blood, all he saw was a vision of these young ladies crumpled up in a heap. Moving his hand forward he reached for the door handle, but a familiar voice stopped him dead in his tracks.

"Don't touch the door, I think there maybe live cables floating around."

Paul pulled back his hand quickly as he remembered that overhead power cables supplied their electricity.

"The wife has called for an ambulance, in fact she has called for all three services." Continued the landlord.

"Great, the ambulance station is only half a mile up the road. I don't think we should touch anything until they arrive."

At that moment they heard a piercing scream from out of the tangled mess of arms and legs.

"Don't move! Help is on its way," instructed Paul...

When Jason and Tom arrived, they took one look and knew that they would not get away with only one ambulance. Tom reached forward and picked up the hand set. "Can we have at least one other vehicle as quickly as you can dispatch, please."

Jason in the meantime had moved forward and started to investigate the site. He was an old hand at this and would never let himself be panicked into rushing forward without making sure that it was safe to do so.

It did not take long to discover that the crash had brought the power lines down. Live cables were merrily dancing about in the breeze, the shooting blue arc light flashing as they touched the damp ground.

"Everyone stand back and keep clear! There are live wires about and you all run the risk of electrocution," yelled Jason.

The night sky lit up as the fire engine turned the bend of the road, its blue lights illuminating the scene. There was a squeal of brakes as they took action to avoid hitting the man, still wandering aimlessly in the road.

"For Christ sake get hold of him before he gets himself killed," Jason yelled back over his shoulder as he walked towards the Fire Officer.

He pointed to the power cables still dancing in the breeze. "Can you get those under control? I dare not risk myself or my partner getting near while that lot are jumping about." He had considered the implications of trying to get in and treating the people trapped in the car. But he knew that if one of those cables touched the metal frame of the vehicle both he and Tom could have become casualties.

The Firemen very quickly made the cables safe and the two paramedics set to work sorting out the tangled mass inside the car. One of the women was dead. Her chest and larynx had been crushed and on closer examination he found her neck was broken. He imagined that she died almost instantaneously. Sadly she was causing an obstruction by restricting access to the others.

It was decided that her removal was the best choice.

This once voluptuous red head, dressed in a blue silk top and white, blood-soaked skirt lay with her head perched on the back parcel shelf. Her lifeless eyes were wide open and staring up at the roof of the car. Some mother's daughter, who would no longer feel pain or joy, had lost her chance to live to old age in a split second.

Jason indicated to the firemen to ease her out of the vehicle and lay her on the ground. The dead had to make way for the living and they could not help the others until she was removed.

Sounds from her friends now filled the air as the pain and bewilderment seeped into their brains.

Once the dead woman had been removed they concentrated on the remaining three casualties. One had also suffered some sort of spinal injury, as she could not feel anything from her waist down. Casualty three had multiple fractures, and what turned out to be her sister had lacerations to her upper body and a fractured femur. It was going to take them some time to sort out the best way to extract them from the wreckage.

Blue lights lit up the sky as the police and second ambulance appeared round the bend in the road. Although the police had closed off the road at both ends, it was safer if all the vehicles displayed their warning devices. The moonlight suddenly faded, disappearing behind a cloud and throwing blackness over the scene. "I can't see a bloody thing now," exclaimed Jason.

There was a whirring of a motor as the fire service started their generator and soon concentrated a field of light over the whole area with their overhead floodlights. Everything lit up like a bright summer's morning and Jason could see the full extent of the damage.

Casualty two had Jason worried, for he suspected a bad spinal fracture and with the others still struggling to free their tangled limbs, she was very vulnerable. He had to try and restrict their movements around the back seat and he knew it could not be achieved easily. How do you ask someone that is in pain and uncomfortable to keep still?

But this is exactly what he did. Once he had told them the true implications that their friend could spend her life in a wheelchair if they moved wrongly, all three remained still while the work to free the tangled limbs took place. 'There was always the possibility that she would be paralysed anyway.'

Slowly, with the help of his colleague, Jason and the other crew started to untangle the limbs, noting the extent of damage as the worked. Casualty three had fractures to her arm, leg and hip. Her sister had a fractured leg and a couple of nasty open lacerations to her upper body. Each movement took time as fractures were splinted and wounds dressed. Drips were set up and pain relief administered to those in need, until one by one they prepared them for removal. All three women were marvellous; they fought their own pain and stayed calm without any fuss.

While the firemen cut away the roof of the car, the ambulance crews did their best to keep the casualties still. The main problems were the restrictions of movement in the cramped compartment and the patient's potential injuries. Oxygen, Entonox and Nubain were all administered to eradicate as much discomfort as possible.

Soon the roof was lifted away by the firemen and they had more room to work.

It was time to start getting these people to the warmth of the hospital. This would get them treatment that could not be administered at the roadside, the two ladies with fractures to their limbs were taken off to hospital by the second ambulance crew, leaving Jason and Tom to finish setting the R.E.D. Board into position so that they could safely extract the spinal patient. Her tight fitted dress made it easier; the silky material helped the straps of the spinal board slide into position.

Everything was going well until the straps were being tightened. She was a big girl, her large cleavage centring her brimming breast causing Jason considerable problems when packing out the hollows of the straps. Jason cradled her head and shoulders in his arms while Tom guided the lower half out of the confined space of the car and onto the waiting stretcher placed alongside.

He suddenly realised that he was soaked to the skin. With all that had been going on he had not noticed that it was raining. Although he had only been in a crouched position for a short while, there had been no rest from the cold deluge.

"We'll bloody drown in this lot! he said. He felt miserable as the wet rain dripped down the back of his coat collar and onto his neck. As the water hit his glasses it masked his vision, causing him a little difficulty. It was times like this he wished that they would invent wiper blades for spectacles.

They tried to shield their patient lying on the trolley but the rain gushed down in unsympathetic torrents. Blood from small glass cuts diluted its redness with the heavenly fluids from above before being washed away. They had a deep feeling of compassion for the patient, for if they were wet and miserable what must she

179

be feeling? Both men were frustrated working in these conditions but they had to move slowly. They could not rush towards the dryness of the ambulance for fear that any awkward movement could have fatal consequences.

Once they had finally loaded the young lady onto the vehicle Tom slipped off and discreetly arranged with the police for a further ambulance to pick up the deceased lady still laying on the cold ground.

The journey into hospital, although slow, was uneventful and her condition remained unchanged.

The police took the driver who had caused the accident by showing off to his female passengers to the hospital. They had arrested him on scene and would detain him at Her Majesty's pleasure after he was released from the casualty department.

This had been a night of road traffic accidents and the two paramedics were getting tired. "God, I need a break from this," exclaimed Tom.

"Well, if they give us the chance we should try and get back to station. That way we stand a chance of a prompt finish."

Tom drove into the casualty tunnel where staff were standing awaiting their arrival. The back doors were opened up from the outside by casualty staff, questions firing from their lips as they moved forward.

"Is this the back injury we have been waiting for?"

"Yes, this is Jenny. Loss of sensation from the waist down. Only other injuries are minor glass cuts,"

They wheeled her into the trauma room where the emergency team was waiting to begin their examinations. Once again the same questions were asked of the crew.

"How long had she been trapped. How was she found? What was her condition and had it changed on route?" Standard questions and procedures that were practised by all, but necessary in case the smallest detail got overlooked.

One tiny snip of information could make life or death changes.

It had seemed like hours that they had been involved with this call but it was only four-fourteen, less than an hour had passed. Tom and Jason handed their patient over to the casualty officer and went to find out how the others had progressed. Both the other two ladies were now in a stable condition and lucky that they had not suffered any internal injuries. None of the three were aware that their friend was dead. They all assumed that she was being treated in another department as she had been taken out of the car first. No one had the heart to tell them the truth.

The male driver was going to be kept in under observation because there was a possibility he could have suffered a head injury. But he would remain under police guard until he could be removed to the local holding centre.

The paramedics dragged their tired, aching bones back to the vehicle almost dreading calling up the controller in case he found them something else. Luck was on their side this time and they were instructed to return to base for a well-earned cup of tea ...

Back on the ambulance station Jason uttered a soft groan as he shifted his weight; he could not sit in the one position for much longer as his knee joint was giving him grief again. He looked at his wristwatch: only three more hours left before they finished the shift and could head for home. 'There has to be a better way for him to make a living than this,' he told himself. He bent forward and massaged his painful limb while at the same time glancing across at Tom, who was sat bolt upright fast asleep and gently snoring.

The light outside was gradually beginning to brighten as the dawn broke. Shadowy contours of the surrounding buildings showed their stark lines as the sky eased slowly from the darkness.

A brand new day was about to begin. He settled himself back in the easy chair, glanced up at the clock on the wall and closed his eyes ...

181

Jason woke quickly in the partial darkness of the station for he had not been in a deep sleep. A thin ribbon of sweat trickled into his eye, causing him to blink. Tom must have turned up the thermostat on the heating system. Although it was freezing outside, it was hotter than hell in the crew room. He crept across the floor towards the kitchen area, as he did not want to disturb his sleeping partner. Easing a drinking glass from out of the cupboard, he filled it with cold water before gulping it down in just two slugs.

Still his mouth felt dry; he needed to get some fresh air into his lungs for the central heating had dried all the spittle from the back of his throat and he could not swallow. He made for the garage door; it made a creaking sound as he pushed it open. Tom stirred slightly, then turned before slipping back into a deep slumber.

A split second later the alarm sounded loudly, causing Tom to jump upright with shock. Reluctantly Jason picked up the handset and responded.

"What are people doing walking around in the middle of the night?" exclaimed Tom, showing his frustration at being woken so suddenly. He looked a mess, eyes narrowed and bloodshot, hair sticking up on one side where he had laid his head. In fact, he looked like a steamroller had run over him. He move quickly towards the sink, turned on the cold tap and splashed his face a few times with the cold water, desperate to wake himself before racing down the road at sixty plus miles an hour. "Why the hell was I not born rich?" he muttered querulously.

Tom opened the driver's window; the cold air blasted its way through the open gap and its freezing flow shook them both into a state of alertness. Jason sat in the attendant's seat, his hand draped loosely over the medical bag he held on his lap.

They approached a surprising number of cars running in front of them. Although sirens were not used during the twilight hours, Tom reached forward for the blue light switch and lit up the morning sky. Most of the cars moved over to let them pass, but the car in front made no attempt to stop or slow down. In fact, the driver increased his speed trying to stay ahead of the ambulance. He did not get far as a red light forced him to stop abruptly. The passenger in the car tried to look away embarrassed by the situation as they flashed past.

They had progressed a couple of more miles further down the road when they spotted a set of headlights flashing a signal at their approaching vehicle. Tom eased his speed as they drew nearer, making sure that this was indeed the right location.

Jason was dismounting from the cab before the ambulance had fully stopped.

He walked towards a couple of guys standing on the edge of a steep bank; it must have been at least a ten-foot drop to the bottom. Looking down he observed the remains of a car on its side. There were signs that the car had struck a large gnarled tree; pieces of bark and torn branches littered the ground around its base. The impact must have been tremendous for the tree was not only split and cracked but it was almost toppled. Its roots, lifted up from out of the ground, had left a small crater, exposing the roots, and he could see that it would take very little force to topple it completely.

"Has anyone been down there yet?

They both replied at the same time, 'No.'

"Christ, this is going to be bloody awkward"

Jason started making his way down the steep bank, hanging onto the undergrowth with one hand and clutching his medical bag with the other. Slipping and sliding he finally reached the bottom of the grassy bank, moving directly towards the wreckage. He flashed the beam of light from his torch through the window and into the car's interior. It looked empty at first, no signs of life, then he caught sight of a body curled into the foot well of the car. Forcing open the door he was immediately taken aback by the ferocious smell of decomposing flesh from within. He controlled his urge to vomit and on closer examination of the body he found it to be black and bloated; insects were swarming over its rotting form gorging on this prodigious feast.

"Oh God, poor sod." He wondered how long he had been down here and did he die immediately.

He could not stand the pungent smell any longer; his heaving stomach began to churn as the waves of nausea swept over him. Quickly he shut the car door and gulped the cold fresh air into his lungs. Then, after taking a few seconds to compose himself, he looked upward and yelled to Tom who was awaiting instructions.

"This poor old bugger has been dead for days. There is nothing at all we can do for him. Can you contact control and get the 'local plod' here as quickly as they like?"

Tom signalled that he had understood and turned towards the ambulance.

Jason stayed at the bottom of the bank to have a good look around, making sure that there had not been another casualty from the wreck. The last thing he wanted was to overlook a cadaver lying in the grass somewhere. He was aware of the need not to disturb the scene too much, knowing that the police would want to investigate the area in depth.

The sickness that he had felt in his stomach had passed after he had witnessed the corpse swarming with bugs enjoying their meal. In fact, it had given way to ravenous hunger; he had forgotten the last time he had eaten something and now his belly craved substance.

He gave himself the once-over inspection to make sure that he had not suffered any injuries on the decent down the grass bank. There was a fat raindrop that slapped into his glasses just before the heavens opened up and the rain came down in bucket loads turning the roads into rivers of water. He threw back his head and shoulders breathing in deeply the cold wet air before attempting the climb back up the now muddy slope.

What he suddenly felt was a sort of premonition that something terrible was about to happen, a surge of fear sent a shiver up his spine. Without warning there was a loud cracking sound above his head.

Instinctively he dropped into a crouched.

Only a split second passed but it felt like time had stood still. Then he was aware of a bulky shape hurtling down the bank straight towards his position. Without thinking, he threw himself to the right as the large object crashed past his body, just missing him with inches to spare. It was like something in slow motion: every detail vivid in his mind as he lay still on the ground willing his heartbeat to slow its pace. Adrenaline coursing through his veins caused a pounding in his ears and he felt that they would burst at any moment.

He looked across at the large shape silhouetted in the half-light. The tree, already lifted partially out of the ground, had crashed down from the top of the bank after the rain had washed away the holding soil. 'Fuck, that was bloody close,' he told himself.

Tom yelled down from above, "are you all right?"

"Yes, just about, that was too close for comfort."

Looking towards the tree, its shape loomed menacing in the torchlight where it had fallen with its branches spread across the bonnet of the wrecked car.

It was almost as if it had reached out in revenge for being uprooted by the metal monster. This had been a day like many others, except on this day he had faced his own shadow of death.

Jason started up the muddy bank once more, but he soon knew that he was not going to make it back up that slope without help.

Seeing his partner's plight Tom threw down a rope.

His medical bag was hoisted up first, before Jason made his ascent to the road. Many hands helped him scramble up the last

185

couple of feet, as the effort had taken its effect. Once on the firm surface Jason took a look at himself in the wing mirror of the ambulance. What a bloody mess! He was covered in a thick layer of mud that was slowly washing off with the rain. There was no trace of whiteness, the thaw had come and completely washed the snow away.

The police turned up a short while after. One of them looked over the edge and whistled through his teeth.

"Must have hit the tree and brought it down on top of the car."

"Like hell it did, the bloody thing tried to take me with it." Jason explained what had happened and what he had found in the wreckage before handing over to them. It would be down to a police investigation now to determine what was the cause of this fatal accident.

Tom stoked up the engine and headed back to base for a well-earned finish and rest.

The cold damp of the morning bit deep into Jason's bones sending an ache across the small of his back. He turned up the collar of his fluorescent jacket trying to keep the chill off his neck. The night was slowly fading, warming to the hazy light of the morning and nature was waking to the dawn. People would soon be stirring from their warm beds, dreams set aside as they scampered around frantically getting ready to attend their designated work places, or the lucky ones that could sit back and relax enjoying the national holiday. Jason gave a shudder as the cold swept through his body; he always felt the cold more when he was weary. Without a doubt, being shut up in that cramped ambulance all night had done him no favours. He pondered the night's work: then stopped himself and thought, "What the hell, it's a new day and a brand new year and I want to get home" ...

186

On arriving at the house everything was still and he crept silently through the hallway, not wishing to disturb his wife, who he assumed would still be asleep. He made a hot drink and settled down in his chair to unwind, the adrenaline still coursing through his veins. He would be on a high for some time yet and this would stop him from sleeping if he went straight to bed.

Looking out of the conservatory window he watched the birds scouring the ground for food. He had a soft spot for all the feathered species that flew in and out of his garden, for they gave him many hours of enjoyment as he observed their funny antics. His garden was a source of immense pleasure; he loved to sit and plan, changing layouts in his mind; some he would put into practice and others would be forgotten. Although he lived close to a busy motorway, the traffic noise did not disturb the tranquillity. Nature had adapted to the hustle and bustle of the ever-growing human population and the wild life had also accepted the changes to their habitat.

Jason closed his eyes and went over the previous night's work in his mind, analysing each job in turn, looking for anything that could have been improved or handled better. His thoughts were disturbed as he heard movement in the hallway; his wife was awake and had got out of bed.

"Morning, Jay, did you have a good night?" she asked.

"Not to bad. It was busy though: kept us out for most of the night," he replied.

He did not mention his close shave with the falling tree; some things were best kept secret.

"Happy New Year, by the way. I've left the bed nice and warm for you. See you about midday and I will talk to you then"...

CHAPTER FOURTEEN

The dreams were back, caused by his state of mind and the dysfunctional confidence that he felt sometimes. Theses constant depressions were a warning that he could not cope with the job for much longer. He could not stand to watch many more grieving families collapse after the death of a loved one or listen to the cries of a distraught mother who's child had been crushed or maimed in some tragic accident. Too many times he had watched as they buried their faces into hankies, heard them sob as the tears filled their eyes and listened to the pitiful pleas as they sought miracles. These were some of the faceless shadows that haunted his dreams, reaching into the very depths of his soul as if somehow he held himself responsible for all the misery that they had suffered.

Training school teaches you how to cope and become detached from the countless tragedies that come with the job. But after twenty-two years he could not hold back the tide of grief. He was not able to hide it away in some dark corner of his mind as he did when he first joined the service. If he let his employers know that this was how he felt and that these were the thoughts that passed through his mind, they would without doubt try hard to dispense with him quickly and quietly under some pretext or another, for they would deem him unstable.

His GP knew the stress was taking a wicked toll and had tried many times to get Jason to throw in the towel and seek early retirement on medical grounds, but he resisted every time ...

He tried to scream, but he only produced a low choked gurgling. His voice no longer seemed to want to vibrate the vocal cords. The conversation was taking place in his head but that was as far as it wanted to travel. Dry cracked lips felt parched beyond belief and his tongue seemed paralysed and numb. The dreams were back again.

'This is ridiculous, how can this keep on happening to me?'

Seemingly he was floating, then standing looking down at the form at his feet. It looked human, but there was no face, no skin or eyes. Just the monstrous shape, barbecued and blackened, cooked meat that showed the outline of bones. Taught burnt flesh just above the surface of the gaunt blacken skull suggested that this was once a man, although you could be forgiven for not recognising this misshapen mass as such. Fires had billowed and roared into flames that had consumed everything in its path. The horrible things that had been done to this unfortunate human would make the blood of anyone run cold.

Jason tried to extricate these grotesque visions from his dreams, dreading the next episode and the fearful sights to come.

The picture changes: the body of a woman stares up at him with dead eyes. He puts the stethoscope to his ears and starts to check for breath sounds as he squeezes the Sussex bag. No breath sounds from the right lung, none from the left. It was not the chest that was rising. He had intubated the 'Oesophagus'. "Sod it!" he exclaimed as he quickly deflated the cuff on the endotracheal tube, and started again. He could not understand how he had managed to miss; the vocal cords had been clearly sighted. He re-inserted the tube correctly and checked with the stethoscope to make doubly sure that it was correctly sited.

He chastised himself. "You let yourself intubate the oesophagus, you did not check for breath sounds, you let the emergency cloud your judgement."

A voice from the back of his mind reminded him that he was human, not a bloody machine, anyone could make the odd mistake. This was typical of Jason, cracking down harder than anyone else could ever do as he analysed everything that he did. The jumbled scenes continued as his disturbed sleep kept his mind in overdrive.

Constantly he wiped away the thoughts of his wrongful actions, only to have them replaced by the vision of a man who had

189

suffered traumatic amputations of both legs. The poor man was dragging his injured body around the room with his arms, leaving a large wet trail of blood in his wake, pleading with Jason for help, expecting the paramedic to perform the impossible.

A sudden urge to run swept over him, to get away and leave it to someone else to take the responsibility. But he knew that running would not be an option. The patient needed help and that had to happen now!

Waking with a start, he sat upright in his wet bed; his sweating body had made him soaking wet and as the cold air hit the heat of his flesh it turned icy. He was physically shaking either from the coldness of the room or the tenseness of the dreams.

'A psychoanalyst would have a field day trying to make sense of my dreams, they would haul my arse up before the college of psychiatry as a show piece,' he thought to himself.

Slipping out of bed, he put on his dressing gown and walked to the window and looked out. The rain was falling as a mixture of sleet and cold rain; people were hurrying past to get to the warmth of their own homes. The ticking of the clock on the side of the bed told him that he had only been sleeping for just under five hours ...

After a good meal and a few hours relaxing in front of the box stuck in the corner of the room, he heaved his weary body out of the chair and made his way to the bathroom to get ready for another exciting night on the streets of Southsea.

Standing in front of the mirror he took a look at his tired face staring back at him. 'God, I look a mess,' he thought to himself.

His mind drifted as he thought of the previous year and he remembered one of the calls that they had dealt with. The young woman who had jumped from the top floor of the block of flats, smashing every bone in her body. What is it that drives someone to end his or her own life in such a dramatic way? Experience had taught him that these poor lost souls reach a precarious moment in life where it takes insanity, desperation or pure bravery

190

to face death in this way. A slight shiver swept through him as he recalled trying to lift what was left of that poor wretched woman off the hard concrete floor. Without the bony skeleton to hold her body together she was just like a bag full of water. They were to discover later that she was over four months pregnant and only eighteen years old.

Olive stood watching from outside the door: he looked more tired that she had ever seen him look before. His eyes stared straight ahead, as if transfixed, seemingly engrossed in some deep thought. Jason's body may have stood there in that room but his mind was far away. How she wished that he would stop being so judgmental towards himself or, better still, pluck up the courage to take the plunge and retire. But she knew that it would take a mighty shove to get him to make a complete detachment from the job that he loved to hate.

Both Tom and Jason had to live with the self-questions and doubts that haunted them, hide the sadness of those that are beyond help and take the responsibilities of bringing new life into this hard and cruel world. It was their way of debriefing the mind; any mistake brought doubts in both man's ability whenever things went wrong.

Anyone that can tell you they are so good they don't make mistakes, you should worry about them, for even doctors sometimes get it wrong, for we are humans not robots.

Possessing these advanced skills put a tremendous burden on Jason, he had been much happier when he was a technician. He had often wished that he'd chosen a different type of career. 'The Fire Brigade' or 'The Police Force', both offering better pay and working conditions, or maybe as a high flyer with a large pay cheque at the end of the month.

Putting the final touches to his uniform he made one last check before saying goodbye to his wife and making for the front door.

As he drove the few miles towards the ambulance station he observed the steady stream of cars and lorries making their usual dash for home. Most would soon get ready for a night out on the town while Tom and himself would be out working picking up the aftermath. He wondered what lay ahead of them this evening.

Ten years ago the only bad nights used to be Fridays and Saturdays, but these days every night was the same. He had seen the number of calls increase year on year, but the amount of vehicles had actually been reduced due to cut-backs. The pressure was slowly putting a strain on everyone, from ambulance crews to hospital staff, even the porters and cleaners felt the demands increasing.

He swung into the station, parked the car and with a sigh dragged himself out into the damp failing light. 'Here we go again, suppose it would be too much to ask for quiet night,' he thought, as he looked skywards...

Chapter Fifteen

Angel and Sam sat in the station crew room watching the television while awaiting the return of the vehicle. The previous crew must have been given a late job, which would cause a delay in the change over. It was a Friday night and the first of seven duties to look forward to before getting any time off again.

The first night was always the worst. Not only was it on a Friday, one of the busy shifts of the week. But it was also made hard because of the trend of not being able to sleep properly; you still got up early in the morning meaning that you then had to stay awake until at least eight o'clock the following day.

Friday and Saturday nights were bad, not only do the run-of the-mill calls come in, but the users of Clubs, Pubs and Discos also expand the pressurised service. This is reflected in many ways: mostly drink- related problems, causing many of the Traffic Accidents on our road system. Drinking also is responsible for many fights, domestic assaults, sudden collapse and just plain old feeling unwell through over indulgence.

There is a new, much more serious problem that has raised its ugly head over the last few years. This is a new kind of drink-related assault, one of the worse kinds being that of the 'Rat Pack': gangs of young men and women that walk around towns at night just looking for victim's to take their frustrations out on. No one in particular it could be anyone, it could even be 'You'. All that is required is that you are there in front of them. The chosen victim can be on his way home from work, saying good night to a girl friend or just coming out of a pub. No matter what the reason, it would be a case of being in the wrong place at the wrong time.

Injuries that are delivered to these victims are not normally that of a minor nature, most suffer lasting damage or even death.

193

The aim of this sick game is to inflict as much pain and injury as possible. It has been known in some seaside towns for this type of assault to happen up to five or six times in the same night, and believed to be the work of the same gang.

There are still many unsolved murders from these kinds of incidents. The cause of death in most cases was due to that of massive head injuries, resulting in coma and brain stem damage. The gangs that were responsible seemed to get a quick buzz out of orchestrating this type of attack and the consequences to their victims did not deter them at all. The fact is, the more they performed this savagery, the more they would keep looking for more blood and innocent victims to ravage.

Add all this to a normal working shift, plus the fact that after eleven o'clock at night only about five Ambulances remain to cover an area of some twenty six miles in circumference, that is about one fifth of the vehicles that are on the road during the day. There is also added pressure if one of the crew that is due to cover a vehicle reports in sick and they cannot cover the his duty by means of overtime. This would mean that the remaining crews having to work much harder and faster to make up the shortfall. It is a fact that there have been times when the service has been reduced to only three Ambulances out of five that have been fully manned on the road on a Friday and Saturday night, placing extreme pressure on the remaining crews. They would be arriving at the local hospital to be greeted by some Nurse telling them that there was a phone call from their control operator, who expected them to drop everything and go out on the next call. This caused friction at the best of times; all that it did was anger the crew concerned ...

Angel and Sam had settled themselves down into the rest room chairs while awaiting the return of the late-finishing vehicle to arrive back on base. The television was not very interesting and it was

194

pointless trying to get involved in a film, as they would never get to see the end. Sam got out a book while Angel started on her crossword from a magazine. They spent the time talking about their family lives and what they had got up to on their days off. Angel had two daughters and a son who would make her life unbearable at times. Her youngest girl was the one that gave her the most problems; she always seemed to be up to mischief and gave her mother more headaches than the other two put together.

Sam had been working with Angel as a partner for some years now, ever since she and Jason had qualified as paramedics. At that time they needed at least one paramedic on each vehicle and management had split them up and sent them to different stations to achieve this aim. Angel was a lovely lady, liked by almost everyone on the service and although slight in build she could hold her ground with any man on the job.

There was a roar of a motor engine outside in the station yard. A screech of brakes as an Ambulance pulled up alongside the crew room window. Angel and Sam jumped up from their chairs expecting the vehicle to be that of the late crew back from the last call. But they were wrong, it was another crew who had been sent into give cover until their own motor arrived. This was standard practice within the ambulance service as vehicles were dispatched to answer emergency calls, other vehicles would be moved up the line to halfway stages. No one could ever have prescience as to where the next call would come from. It was a practised procedure and rightly or wrongly it had been this way for many years.

Probably almost every member of the general public must have at some time looked at an Ambulance parked on a roundabout or sat on the top of a Motorway bridge. Just sitting waiting for the next call to come through on the radio. There were not as many thought, just sitting wasting time or enjoying a quick cup of tea. In fact, many shifts these days pass without the crews getting

195

any subsistance at all; the demand is so great sometimes they are put in the position of having to work in excess of twelve hours with no substantial food or drink. This increased the risk of mistakes being made through tiredness or the drop in blood sugar levels; ambulance personnel have the same needs as any other human. Fuel, If you don't put petrol in a car, it stops running and if you don't feed the cells in a human it breaks down.

Administration in the health service is top heavy; bureaucracy gone mad and always ready to stand in judgement against overworked and over stretched staff. Regardless of what political power lorded over parliament it remained in a state of under manning and under funded incompetence. The constant increase of paperwork was considered more valuable than patient care, although nobody would admit to it. Accident report forms are to be filled out in detail regardless of time needed for medical treatments; crews viewed this with a negative attitude. These reports were tedious, but recognised as a necessity, provided they did not cause neglect of patient care.

Take a road traffic accident: the trauma created around the scene of any accident can be totally mind-blowing. A paramedic's brain is racing at an alarming rate, as he tries to combat the injuries, entrapment and movements all around him. There could be more than one patient to deal with as he assesses the situation. The last thing on his mind while making a diagnosis is filling out a report form.

Contrary to the beliefs of the administration, these forms are not completed correctly. This is not because the person filling out the forms are irresponsible or lazy; it's because he or she is human. Mistakes and omissions happen regularly in the National Health Service: staff on the ground know it is caused by stress.

The pen pushers would never admit that it stems from the need to justify their positions or the lack of funding ...

There was a crash as Jason and Tom walked into the station doorway. Jason greeted Angel with a big smile and a hug, never forgetting that they had once been such good working partners before being split up. They had been a good team for in excess of a ten-year period and their two families got on extremely well.

Angel would confide in Jason about her family problems and he would do the same, unfolding all his troubles to her.

They had worked strictly on a professional basis, although there were many that did not believe this to be the complete truth. The fact was that when they first started working together, Angel's daughters used to creep round to the Ambulance Station in the evenings to check up on the pair of them. Jason's first wife had also made comments on the subject from time to time ...

"Control said to tell you to put your feet up for a while. The late crew was given a job to go in London about an hour ago, so you will not see them for few hours yet."

"Well, in that case, let's put the kettle on while we have the chance," said Sam.

The other three sat down in the easy chairs and before long they were all talking about different issues taking place within the Service. The local gossip was a prized topic with ambulance personnel; there was always something or someone to talk about and because they could go weeks without seeing each other, there was always news hot off the press to pass on.

It did not take long before the conversation got around to discussing previous jobs that they had dealt with in the past. By being able to do this, ambulance personnel can pass on helpful information and little tips to each other that could be put to good use at a later date. Some ideas that may seem silly to most can prevent a lot of pain and suffering if used at the right time and in the right text. Treatments learnt this way can often be used for all manner of circumstances. Soon the conversation got around to one of the many jobs that Jason and Angel had done many years previously.

197

They had been called to a print works one morning in the height of summer to a collapsed male. On arrival at the incident they were greeted by the works manager, who gave them a brief history of what had taken place before their arrival. The injured man in question did not work at the print works, he was an outside contractor employed to clean the inside of an 'Ink Tank'.

This was what he had been doing just before the collapse took place.

Angel and Jason were guided to the location of the tank, where they both stood with dismayed look upon their faces. The Ink tank that they visualised was not, as they supposed, on the ground but suspended some fifteen foot up on a platform. It was approximately 6'x4'x6'. The whole area was covered with black sticky ink and everything that came near to it was contaminated with a black stain.

When Angel and Jason got to the top of the ink tank they both stopped dead in their tracks. They had spotted a 'Hazchem' warning sign on the side of a cleaning bottle, warning them that they were dealing with a toxic substance that was able to give off gas fumes, and advising the use of Breathing Apparatus before approaching in confined areas.

Jason shouted down to the shop Foreman below and asked him to dial 999 again, requesting the presence of the Fire Brigade, making sure that they were made aware that the ambulance crew had a chemical problem and needed special BA equipment urgently.

Angel had already put her head over the side of the tank and as she looked down into the inside of the tank the fumes hit her nostrils. "This silly sod has no breathing gear on," she gasped.

The man had lowered himself into the metal tank that had just a three-foot hole at the top to allow access. He had started to clean the inside with a solvent solution before being over come by the fumes. He was supposed to be wearing Industrial Breathing

Apparatus but had decided not to because of its bulk, probably thinking that it would get in the way with such a small working area. It would not have taken very long before the effects of the solvents started to work on his respiratory system.

By the time Angel and Jason arrived on scene the man had lost consciousness, the fumes that were being given off by the solvent were acting like an anaesthetic. The problem that the pair had was that the hole was not big enough to allow Jason to climb into the tank and that the man lay directly under the only opening. To cap it all, the man in the tank was approximately sixteen stone of what now would be dead weight because of his relaxed muscles.

Angel and Jason were covered in print ink; it was all over their hands, faces and soaked into their uniforms. Jason leaned into the tank and was just able to reach down to the man's face with the oxygen mask; he held it there as long as possible before he needed to use some of the oxygen himself as the fumes started to take effect on him.

He heard someone talking behind him and upon raising himself out of the tank opening he looked into the face of Fred, one of the local Fire Fighters. Like the police officers, the ambulance crews had a good social understanding with the fire crews. They all worked on varying jobs together from time to time and they got to know each other quite well. There was also a good social and entertainment side that goes handi-in-hand with emergency workers; of course, this includes the hospital staff, for without the nurses no party would ever get off the ground.

Jason gave Fred an update on the situation, explaining that he had found it very hard to give aid to the guy in the tank. He moved aside to let Fred have a look for himself so that he could take charge of the rescue. The 'Tetrachloroethylene' was well known to the fireman, and the consequences that could arise if not handled correctly.

They could not get a fireman inside the tank as the chap was blocking the entrance with his body. "What a bloody stupid thing to do. Who in his right mind would go into an enclosure this size with solvents and no flipping breathing gear? said Fred.

One of the firemen came up with a crude but seemingly logical suggestion; by means of some rope and a thick plank of wood they would try and lift him out. The plank would be used to give them some traction and by allowing, one of the firemen to lay across the wooden board it was hoped that he could reach in and secure the rope under the guy's arms.

His plan was set into action without delay. Although slipping the rope around the man was not a problem, the amount of access was. Along with the slippery ink it made the rescue very difficult and to get any grip created hazards.

While this was going on Jason had to keep checking to see if the man's airway was intact and that his breathing was not being compromised.

The fireman managed to get the rope under the guy's arms and secured; he was then hoisted upwards so that he was now in a standing position and the rope tied off to stop him slipping back into the tank. Other members of the fire crew had been rigging a pulley and hoist system so that he could be heaved completely out of the tank.

Angel and Jason were making sure that the man's airway was still clear and that he was breathing all right. Jason requested that another Ambulance be called, for this rescue had taken some time now and the oxygen was getting very low, also it would be much easier to have someone not contaminated by ink to drive the vehicle to hospital ...

Fire crews worked quickly, now gently guiding him out of the tank a little at a time. The oxygen and the movement slowly started to take effect. He responded just enough for him to give some assistance to the firemen making the extraction. Down below the second Ambulance had arrived and they were busy setting up the stretcher ready to receive the patient once lowered to the ground. Fire crews gently lowered him down via the pulley system to the ambulance crew waiting to give him their attention. He was covered in ink from his head to his toes and they could not believe the mess. All the people concerned looked as if they had been involved in a school rag week or auditioning for a series of the black and white minstrels. Thankfully everyone saw the funny side of things and had a real good laugh about it.

Angel and Jason had set out that morning with sharply pressed slacks, white shirts and shining shoes. When they stopped and looked at each other after the job was completed all they could do was burst out laughing. Gone were the white shirts and neat blue trousers. They were covered in a black, sticky, gooey mess, to say that they could see the whites of their eyes was an under statement.

It took almost four hours to clean up both the vehicle and themselves, making the ambulance unfit to be on the road until all traces of the ink were gone. They had to scrap their uniforms for they would never be the same again.

The man was released later that day suffering no ill effects, but not before his 'fortune had been read by the Fire Officer' over the correct use of breathing apparatus when using chemical agents...

Like all good things, they have to end. Control rang and instructed them to return to their own base station as they were now fully covered again. They departed but not without Jason's usual hug from Angel.

Tom turned the key in the ignition, gunned up the engine and headed the vehicle back towards the station.

They had not been mobile more than four minutes when they spotted a woman frantically waving her arms, then pointing towards a dark shape lying on the ground.

"Call it in Tom, I'll go and have a look."

The woman was at the door before Jason had a chance to open it; she was shaking and deeply concerned about a man who had collapsed. "You didn't hang about. I only rang a couple of minutes ago. You better come quickly, I think he maybe dead."

"Sounds like there is already a vehicle on the way. Tell them we'll deal with this call."

Jason grabbed his medic bag and dropped down beside the body on the pavement. "Can you hear me, mate?" there was no response.

Feeling for a pulse he breathed a sigh of relief when he found one bounding under his fingers. 'Thank you, Lord,' he thought.

He shone his torch to see if there were any obvious signs of injury and a body scans. It was when he checked for facial injuries that he recognised the man: to the woman's surprise Jason stood up and spoke to the man: "come on, Tony, get on your feet."

Dismayed the woman looked at Jason, shocked at his seemingly uncaring approach.

Tony Rice was one of their regulars, who, if he had attended drama school, would have most likely been the next Noel Coward. He was well known by most of the local crews for his Oscar – winning performances. Tony knew every trick in the book, from throwing a fit to faking a full-blown heart attack. This man knew more about trauma than some of the nursing staff that cared for him. He was so good at pretending to be unconscious; he could let a paramedic insert an oral airway without gagging on it. Unlike some of the other regular play actors, this one was not aggressive.

"Tony, its Jason. Come on, don't waste our time, I have seen more collapse cases than you have had hot dinners. You don't roll your eyes under their lids or swallow like that if your unconscious, mate."

With that, Tony promptly stood up and gave Jason a mouthful of abuse, then walked off.

The woman that had flagged them down stood with her mouth wide open watching her dead body amble off muttering under his breath.

"I don't believe that. I was so sure that he was in a bad way. I am sorry to have wasted your time."

"Don't worry, you're not the first to be fooled by our Tony: he is one of the best actors we have and I can assure you that there are a few of them in this area."

"Why do they bother?" she asked.

"Mainly because they can pick a warm spot to sleep in the casualty unit if they find a crew that doesn't know them," Jason explained.

Feeling guilty, the woman continued on her way, leaving Jason to complete the paperwork on Tony.

"Sad really, to end up in that state. What kind of life can that be?" said Tom as he kicked the motor into gear and headed back to station...

They had been back on the road for only a few minutes when Jason started to twist and turn in his seat because of his knee problem that had been playing him up for some time. There would be no warning, just a sudden pain that felt like a knife had been stuck into his knee joint and then twisted. The pain made him feel totally uncomfortable and no matter what position he placed himself in, it could not be eased.

Tom looked across at Jason with pity aware of the problem that he had. "Are you alright?"

Jason nodded his head and tried to manage a smile but, unable to relax, the tension was reflected in his face and the creased lines showed that the pain was real. Perspiration ran off his brow in steady streams down to his neck, making the shirt collar damp. Reluctantly he had asked for help from the hospital, not knowing what the cause of the problem was, although he did have a rough idea. Accepting the results with relief, he had been almost happy to hear that it was just a misplaced joint that just needed realignment. It was a big weight off his shoulders, 'I am not sick, there is nothing wrong that can't be fixed, he thought.' Although he would have to undergo weeks of physiotherapy and possibly an hour under the surgeon's knife, he could live with that; better than some of the things that had crossed his mind over the past months.

The light of the street lamp pierced the windshield and passed through his body; then, almost as if by some miracle, the pain eased away. It was embarrassing to have this weakness show up, but the pain was so bad at times he could not physically hide it. He gave Tom a quick glance and grinned, settled back in the seat and looked at the road ahead, pausing to collect his thoughts. It was not easy to stay in a job that caused him so many problems, and then he remembered how good it used to be.

Suddenly the radio burst into life, causing the pair of them to jump out of their seats.

"No bloody peace for the wicked, we must have been a couple of real bad sons of bitches at some point," retorted Tom.

The vehicle was immediately aimed towards the location of the call given by the controller. Adrenaline started to pump through both bodies as their minds worked overtime. Heart rates increased with anticipation of things to come. The past few minutes were gone and forgotten for they had to focus on the call that they were to attend. They had been called to a disco fight that involved a stabbing, causing a neck wound.

Tom pushed the vehicle along at top speed, desperately surveying the road ahead and trying to force his way through the traffic. Jason had every confidence in his partner's ability, knowing that he would be aware only of the road and the task ahead. Sitting in the passenger seat, he looked at the road in front, trying to watch out for sudden, unforeseen dangers. Driving at this speed, the more pairs of eyes to watch the better.

Suddenly Tom hit the horn and started to cuss out loud as he swerved the ambulance to avoid the car in front. "Stupid, daft shit," he hissed through his teeth at the driver he had almost hit up the rear.

The driver of the Rover in front looked up, surprised to find that he had drifted out across the white line. Tom's quick reflexes had saved a nasty accident, not to mention yards of paperwork. Had he hit the car it would have been classed as his fault by law ...

The disco had started at eight. Everything was normal: lads were propping up the bar as usual and the girls were putting in their requests for the top songs with the local disc jockey. Friends that just wanted to catch up on the local gossip gathered in small groups. Time just seemed to fly by with everyone enjoying the night's entertainment, until a couple of hours later when the fight started. Drinks had been flowing fast all night and it was almost too good to be true that trouble had not erupted before now. The good humour in the crowd suddenly changed, a small fight started between two of the lads. Verbal at first, then the punching and kicking, laying into each other with heated resolve. In all probability over some girl that they had both taken a shine to. The fight had started with just the two but before long many others had joined in the fracas and the fist were now flying in all directions with bodies everywhere.

Then it turned nasty: someone smashed a pint glass and stuck the jagged sharp edge into the side of another's neck. Almost immediately the fighting stopped and the crowd moved forward to stare down at the body on the ground, gazing at the gaping wound.

The lad on the floor was now still, the hot blood in his veins cooling to the iced cold fear he now felt. Blood oozing from the jagged hole in the side of his neck felt warm as it ran down to the rear of the head and lay in a pool. A throbbing pain nagged

205

constantly, causing him to grimace as it increased its grip. He was aware of all that was going on around him but not able to move from the ground where he lay. His head swimming and the feeling of nausea swept through him. Now he was fighting to stay conscious as the blood flowed from the wound.

"Call for an ambulance!" came a cry from the crowd.

"Do something! look at all the blood!" screamed another ...

Walking into a dancehall or a pub was always hazardous where the booze had been flowing. To locate the patient was hard and they had to rely on someone being sober enough to show them where to go. Forcing a pathway through the crowd with all the equipment caused problems as some were still in an angry mood, looking for any excuse to take their frustrations out on anyone that happened to get in the way.

While Jason and Tom worked on the lad with the cut to his throat, one of his mates started the fighting all over again. Fist and verbal abuse were flying everywhere and it was not just the lads fighting now, the girls had joined in. They were more vicious; pulling hair, long fingernails tearing into soft flesh and the verbal that was rendered from those sweet young mouths would make the vicar cringe with dismay.

Tom's uniform was smeared with blood as he crouched along side the lad, his coat bottom sweeping the pool of blood as he moved. "I can't stop the bleeding it just keeps seeping through," he yelled at Jason.

Adrenaline was coursing through his body as the tension mounted. Exhausted with the effort, his hands started to tremble as he put one more pressure pad in place. He pushed down with his hand, trying desperately to stem the flow of blood.

Both minds now racing, Jason thought of something that had worked once before on a previous call. Looking up at the under manager he asked. "Have you got a bath towel on the premises?"

The manager flew off in the direction of the bar and a couple of minutes later came back with a collection of towels.

Selecting the most appropriate, Jason rolled the bath towel loosely and draped it around the lads neck like a scarf and crossed at the windpipe. Leaving Tom to watch the wound, Jason set about securing an intravenous line to give fluid access.

His heart was beating like a drum, head pounding and stomach tight like a clenched fist as he finished assembling the drip unit. The flow wheel of the giving set was opened to its full capacity to allow precious fluids to replace those that had been lost. He squeezed the bag to force the fluid through quickly trying to stem the falling blood pressure.

In a flash of anger Jason snapped and screamed out to the crowd: " For Christ sake, give us some room to work."

Just then the Police arrived to stop the fighting.

Jason felt the pressure, it was not like him to lose control but the pushing crowd made conditions awkward. Making use of one of the police officers to assist in getting the stretcher from the ambulance, the paramedic continued. He put in a second line so that they could double the fluid access, the patient had lost a large volume of blood and the need to get him stable enough for the trip into hospital was crucial. Tom wasted no time in fetching the equipment from the vehicle, and then assisting his colleague stopped to pick up their patient and rush him into the ambulance.

Both men straightened their backs as they took the strain.

"One, two, three lift." The stretcher was heaved up and into the back of the vehicle.

They requested that the police gave them an escort all the way to the local hospital and that one of the officers drove the ambulance to allow the two paramedics to work on the lad on route.

Flashing blue lights lit up the night sky, sirens cut through the silence as the police car and ambulance raced towards the casualty unit. Alerts had already been made so that the hospital had time to prepare for their arrival.

In the back of the ambulance they worked in a frenzy of activity, one managing the airway and the monitor, constantly checking on vital signs, oxygen flowing at full capacity to feed vital organs. The other squeezed the crystalloid solution through the drip unit, keeping slight pressure on the towel dressing. The strain showed on both faces of the paramedics and sweat was dripping from everywhere as they worked. Each pushed their skills to the limit as they fought to recall the correct procedures. Time was running out and the possibilities of keeping the patient alive were slim. Racing minds and the sheer physical effort was taking its toll on the crew; they both knew what the outcome might be but they had to give it their best shot ...

The red stand-by phone burst into life. This was a direct line from ambulance control used only for emergency calls. It was picked up by a male charge nurse, who immediately sprang into action: flicking the switch of the loudspeaker system, he uttered just three words "Stand-by to resus room." He repeated this once more before making his way to the emergency room, shouting instructions as he went.

Within minutes nursing staff and casualty Doctors were busy with equipment checks: electrocardiogram machine, emergency trolley, drug cabinets and resuscitation units, making sure that all were in a state of readiness. An alert call was phoned through to the surgical team with a request that an attendance was made in the emergency room as soon as possible to deal with any complications.

All casualty personnel were now ready and positioned in their allotted places awaiting the arrival of the ambulance. A silence filled the department but in a few minutes it would be broken with a frenzy of action, each member of the team knowing exactly what was expected, for they had all performed in situations like this many times before.

A tall man stood tearing at a sealed paper packet before carefully lifting out a pair of latex gloves. He dipped his hand into each glove in turn, stretching the thin rubber over his fingers. Mr. McKee, the surgical consultant on call was an ex- army major who had joined the hospital direct from the Royal Army Medical Corps. As previously mentioned, this was a man of strong will and his expectations from all that worked by his side were one hundred per cent plus. To characterise his ability one would say brilliant: he had been born to be a surgeon and was now at the height of a very successful career. To watch him work had inspired many an intern student. His skilled fingers were like a Swiss clockmaker, precise, gentle and firm always in control. His techniques were exquisite to behold; he handled equipment with precision and calm determination. The emotional euphoria would show through whenever he felt that something had gone really well and that his skills had made some difference. He lived and breathed trauma. The more he dealt with the demands on his skills the slicker his knife hand became. McKee could be frightening and was used to having his orders carried out absolutely to the letter. Off duty he was the life and soul of the party, mixing with any member of staff treating them as if they were his equals ...

The plastic doors of the emergency room burst open, information being passed in a flow of words as the paramedics advanced towards the awaiting teams.

"Wound to the throat caused by glass; GCS five; blood pressure 90/50: pulse no longer palpable, respiration has been assisted. He has had two bags of crystalloid squeezed through, now has two new bags situated. He was conscious just before arrival. One, two, three lift."

Questions were fired at the paramedics as they lifted the patient onto the resuscitation trolley, medical teams trying to build a picture of the events leading to the arrival at hospital.

Dressings were removed, revealing the mutilated flesh; they could not believe the destruction of the tissue the beer glass caused. Mr. McKee moved forward to take a closer look, then in a second he started to give out orders in a calm and professional manner. Each member of the casualty unit, working as a well programmed computer, knowing precisely what was expected of them.

The surgeon made an emergency repair by clamping the torn flesh together; giving much needed time to get him up stairs to the main operating theatre. Closing the jagged edges of the wound had stemmed the haemorrhage but the man's condition was critical and his chance of survival was not good. They needed to operate quickly.

The surgeon had been giving a running commentary as he worked, preparation was almost complete for the forthcoming procedures. Work on the patient had taken almost thirty minutes to get the haemorrhage under control.

"Can someone contact intensive care. If this fellow makes it, we are going to need one of their beds"...

Jason and Tom had cleaned up and stowed away the equipment that was used, each item being returned to its rightful place ready to be used again.

Both paramedics were sure that the patient was in the best possible hands and if anyone could save him it had to be Mr. McKee and his surgical team...

CHAPTER SIXTEEN

The lone vehicle sat silently on the stand-by point; all lights were off except for those inside the cab. Jason shifted his leg; the ache in his knee was like a bad tooth constantly nagging away at him. He cursed as the waves of pain shot through the troubled limb with a sickening persistence. Outside the sky darkened as the approaching storm clouds crept ever closer. They could almost feel the atmosphere change even from inside the cab of the vehicle.

Then suddenly it hit! One moment it was just the dark threat of rain, the next heavy clouds spilled out their deluge towards the earth. It had attacked with such violence that the watery drops were like spent slugs from an airgun as they hit the windscreen, totally obscuring their vision of the world outside. Tom set the wipers into motion trying to remove the heavy downpour from the glass screen up front, but they did little to stem the pounding rain. After a while Tom gave up and switched them off again. They sat listening to the rain drumming its continuous rhythm on the cab roof above their heads. "I hope we don't get a road traffic accident now or we'll get bloody drenched in this lot," muttered Jason as he sat watching the fall of water outside ...

Mike James was a tall man in his mid-thirties; he had worked hard and built up a nice comfortable little business. Not that he was well-to-do he was comfortable in as much that he had a good turnover of profit, a nice house, car and a loving family. He felt tired as he turned the key in the door of his office. It had been a busy day and he longed to be home with his feet up and a tall drink of beer in his right hand. The work seemed to take all of his energy lately and he always felt exhausted by the end of a long day in his office. Most nights he would be asleep within an hour of arriving home, totally drained by the mental effort it took to run the business.

He pulled the car keys from out of his pocket, opened the Jaguar door and eased his weary body into the soft leather seats. 'Perhaps its time for me to take a holiday somewhere in the sun, away from all this stress,' he thought to himself as he turned the key in the ignition.

He had not taken much notice of the weather until he started for home. The storm was in full swing, wind, rain and sleet, all took turns to batter the Jaguar as it sped towards Mike's house. The pouring rain made visibility difficult and put a strain on the driver's already tired eyes. He switched on the radio to try and keep his attention focused on something other than wanting to close his eyes and sleep. The radio chat-line was talking about marriage and the family causing Mike to think immediately of his own, waiting patiently for his return home. His wife would be waiting to serve the meal that she would have laboriously prepared; it would not be started until he walked through the door and the children had blurted out their day's adventures...

There was no warning! The motor cycle appeared from out of nowhere. He stamped his foot on the brake pedal trying to miss the obstacle in his path. He turned the steering wheel hard over but he knew it was to late. His body set rigid as the muscles went tense and his fingers gripped the wheel until the blood drained from them and they turned white.

The car skidded. Turned and rolled as the vehicle lost its traction; it continued to twist and roll over and over, its contents flying around in the enclosed space. Mike James unresisting body was tossed from side to side, shattering bones as his arms and shoulders were crushed by the car's metal structure. Time was almost at a standstill but then the twisted and torn metal began to dig and rip into his soft flesh. It sent splatters of red blood-soaked matter in all directions, sticking firmly to the car's interior. Mike's upper body was forced forward and his head made contact with the front glass of the windscreen with a sharp crack!

It was very similar to the sound of a hammer knocking a fence post into the ground thwack!-before slamming him back into the seat and coming to rest with an abrupt halt. He had no time to cry out. The outer casing of his skull had broken and splintered like a crushed egg. Sharp shards of bone sliced their way into the soft spongy tissues of his brain and his pelvis snapped like a dry twig almost simultaneously. The Jaguar seemed to hang in the air like a dragonfly before falling back to the ground and coming to rest ...

Headlights lit up the scene showing the carnage caused by the crash in panorama. The front screen had fragmented into a thousand tiny pieces of glass. Both paramedics tugged and pulled at the remnants of the car door. Mike looked up at the blurred figure that was peering through the opening. The face beneath the white helmet looked at him with a deep concern just before what was left of Mike's senses let him down and the interior of his car seemed to spin as he lost consciousness.

Jason moved next to the man in the car. The soft leather seats were covered with fragments of broken windscreen glass, making movements awkward.

The back of his neck was getting wet as the rain found a newly formed crease in the car's roof, allowing a steady stream to flow over his safety helmet.

"You're going to get soaked!" exclaimed Tom.

Jason believed his comments had come too late: the rain had drenched him as it ran off the newly formed gully. His eyes blinked against the water as it hit his spectacles and slashed back at his face. He lifted the lid of each of the driver's eyes and was relieved to find that both pupils were equal, although dilated but at least he was breathing. The wound to his head was extremely worrying; bone splinters were clearly visible through the wound and he could not be sure at this stage if the blood in his ears had formed from the wound or an internal source. The arm was crushed; splintered bones just below the surface of stretched muscle and periphery of skin swelled under the pressure of a growing haematoma.

Jason was suddenly conscious of the slippery wetness against the rubber-gloved fingers. "Lets have the torch a little closer." His gloves were covered in red gooey blood, thick and congealed. "Ok, we need to get a close examination of this guy fast!"

The Fire Brigade arrived in their rescue tender, normally dispatched when there is a report of persons trapped in a road traffic accident. Their officer approached Jason and asked what the situation was. Jason quickly brought him up to speed and requested that they cut the driver out fast, bearing in mind the safety aspect. He informed the Fire officer of the type of injuries that they were up against and although speed was important, they would have to follow the instructions given by the medics.

They moved in with their heavy-duty cutting equipment, starting on the roof of the Jaguar, cutting into each door pillar in turn. The sound from inside the car was frightening as the cutter and spreaders bit deep into the metal wreckage.

Jason was mindful of patient care, while at the same time keeping an eye on the progress of the fire crews, controlling what they were doing. Ripping back the Velcro strap from the cervical collar he managed to place it around the injured driver's neck before attempting to intubate the airway. It had been difficult trying to manoeuvre the Laryngoscope in such a confined space. On his second attempt he was able to slip the endotracheal tube firmly between the vocal cords and connect it to the resuscitation bag. Jason could have done with an extra pair of hands but because of the cramped space there was only room for one other than the driver.

Suddenly the roof popped off the car! The cold rain dropped onto the occupants, causing an extra problem; they quickly covered the driver with blankets and a waterproof sheet. There was a lot more room to move about now and Tom was able to get closer to assist Jason.

214

Wounds needed to be dressed, the airway maintained, and still they had to get him free from the wreck and into the comfort of the ambulance. The problem now was that the engine compartment had been forced back into the cab space and was holding the driver's leg fast. The paramedics were unable to tell what injuries had occurred to the trapped leg.

"Let's take things nice and easy, lads," instructed Jason as he raised his hands to signal the firemen to begin cutting the front bulkhead away.

Tom meanwhile was giving the driver further visual checks to make sure that he was remaining stable, if you could call it that, while gently squeezing the Sussex bag assisting with the breathing.

Sounds of crunching metal filled the night as the fire crews worked feverishly to get the patient free from the wreckage, but it was a slow job and they dare not make a hurried mistake. They were almost at the point of extraction: this was the danger period. Unknown injuries or unseen wounds and internal injuries can suddenly appear at the release point. Tom kept a visual watch and airway management on the top half of the driver, while Jason kept an eye on the trapped leg that was just about to be freed ...

The accident unit had eased at last, it had been yet another busy night at Southsea Hospital. The nursing staff had been put under a lot of pressure all night. As fast as one cubical was cleared, another patient brought in by an ambulance crew had filled it. Cardiac, respiratory and trauma had constantly flowed in and out of the unit, keeping the doctors and nurses running on adrenaline overdrive. But for now there was an eerie silence that made it hard to believe that frantic activity had taken place just a short time previously. Now was the time for some of the staff to take a chance and slip into empty cubicles for quick forty winks or to make a well-earned cup of tea. A skeleton staff of nurses worked quietly on to replace equipment used on previous patients, or kept a close eye on the remaining few that still lay behind closed curtains. Only three patients remained on the unit, awaiting transfer to a ward. Occasional sounds echoed into the stillness of silent corridors, expanding every little squeaky noise into a loud groan.

An old man in cubicle two sat up and coughed loudly, flexing the muscles of his throat as he struggled to bring up the phlegm that was stuck fast and disrupting his breathing. He started to panic as he convinced himself that he can't breathe properly.

Once again the silence is disrupted as the nurse's move towards the cubicle and their shoes squeak on the polished floor. The short respite is over and the department is active again as the phone rings on the emergency line. Another stand-by call from ambulance control puts the nursing sister on alert and she rapidly jots down the details. "Road, traffic coming in! Its been trapped for forty minutes. Serious head injury, intubated and is unconscious. Can someone bleep the crash team?" she yelled without stopping to take a breath"...

The Fire Brigade cut away the last piece of metal from the trapped leg. As the pressure of metal plate was released, a jet of dark red blood shot its crimson stickiness from out of the now open leg wound. Jason had been prepared for such an incident; he immediately slapped a dressing over the wound and squeezed with a gentle but firm pressure. It only took a few minutes to complete the extraction from the vehicle. The driver was gently eased onto a spinal board and head pads strapped into place. Because of the head injuries the paramedics had to assume that the cervical spine had also been damaged and was the site of a possible fracture. This meant that extreme care would be needed during the journey to hospital. The driver was still unconscious. As a precaution Jason had stroked the sole of patient's foot, observing the big toe's upward bend: a good sign of 'Babinski's reflex' (possible presence of an upper motor neurone injury).

216

Although the roads were quiet, the police had offered to give the ambulance crew an escorted ride to the casualty hospital. There was not a lot more Jason could do other than constant observations, maintain the airway and keep a close watch on the monitor screen.

Suddenly, the monitor changed, the saturation levels were dropping.

"He is completely unresponsive," Jason whispered across to Tom. "I can't get a pulse anywhere except the carotid and that's barely audible, very weak and intermittent."

He shone his torch into the patient's eyes, first one then the other; both were now blown, widely dilated and fixed. "Fuck, fuck, fuck," hissed Jason as he grabbed the Sussex and started bagging the patient. Starting resuscitation was his only course of action, he knew that he had to try and stabilise the patient until they could get him to a surgeon.

As Tom drove like hell along the coast road it was dark. There was no moon and where the beach reaches out to the sea it was black. The darkness had swallowed up the light, save for the odd boat's mooring lamp where they were doing a spot of night fishing just off the shoreline. This road was one of the major routes through three towns.

During the winter it is used only as short cut to get from one end to the other. The summer is a total transformation as holidaymaker's flock into the area by the hundreds to laze, stretched out on their towels, trying to collect a tan from the heat of the sun.

Unbelievably people were still walking their dogs along the beach pathway, looking up at the flashing blue lights as the ambulance speed passed.

On arrival at the hospital Tom drew the vehicle to a halt behind another ambulance. The back doors burst open; Jason had stopped the resuscitation just long enough to help Tom unload the stretcher.

"I'm afraid the patient deteriorated on route and has been expired for at least five minutes. Both pupils are fully blown and dilated," Jason explained to the casualty doctor as they moved forward into the resuscitation room.

There was sadness between the two paramedics as they left the department. Death is the ultimate end and whatever the individual believes about the existence of life after death, it is no comfort for the deep despair felt by the mourners of the departed or indeed those that have witnessed that death.

Outside, after the patient had been handed over to the medical team, they stood talking to the another crew. Tom sucked the smoke from the cigarette that dangled from the corner of his mouth, while Phil the driver played out one of his smutty jokes. He would come up with a ditty or dirty joke on a regular basis. Jason would always find them amusing, but he could never remember fully what was said or how they had been delivered when he tried to repeat them at a later stage ...

CHAPTER SEVENTEEN

On the way back to station they stopped the vehicle outside the local chip shop, hoping to get something to eat. Jason jumped out and got as far as the shop door when the radio went off again. They had a call to a person reported behind locked doors and that the police were also to attend. The call had come in from concerned neighbours who had not seen the owner of the address they were heading towards for some time.

The old man that owned the house lived alone and was an ex-stroke victim; his neighbours were used to going into the house on a daily basis just in case he needed anything. Today they could not get any answer and the doors had not been left unlocked as they usually were ...

The old man sat in his chair huddled up in a blanket to keep warm, coughing and sneezing. His body gave a little tremor, his shaking hands fumbled with the box of pills taken from the small table alongside his chair.

He was a pitiful sight to see, sick and crippled by age, captivated by a right-sided stroke that had left him with wasting muscles and anticipation of death. Since his wife had died, this once proud man had sunk to the depths of despair. He had been a handsome man standing tall in his regimental uniform. Serving in two world wars, he had returned home to his wife with a chest full of gleaming medals. This was the prime of his life, full of hope and desperate to get back into to the abandoned civilian way of things. He had some money in his pocket and a brain full of ideas. With the help of his wife he could start a fresh and try and put the horrors of war behind him.

No matter how many times his wife had asked about the past years, he refused to talk about his memories or the hardships that he and his comrades had endured. She tried hard to explore his

219

innermost thoughts, for the nightmares that he had each night told her he was a troubled man.

Ken had tried to dismiss the scenes from his mind but they kept haunting him night after night, seeing the faces of fallen comrades staring at him, their dead bodies torn and shattered; limbs that had been blown away by cannon shells and mines, leaving behind ripped and jagged flesh. He questioned why he had survived and so many others had died never to return home again.

The dreams had improved slowly over the years, but they never really left him; he could not forget the horrors that his old eyes had witnessed all those years ago ...

The weather had broken and given way to light rain. There was little traffic on the roads but Tom kept the ambulance at a steady speed, mainly because of the twisting country lanes but also the rain had made the surface slippery in places. Jason checked the map to make sure they were heading in the right direction. Once they had left the main road their route had become more complicated; they were looking for 'Star' cottage that lay off a long, winding lane. Houses were few and far between; it was one of those places that, because they were so isolated and obscure, missing the cottage would have made diversions long and time consuming.

The lane narrowed, making driving conditions more difficult as it filtered into single lane traffic. There was just enough room to get one vehicle through at a time. Potholes filled with water made the suspension work overtime, causing Jason to hang onto the door handle tightly for support. Tom slowed his speed to compensate for the state of the rough track, apologising for the bumpy ride, nervousness in his smile as he glanced across at his partner.

They came upon an old signpost, cracked and weathered with

age; it told Jason the cottage was directly ahead of them. "Ok," he said out loud, "dead ahead it is, then."

It started to rain heavily and the dark clouds shut out the moonlight; wind and rain gusted against the windscreen of the ambulance, making trees seem like weird images dancing before them as they drove forward. Suddenly Tom stamped hard on the brake pedal, praying the vehicle would not skid on the muddy surface of the lane. In the beam of the headlights loomed a large iron gate that blocked the access beyond. Tom had been lucky to avoid a collision with the metal object that now blocked their route.

The frustrated crew had no choice but to walk the rest of the way, through rain, wind and sticky, oozing mud, armed with box loads of equipment that they might need once they had arrived at the front door. Their breaths were coming in short gasps as they struggled along the muddy lane towards the cottage. Leafy branches hung from the trees on either side of the lane creating a dark archway; the undergrowth was thick and it was obvious that it had not been tended for some time. When they arrived at the house it was well illuminated, lights blazing from every room. At the front door of the cottage, Jason looked back, staring down the black empty lane, and he could just about make out the white shape of their ambulance parked some distance away. It was at this point that he saw the blue lights of the police car forcing its way up the lane. "Well, at least we have some help if its needed," he remarked to Tom.

The front door was locked and they were not getting any joy from the doorbell.

"I'm afraid it looks like a job for our friends in blue. We will just have to wait a little longer until they get hear. I've a dreadful fear of what we'll find when we get in," said Jason ...

Distressed breathing made him feel uncomfortable: the tight little pain in his chest was annoying; sweating and trembling his body gave a shiver, 'must be coming down with the flu,' he thought to himself.

Suddenly he felt very tired. 'Just a few minutes sleep and I will be all right,' he thought as he settled down into the chair, closing his eyes. His mind drifted a little, the tight pain in his chest still giving him problems. The memories started to flood back: first the German air raids scenes of fallen comrades arms and legs blown away, leaving torn and twisted bodies on the blood-soaked ground.

He remembered when the torpedo hit the troopship: all those young men struggling in the cold sea; the oil that had finished off so many as they sucked it into their lungs. Ken and some of the men had been picked up by a British naval frigate only to find themselves back in the water once more after an enemy dive bomber had dropped its explosive load directly down the funnel of the rescue ship. Many men died that day, drowned or consumed by the lake of burning oil before the ship was sucked below the surface of the sea.

The horrors slipped away and he saw his wife standing before him. She looked the same as the first day that they met when they were both just eighteen years old. Her tall slender body, eyes of blue and long red hair had dazzled him from the very first glance; she had a face like an angel and her smile melted the coldest of hearts. She had been a loving wife and mother to the two children until cancer struck. Within four months she was gone, leaving a gaping hole in the family. It had broken his heart when the end came even though they all knew that she was surely dying.

He remembered her tears the day that she was told about the cancer and that there was nothing that could be done. She had realised that they all needed to accept the fate that had been dealt. They had said their goodbyes long before the end finally came and it made death more tolerable. But it did not prepare him for the large gap that she had left in his life; things were never the same after that.

The pain in his chest became more acute, making the sweat stream out of the pores of his skin. Ken had never worried about his health; in fact he had only seen the inside of a hospital once, after the rescue ship had been torpedoed during the war. Suddenly the pain his chest became unbearable; he felt paralysed as the fear took a grip, straining to catch his breath and fighting off the waves of nausea that swept his body. It was an intermittent pain, sharp at first then a dull ache. Suddenly the pain came back as a crushing, searing invasion of his body; the clammy feeling swept across the surface of his skin causing a feverish sensation. The old man tried to cough but that just made the pain more intense. It took extra effort to inflate his lungs, and his chest felt as though hot liquid had been pored into his throat before being allowed to cool. Trying to get up from the chair, he found that he could not move; his body felt like a ton weight had been placed on his chest.

He was no stranger to death; he had seen more than most during the war years but now he experienced the full terror for the first time of what death felt like. Now his body was so cold and the paralysing state left him helpless. His pitiful attempts to breath worsened as the situation became almost impossible. Totally paralysed he could do nothing and he knew that he was about to die; there was a strange buzzing in his ears, his brain fighting to keep on going. Then a bright light illuminated the inside of his skull; he could see a dark shadow at the far end of the light, arms out stretched and beckoning. The shadow reached out and took his hand. He looked up at the face that he had never forgotten and walked with her towards the brightness ...

Tom and Jason waited for the police to smash the small pane of glass by the front door lock; it took two blows before the glass gave way. The police officer put his arm through the newly found hole and released the door catch from the inside. There was a

223

low thumping from within, a continuous beat. Jason realised that it was the pounding in his own ears as the blood rushed through dilated veins, pumped by a quickening heart. Armed with the defibrillator, paramedic bag and drug box, along with the portable suction unit and oxygen bottle, they rushed through the door ready to start immediate resuscitation.

Once inside it did not take long to locate the owner of the property, still seated in his chair with his head bent forward so that the chin lay on his chest. His skin had a lifeless blue tinge to its surface and the smell of death was apparent.

Jason gave him a quick examination but it was obvious that he had been dead for some time. "Not much we can do for this poor old fellow," he said.

"Would you say natural causes?" asked the police officer.

"Yes, there would be little doubt at all. Looks like the old boy had a massive heart attack; hopefully it would have been quick," Jason replied.

The interior was neat and tidy with expensive furniture and ornaments adorning the rooms graced with pastel colours. Tom looked up at the display box on the wall, along with a picture of a soldier in full dress uniform. The box housed a line of military medals. "Looks like the poor old sod went through it during the war." There was that same look that Jason had seen so many times in the past, the look of relief leaving almost a faint smile on the dead man's face.

They tried to lay the old man down but rigor mortis had set the body solid. A blanket was placed over the old man while they waited for the doctor to arrive.

Jason started to fill out the report form while answering questions from one of the police officers, who was also making notes of what they had found.

There was sure to be a coroner's inquest if the old man had not seen his own doctor in the last two weeks. Neither the police nor the paramedic's wanted any complications to rise up in a coroner's court through the lack of detail.

When the doctor arrived some five minutes later to certify death, Jason and Tom respectfully departed from the house, leaving the doctor and the police to make arrangements for the bodies removal. They walked back to the gate where the ambulance was parked in the muddy entrance. They both climbed aboard and Tom put the vehicle into reverse gear. He eased the motor down the lane, putting distance between themselves and the location. Jason set about finishing the required paper work while Tom eased the motor down the lane and onto a main road.

The crew pondered on the old man's last moments. "Sad way to go, that; all alone with no one to say goodbye to," remarked Tom, who had become aware that he was gripping the steering wheel so hard the tips of his fingers were going numb. Like his partner, too many traumas too much life-saving demands and fatigue were turning him into a physical wreck. Jason just sighed as his thoughts turned to the old man dying alone like that and it made him sad that no one was there to help him through the last moments...

They were instructed to return back to station for cover. Making the most of the opportunity to get back to base and the chance of a drink. Tom put a little more pressure on the throttle. If there was any chance at all It was grabbed, for they might not see the station again for the rest of the shift.

The drive back took just eighteen minutes, Tom parked the vehicle in the bay while Jason made for the duty room and switched on the kettle. He crossed his fingers and said a little prayer: for some reason the flicking of the kettle switch sends a jungle drum message through to the control supervisor; this seems to be the case on all ambulance stations.

Halfway through the cup of coffee the station alarm bell rang,

225

causing both men to jump up with a start; Jason had almost knocked the cup off the table. He could never get used to that bell. Why they made it so loud he would never understand; in fact, it had often crossed his mind why the residents close by had not complained. Their brief rest now shattered, the remainder of the long awaited liquid was flushed down the sink before making their way to the ambulance.

The weather had changed and the air was full of foreboding as they heaved their tired bodies into the vehicle.

They had been given another emergency call, this time to a house fire with persons reported trapped. The call had come in via the Fire Brigade, requesting that a paramedic unit attend as there was at least two or more casualties involved.

The cool breeze of the early morning air suddenly changed to a squall. Wind picking up, followed by the pitter-patter of the rain, fine at first but developing into heavy drops of water. Storm clouds flashed across the sky. The wind started to pick up to a strong gust, driving the rain onto the windshield of the vehicle almost to the point that the windscreen wipers were no longer effective. This weather could only slow down their progress. Driving in these conditions created innumerable hazards. They had always been taught that safety was paramount, better to get there a little late than not at all.

Jason and Tom were both seasoned paramedics and they were so used to working in these types of conditions. After a while travelling the same roads so many times they learned every bump, curve and drain cover there was to know.

Traffic was already, building clogging roads, making the progress slower still. Tom eased his way forward trying to influence the vehicles in front to clear a pathway. The two – tones blasted out their vociferous sound, interrupting thoughts and dreams of home and causing panic amongst the startled drivers. They hated using blue lights and two – tones this early in the morning, knowing that it would disturb the peaceful sleep of those still in bed, but this was a fire-call.

Responding to a fire-call was always distressing for all that attended, because, if no one had been hurt, there was always shock and dismay, at losing one's home or personnel belongings, which in some cases had taken a life's work to obtain. That was a terrible sight to behold.

Then the grip of hopeless fear takes over. "Where are we to live now? How can we replace all that is lost?" Followed by the realisation that life would not be the same for a very long time.

Still with a fine sprinkle of rain on the windshield, conditions improved and the ambulance was able to make better progress towards the location of the house fire. Years of experience had taught them how to manoeuvre a large ambulance through heavy traffic to their advantage. Once clear of the bottled-up roads Tom kept in the centre and each time he caught up with the vehicle in front, he waited for a gap before squeezing through. Then he picked up speed again.

Two pairs of tiny eyes stared at them from the back of the car in front. These children smiled and waved, excited at the prospect of being chased by an ambulance. Bright eyes gleamed as Tom slapped the gears and roared around the slowing vehicle. Then they were gone...

Her death was cruel and unjustified, caused by the tiredness that had overtaken her body and the cigarette that fell from her fingers, spilling its hot fiery ash onto the bedding where she lay. A slow, suffering, painful death just for the sake of one small pleasure.

The smouldering embers burst into flame as she dreamt about her youth, the days when she would turn many men's eyes to her beauty. She had once stood upright and proud, a beautiful creature admired by many suitors; accompanied by an attractive smile and grace, many sought her heart.

227

Black, hot, acrid smoke filled the room; choking black plumes filling every crevice; she could feel the heat now, as she became aware of the surroundings. Flames licking at her flesh made her scream out with the pain they inflicted upon her; relentless, wicked, burning flames. But she could not move away from them, because she had suffered a stroke that had left her paralysed a couple of years earlier.

Failing health had caused significant deterioration; her legs were ulcerated, and a mass of running sores that had entangled into the material of her mattress acted as an adhesive. Rotting cavities oozed their sticky wetness from stretched tissue as it ate through her infected flesh.

She tried to beat back the flames with her good arm as the fire billowed out of control. Her lungs started to fill with the black acrid smoke, forcing the last pockets of oxygen to become undermined. She felt the strangulating tightness in her chest, trapped by her own body which stopped her from leaving the bed. The dizziness that followed almost gave way to relief compared to the pain from her scorched airway. Fear now gripped her like the crushing band that she felt in her chest, squeezing the blackened lobes of her lungs. As breathing became laboured, her pounding heart rate started to increase, faster and faster until ...

Total blackness releases her from the torment.

Flames fan out licking at the shrivelling flesh as it shrinks back, melted by fire. She will not feel the pain anymore or smell the human flesh that is burning. Blackened as it cooks and sizzles, contorted muscles turned to charcoal. For she has gone for that long last sleep ...

Smoke, thick and black was pouring out of the doors and windows; neighbours were trying desperately to enter the front door but were beaten back by the searing heat and thick smoke.

228

The Fire engine stopped outside the burning building, firemen rushed forward; playing out the hose reels as they went. They sent up the platform ladder to rescue two from the roof. Fire fighters working like a precision instrument rushed backwards and forwards, each knowing just what he is expected to do. Breathing apparatus packs were quickly taken from the storage locker and strapped to the backs of the chosen crews. They spend hours of practice to get it all together like a well-oiled piece of machinery. These were the guys that had to take the most risks for they would enter the seat of the fire. They would face the noxious thick smoke and burning flames.

Blue and orange started to show through the top of the roof slates; these were quickly tackled with water jets. They would continue until they gained control and stopped the spread of fire. Steam rose up into the morning sky as the jets of water hit the heat of the flames. Without warning! The sounds of exploding glass filled the air as the heat on the glass caused it to fracture.

One of the women on the roof was an asthmatic and having breathing problems. She refused to leave the roof because she feared the height as much as the flames, causing her to panic breath and trigger her medical condition. The other woman shouted, "My mother is still trapped inside. She can't walk, she's had a stroke." The fireman tried to get more information but was greeted with more screams of grief. "You have to get my mother out! She's trapped in bed!" She pleaded.

A group of firemen moved an extension ladder towards the upper window; one of them ascending soon after it was secured ...

The Ambulance arrived below and after the problem was explained Tom volunteered to go up the ladder to medicate the women and get them calmed down before the extraction from the roof took place. Both ladies were terrified, their faces covered in black soot from the acrid smoke. Tom gave one woman a

'Nebulizer' inhalation of 'Salbutamol' to open up the airways and to help her breath easier. She asked if they had managed to get her mother out. But Tom could not give any answers for he did not know at this time. He tried to give her reassurance that everything would be fine and that the Firemen would get her out. But he was unaware that the mother had perished in the fire.

The damp night air suddenly filled with the sound of piercing screams. Relatives had been informed of the family death. It is the relatives, mourning and crying, who are left to remember their loved ones. It is much too late to say that you loved and cared for them, for the words fall on deaf ears now. Only the memories remain. Worlds fall apart and each is asking the same question. "Why?"

Mourners are the ones needing a shoulder to cry on. Somebody to support them in their time of pain; these people are left to remember their departed ones. Jason felt lost and empty inside as her pitiful tear-stained face looked up at him and the tears continued to fall from her eyes.

Too many times had he found himself in this situation and it always made him feel the same. He had lived with their emotions, their perpetual misery when a family succumbs to death's beckoning call. Most ambulance men and women know what it is like to suppress their own feelings as they try to remain professional at times such as these. The smell of burning flesh hangs around for hours; it seemed to cling to the very fibres of their uniforms. Looking at the charred bodies did not cause any lasting effects, because after a while they just got used to it. Like the Firemen, they had to get used to the sight of burnt bodies quickly or they would not last very long in this line of work. Their job was to stay mentally alert. If the sight of a corpse upset their performance then they would be no use to the living or the dead. When someone needs a doctor or a paramedic, they don't want one that is going to pieces as they try to deal with their own emotional problems.

Although it was part of their job to deal with death, there were some calls that stayed deep in the memory and left their mark forever. Most would do their best on all calls and try hard to prevent deaths like all ambulance personnel, but they could only do so much and it was hard when the families expected them to achieve the impossible. For some reason when they see two paramedics walk through the door they think that they carry a bag full of miracles. But these are desperate people, trying to clutch at straws, and in most cases are left disappointed ...

Rays from the sun flashed across the surface of the morning sky, the orange and the reds mixed with the purples of cloud as they returned to station. From the inside of the ambulance one would believe that they were looking at a summer's day, until you took the trouble to observe the exhaust from the car in front, the hot fumes hitting the frosty air leaving a grey vapour trail behind. Tom eased the vehicle towards the coast road, back to the warmth of the stations crew room and the promise of hot drink and hopefully to finish the shift.

As they entered the golden mile, the name given by the locals to describe a section filled with arcades, restaurants, and pubs, the street cleaners were just finishing the daily clean up operation.

When Jason was a lad, the seafront bustled with activity, but only between Easter and the end of October. It would be packed with people from all over England enjoying their holidays, but mostly with coach loads of day-trippers from London. Now the seafront was used twelve months of the year, since the introduction of the disco clubs and the fun palaces filled with computer games machines. Local youngsters use it constantly in the winter as a meeting place where they will hang around in-groups until three o'clock in the morning before sloping off to bed. If you drove along the coast road at this time in the morning, no one would blame you for believing you had just entered a riot zone. Chip wrappings, discarded half-eaten burger buns and paper bags of all sizes would be scattered around the ground for as far as the eye could see. This was the frenzied feeding time for seagulls, swooping in from the shore to harvest the discarded remnants of food that littered the ground. They had two hours to gorge themselves on the feast before the street cleaners arrived to clear the roads of rubbish; by six o'clock the streets would be left spotless. Morning commuters would be oblivious as they made their way to work.

This is the scene at almost all-coastal towns throughout England, and unless you are on the road all-night or making an early start, it is hard to describe the vision of disregard. If these same people found rubbish of this magnitude outside their own front doors, there would be uproar.

Tom parked up for a short while and stopped the engine. It was a cold morning, now calm with not even a whisper of wind. The tides continuous rushing forwards and ebbing of the waves were the only sounds to be heard. Their rise and fall, as they crashed down onto the beach, gave a peaceful awareness.

They were enjoying the tranquil settings when their peace was shattered by the sound of the radio going off in the cab.

"Sorry to do this, but you are our nearest vehicle to a cardiac arrest. Make your way to the Airport car park. Report patient not breathing. Control out."

"Bloody hell, that's all we needed this time in the morning," exclaimed Tom ...

It was two twenty in the morning as Ben Slater and his wife boarded the aircraft at Corfu Airport. He looked as if the holiday had done him the power of good; sporting his newly acquired bronzed tan, he looked like a Greek native. They had been stranded at the airport for over three hours, due to a delayed departure, causing Ben to lose his temper more than once. "No bloody organisation in this place. They treat you worse than sheep," he screamed, expressing his dissatisfaction so forcibly it had caused his blood pressure to rise.

His wife tried her best to look as if he belonged to someone else, cringing at all the fuss he was making. Sometimes she wished that he would just shut up and have a little patience, not get upset every time things go wrong. Once safely on board flight AX840 he settled down and thought of the stories he would tell the lads back home.

The take off was perfect, no bumps or shocks as they left the ground while the girls on the flight deck were calmly going through the crash drill. Ben sank firmly into the seat and relaxed; within minutes his eyes became heavy and his thoughts turned to home. "Not long now and we will be back in dear old England."

One hour into the flight had passed when he woke with a start; his surroundings were lost for a brief moment. "Would you like tea or coffee, sir?" asked the stewardess standing by his side.

He looked up at her beaming smile and realised she had been talking to him. "Oh, coffee would be fine, thank you."

Refreshments were followed a short while later with a small, pre-packed meal that most enjoyed before settling back for the final part of the journey.

Eighteen minutes later Ben felt an uncomfortable tightness in the centre of his chest but dismissed it as indigestion. Through the remainder of the flight and without being consciously aware, he kept rubbing the middle of his breastbone and occasionally grimaced as little waves of pain swept across his chest and shoulder.

The flight touched down at Southsea airport at five-fifty am. It took a further thirty minutes to disembark, pick up their luggage and trot through the customs hall.

Once outside the airport departure lounge they headed for the car park. Pains in Ben's chest were getting more frequent and sharper; he knew that something was very wrong. No indigestion pain could cause this amount of discomfort. He drew breath in short gasps. His chest started heaving under his shirt as the tightness started to encircle him like a band of steel cable. As he lowered the cases alongside his car a crushing pain swept across his chest and down both arms. His eyes were bulging and the veins in his neck and forehead puffed up, giving the impression that he was about to explode.

The last thing his wife saw him do was vomit, choking on it as he fell forward hitting the ground before he stopped breathing...

Rush hour traffic was causing problems as they raced towards the airport; Tom swung the steering wheel forcefully as he began to weave around stationary vehicles. A few miles further on, he suddenly veered, causing the ambulance to bounce up the near side kerb as he avoided hitting an over taking 'Ford Escort' coming from the opposite direction. Tom punched the air with his middle finger, cursing out loud. "Shit, shit! That was bloody close."

When the paramedics arrived there was a small crowd gathered around the body lying on the car park Tarmac. At least two of them were attempting to do some sort of resuscitation, unfortunately they were trying to force air past his own vomit. Jason and Tom took over and rolled the man onto one side to allow drainage; then, sweeping the inside of his mouth with a finger, Jason cleared as much of the vomit as possible. The rest was aspirated with the portable suction unit before fitting an oral airway into position. Though the bag and mask he was given two quick inflations; still no signs of breathing. Check the pulse, but it was absent. One quick blow to the centre of the chest; pulse was still absent.

They started the CPR protocol; Tom on the compressions while Jason managed the airway. Both men knew how important it was to get oxygen circulating around his system to feed the deprived brain of its vital ingredients. The heart had stopped pumping and the only way to restart it was by cardio-pulmonary resuscitation, a sequence of airway inflations by one and chest compressions by the other.

Jason connected the oxygen tubing to the Sussex-bag to increase the amount of air into the lungs, while Tom's straight arms compressed the chest like a piston rod. With all the frantic activity in the car park, they could not believe their ears when some impatient driver sounded his car horn trying to get them out of his path. Thankfully the police arrived and soon put the driver right. Tom asked one of the officers if he would help his partner while he went off to fetch some more equipment from the ambulance.

Jason had just completed four cycles of CPR with the help of the police officer, when Tom finished preparing the defibrillator and drug box. The two paddles were placed against the chest of the man and Tom shouted to everyone that they should stand well clear of the body. A look at the small screen on the monitor, showed that the guy was in VF. (This is when the heart stops beating normally but fibrillates as a result of random electrical charges that fire off uncontrolled, making the heart muscle wobble).

A normal heart has a controlled paced beat, but this dying muscle that was receiving signals from electrical impulses coming from rouge cells in the structure, causing the lack of co-ordination with contractions.

Tom took over the CPR while Jason prepared the equipment for the next stage. Thankfully the police had cleared the area of all the people that did not belong. The last thing the paramedics wanted was to keep tripping over someone's shoes as they move around the patient.

"Right then let's see what is happening now," Jason said as he placed the paddles back onto the guy's chest. The CPR was stopped while they watched the tiny screen; the heart trace showed that it was still reacting the same way.

Instructing the few people that were left to 'Stand Clear' Jason charged up the defibrillator to 200j, looked around to make sure that no one was touching the patient and then pushed the buttons to activate the shock. The body on the ground arched as the electrical charge was delivered. Muscles contracted as they were stimulated, but the aim was to stop the heart from fibrillating by passing the charge of electricity through it and converting it back to a normal sinus rhythm. One paramedic checked for a pulse while the other kept a close eye on the monitor screen. But the rhythm stayed in VF.

Everyone stood transfixed as they watched Jason charge up for a second 200j and repeat the sequence, but still the monitor showed a ventricular graph on the screen.

The man's wife by this time had realised that her husband was in a heap of trouble. She begun to scream uncontrollably as it dawned on her that Ben was dying in front of her eyes and there was nothing she could do about it. One of the police officers moved forward and tried to lead her away from the drama-taking place on the car park floor. But there was no way she intended to move from her position until the paramedics had finished.

Charging the defibrillator for the third time Jason increased the output to 360j; this was the maximum power he could deliver. Too many of these and they would start to microwave the heart.

Once more the man's body arched and quivered as the charge zapped his chest. Checks still showed that the rhythm remained unchanged. Tom took control of the CPR once more, while his partner prepared the equipment to intubate the patient's airway. When ready, Jason instructed Tom to stop resuscitation while he advanced the Laryngoscope, then, lifting the tongue out of the way, he slipped the plastic tube skilfully between the vocal cords before making it secure. Lastly he checked both sides of the chest for breath sounds with the aid of the 'Stethoscope' to make doubly sure that he had not passed the tube down the Oesophagus. This is very rare, but it was standard protocol to check. Once he was sure that everything was as it should be, he asked Tom to continue with the CPR while he tried to find a good intravenous access.

The first drug used was 'Lignocaine', a once only drug to try and stabilise the excitable heart muscle after the use of defibrillation. Flicking the caps off the first mini-jet syringe, he squeezed it down the endotracheal tube closely followed by the second dose. He could have given the drug intravenously using only half the amount, but it defuses faster by squirting it directly into the lungs.

Both paramedics' did ten sequences of CPR to push the drug through the circulation. Sweat poured out of each man as the physical effort took its toll. "Stand clear," yelled Tom as he charged up the defibrillator for another attempt at a 360j shock. Jason had pushed the last of the 'adrenaline' though the intravenous porthole as he heard his partner yell again and quickly pulled his hands away. The last thing he wanted was an electrical charge spiralling through his system. Tom had got carried away with his enthusiasm and almost rendered his mate inoperative. He redeemed himself seconds later when he yelped joyfully: "Hang on! Yes, he has a rhythm; it's looking good."

The monitor showed that there was indeed a clear sinus rhythm on the screen, although slow, it was a good regular graph coming through on the paper roll. Jason had shot forward to check the pulse. "Yes! It was there, although slow, it bounded under his fingers.

"I think we maybe lucky," he said as Ben's chest heaved and took an unaided breath.

"Oh, my God! Thank you, Lord. Thank you boys." The wife was beside herself with joy, she had been given a second chance.

Trying not to burst her bubble Jason explained that they were not out of the woods yet and they needed to get him quickly to hospital for further treatment.

Ben was loaded into the back of the ambulance and straight away put onto oxygen. Tom radioed ahead to the hospital, requesting that an emergency team be waiting on their arrival at the casualty department. Although the patient was maintaining his own output, he was still unconscious and the worry now was, had he suffered any long-lasting brain damage?

The journey to the hospital was thankfully only a short distance away from the airport. When they arrived, they handed the patient over to the emergency team and armed them with as much information possible before transferring him over to the casualty trolley.

Within minutes of the hand over they were able to walk away and the feeling they both had at that moment was fantastic. They had won one back. This was what it is all about; the weeks of practice on dummies in the training school had paid dividends. Most of the time they helped frail old ladies that had fallen over, picked up drunks who repaid them with mouthfuls of abuse, or cleaned up after the neglected, who had been left to sit in their own squalor, living in their smelly environments because they were too weak or not mobile enough to clean up. This is part of the normal routine that they expect as part of their responsibilities as paramedics, but when they are successful with an outcome like Ben's, it all seems worth the effort.

Jason walked towards the booking office to complete the paperwork while Tom sloped off for a quick fix from the nicotine fairy. Ten minutes later Jason handed the papers over to the staff nurse and inquired about Ben's condition.

"He's doing alright at the moment they are still working with him, but it's looking good. If he makes it through, he will be sitting up in bed complaining about his sore ribs. It seems one of you were a little heavy handed on the chest compressions. But don't worry about that you did a fine job."

Outside in the casualty yard they met up with the police officers from the airport. They exchanged information about Ben and built up a picture of what happened before he arrived at the airport car park.

"What are his chances?" asked one of the officers.

"Hard to say, they think he may pull through. You never know, he could be lucky."

"This has been one hell of a week," said Jason.

"Never mind, only a few more minutes and we have a couple of days to rest," retorted Tom.

Back on base the automatic doors of the garage opened up and Tom reversed into the parking bay. While Jason replaced some of the equipment that had been used previously, Tom went to put the kettle on. Silence was interrupted by the soft wooing of a wood pigeon on the roof; the screeching of seagulls stopped it as they swooped in from the sea, searching for food.

Jason walked across to the sink to wash his cup. Looking up, he noticed his reflection in the mirror. He stared at his haggard appearance, shocked to see his mother's face staring back from the reflective glass. He was amazed at the reflection looking back from beyond the peripheral glass. Until that moment he had not realised how much he resembled her image. It was time to go home: the early crew was in charge and both he and Tom were due a well-earned rest ...

When he arrived home he made a hot drink topped with a slug of brandy before collapsing into the soft comfort of the armchair. He felt the tension leaving his body and was able to relax, the adrenaline slowly ebbing away. 'What a relief to get away from the frustrations of work.' All that he really needed now was a long holiday, time to enjoy life and not suffer the constant headaches. If he could get a little quality time away from complications caused by the job, he would have a much clearer view of what he wanted from life. It was ridiculous to continue on like this: he needed new motivation; a chance to examine the consequences and perceptions of his dwindling life.

The depression and bitterness began to spill out, voices somewhere deep in the dark recesses of his mind were telling him to take a long hard look at himself. 'You only get one shot at this life, it's not a trial run,' he thought. He had always put others first: the kids, his job, friends and relatives, they had all been using his space before him. It was not that he did not love them. That was far from the truth. He would lay down his life for any of the children, but there were times when both he and Olive just wanted time – out to do things just for themselves. There always seemed to be some attachment that demanded his attention, always something to be accommodated before he could find time to do what he wanted.

The overwhelming tiredness that he felt was not an exaggeration, he felt totally drained, empty and void of energy. Tears started to ooze from his eyes, he felt disturbed by his own misery and confusion, craving emotional relief. Most of all he wished the nightmares would stop, the need to be rid of those jumbled body parts and confusing voices of the dead that seemed to want so badly to communicate with him from the darkness. For so long now these distorted shapes had filled his dreams; he had felt their pain, their anguish and ultimately their loss.

"Oh, what inspiration a clairvoyant or psychoanalyst could obtain delving into my mind! What satisfaction they would have trying to diagnose my tortured dreams."

"What you doing?" The squeaky voice sounded shrilly from the corner of the room.

His concentration interrupted, Jason looked across to the birdcage. It was 'Ben' the pet cockatoo talking to the polished mirror hanging from above. He watched as the small grey bird eyed him up and down. Jason whistled the whistle that he had spent many hours teaching to the small-feathered creature. Within seconds Ben had cocked his head to on side and issued the same shrill tones, copied in detail. Over and over again it repeated the sounds in abundance before hanging upside down like a bat spreading its wings.

"Bloody mad bird, you're as daft as me." ...

CHAPTER EIGHTEEN

Jason woke with a start as the alarm clock broke the silence of sleep. He felt much brighter this morning after a couple of days rest and relaxation. Just to get away from the hassle of work did his tired, ageing bones the power of good. It was the first day shift and Jason was up earlier than normal as Tom had asked if he could pick him up on the way into work: there was a problem with his motor bike. He looked towards the bed behind him where Olive had wrapped herself tightly into the quilt and looked like a sleeping Egyptian mummy. Moving into the bathroom, he indulged in his daily shower, soaking his body with its refreshing water was his first joy of the day. Once dry he slipped into his uniform shirt and trousers before looking out of the bedroom window. As he adjusted the last buttons he noted that it was a wet damp morning but at least the snow had gone.

He pulled up outside Tom's house and switched off the engine. As he waited for him to get into the car he felt a shiver of unease sweep over him, almost like a premonition of something about to happen, something that he would not be able to control. There was a tightening in his throat and that disturbed him as he loosened his tie trying to make the uncomfortable feeling go away.

"Morning, you old bugger, how are you today?" Tom had broken the spell and Jason was able to dismiss the feeling of unease.

"I'm fine, better after that short rest." He turned the key in the ignition and fired up the engine. "Ok, let's make a start, then."

They headed off in the direction of the ambulance station.

When they arrived on station the night crew was out on a call and the station was silent. Outside the bird songs broke the stillness, they were harmonious with their peaceful sounds. There is something special about the sound of a blackbird singing first thing in the morning; it's a wonderful start to the day.

Jason soon settled and forgot the anxieties that had overtaken him in the car.

Tom had boiled the kettle and was making them both a large cup of coffee. "We might as well make the best of things while we can."

His partner nodded as he bent forward and switched on the television before sinking back into the chair and relaxing.

Time drifted by and then he was suddenly alerted to the sound of a racing engine turning into the station yard. Jason sprang to his feet looking across at Tom who was gently snoring in his chair. Grabbing his partner's arm he gave him a couple of shakes to wake him. "I think they are back ... "

There was a screech of brakes as the ambulance came to a halt. Tom and Jason jumped up and looked out of the crew room window. Outside the ambulance stood motionless with its blue lights flashing and the engine still running; this told the two men on station that there was a job for them to go out on immediately. They collected their personal equipment and made a dash towards the vehicle. Both crews changed over with a sense of urgency, each aware that saving time was critical. The call they were to run on was a 'Road Traffic Accident' involving two cars and a lorry.

"Head 'em up and move 'em out!" yelled Tom as the vehicle surged forward. Jason and Tom, now firmly in the front seat of the ambulance, set off down the road as fast as they could safely go.

The traffic situation in front of them was grim and as usual no one would give way; in some cases the driver's really did not know what they were expected to do. Panic set in when they heard the shrill sounds of the sirens going full blast behind them, causing people to do the most stupid things at times. Progress was slowed by vehicles lining both sides of the road, the owners of some of the parked motors had not given any thought to others

243

using the road and had left their vehicles dangerously protruding outward.

Once conquering that obstacle they were soon presented with another in the form of a discourteous driver. Most of the traffic had moved over to the sides to leave a gap in the middle of the road, all except one car, that is: this one decided to move plumb into the centre and completely block the way ahead.

"Will you just look at that bloody fool? There is always one silly bugger on every job," Tom shouted.

Traffic started to slow down rapidly; this was a sure sign that they must be getting closer to the incident. From this point on they did not have any notion of what they would be up against or the ramifications. When the crew arrived on scene a local Police Officer greeted them. This officer was pleased to see them for he had worked with Tom and Jason many times before. Quickly he gave them a brief update on what had been going on so far and his findings at the scene of the 'road traffic accident'.

"The crap has hit the fan down here, mate. You will have your work cut out to sort that little lot."

"Great. Just what we need, like a hole in the head," came Jason's reply.

"Are you two going to the 999 booze-up next week?" The officer asked.

"Sure, just try and stop us," Tom replied.

Two cars and a lorry were involved in the smash, the lorry driver coming off best with just minor injuries. But the occupants of the two cars had not been so lucky. The driver of a Ford was still trapped inside his car and the Firemen were still trying to release him. It was a job that needed speed but with extreme care. Every piece of torn metal could exasperate the situation and give the paramedics more problems. They had expected to find complete carnage with limbs ripped asunder and gaping wounds, veins and arteries pumping out their precious fluids, but this was not so.

244

"Get me out of this fucking thing," a guttural voice screamed out of the Ford.

Jason squeezed himself into the narrow gap while Tom went to look at the occupants of the other vehicle. "My name is Jason"; we will get you out as soon as it is safe to do so. In the mean time we will do our best to make you comfortable and try and ease some of your pain," said the paramedic.

The driver had not been knocked unconscious, but the impact had left him dazed and a little irritated.

"Do you believe in God?" asked Jason, "because, if you don't my friend, you should do."

Suddenly pain seemed to rake through the driver with a shocking force causing him to feel dizzy. The paramedic tried to explore the driver's limbs and body for broken bones but there seemed to be no imperfections, no slivered flesh and yet the pain kept returning, gathering its intensity as wave after wave shot through his patient's body. The only place that he could not explore was around the guy's lower leg, for that was wrapped in the metal of the car floor.

Jason spoke to the Fire Officer in charge and inquired how long they would be before the driver was freed. He was told it would take about fifteen minutes and that they should have a clear working space for him soon. The paramedic set up a drip to maintain the driver's fluid levels and gave him some Nubain to ease the pain. He could not be sure that the driver had not suffered internal injuries or that the pain was being transferred from a spinal problem.

There was a loud noise as Jason tore back the Velcro tabs of the cervical neck brace. As a safety precaution Jason had put the neck collar on the driver in case of spinal injuries ...

The other car, a Toyota, did not look that bad apart from the usual crunched metal, broken glass and of course, the usual cocktail of mixed motor fluids: the damage seemed light. Its occupants seemed to be restricted to a male driver and a female passenger.

From the first quick survey it looked like the male had injuries to his right leg and pains to his lower back. The lady was complaining of pains to her chest and although it's normal to get chest bruising from the safety strap, she looked a lot worse than this would suggest. In fact, she looked quite ill, there were pains to her chest and right arm, with extremities sweaty and grey.

Tom could not take any chances; the priorities were with this lady. The chest pains and other signs suggested that there was a possible cardiovascular condition, calling for speedy stabilisation and close monitoring of this patient. He managed to attract the attention of one of the police officers and quickly asked him to relay his findings back to Jason hoping that the driver of the other vehicle could be left for a while.

Back at the Ford the police suspected that the driver of that vehicle had been drinking and they wanted to do a 'Breath Test'. Jason gave them the go ahead to do this as there were no facial injuries and the paramedic could not see any harmful reason why it should not be done. They discovered that the man was three times over the legal limit and they arrested him on scene before he was even cut free from the wreck.

From this moment on he was their prisoner and would be accompanied by one of the police officers until fit enough to be charged at the local 'Nick'.

Tom's message had reached his partner but at this precise moment Jason could not leave his own casualty. Circumstances were getting out of hand now: it was obvious that they needed help and fast, although there were many helping hands around, the medical side was sparse. They had no idea how long they were going to be kept on scene and the two paramedics could not give complete care to their patients the way things were at the moment.

The decision was quickly taken to involve another vehicle. Control were asked to send at least one extra ambulance, requesting that there were to be no delays in its dispatch and that the crews were updated on the situation before their arrival. Until that time they would have to manage and hope that nothing unpleasant happen to exacerbate the situation. Because there were two vehicles with patients that needed attention the crew had been split up, working one car each until the arrival of the second ambulance. They both used the assistance of fire crews to give them support and extra pairs of hands. The man in the 'Ford' was still trapped and the Fire Rescue team was still working flat out to get him free.

On Jason's initial examination he had found that the driver's legs were pinned by the metal bodywork of the car; unfortunately he was now in a lot of pain from the lower lumber area of his back. As they worked, poked and prodded around the sharp metal structure of the car's flooring, they could see a gaping flesh wounds on his leg and a piece of white bone showing through where the flesh had been ripped open. Puddles of dark clotted blood lay on the floor along side him ...

Tom had found the driver of the Toyota had a fractured right Femur and pains to his upper back. But it was the passenger with the chest pains that had him more worried: this person had all the signs of a cardiac problem and she was not looking very good at all. He asked one of the traffic police to call on the radio for the estimated time of arrival on the other ambulance; he was worried that this lady was going to have a heart attack at any moment and wished that Jason had been working along side him. They were both professional individuals and more than capable of working alone, but it felt so much better to have your own partner to share the load.

Just as the second ambulance came into view everything seemed to happen at once. One of the firemen came running

247

towards the Officer in charge; there was a very big problem starting to form. The fireman had been working around the lorry when he noticed a leaking substance coming from it. On closer examination he found an 'Hazchem' plate that had come off the lorry due to the accident. (The 'Hazchem' showed a United Nations code for dangerous substances that are transported, the information on that plate gives a series of codes that tell what kind of load is being carried). This one was carrying a code instructing that there was risk of an 'Explosive Reaction' and a 'Consider Evacuation Warning'. The officer in charge considered the implications and then made the decision to evacuate all non-essential personnel ...

The Lady in the Toyota went a blue/grey colour, the pain in her chest was suddenly magnified; acute terror swept over her face, the clamminess of her skin made her feel uncomfortable. Now the pain was crushing like some one had placed a ton weight on her chest, and it felt like a hot knife was cutting into her. She tried to shout but the strength was not there and all she could muster was a faint whisper passing through her clenched teeth.

With uncomfortable embarrassment Tom watched her struggling compassion filling his eyes.

Her breathing became laboured and she felt as if she was suffocating. The sensation of being smothered and the tightness around her chest increased the weakness, and a surge of nausea swept over her, causing a dizziness that she had not felt before. Her brain was in a panic because all the messages received told it the body was dying. Paralysed by the lack of vital oxygen being pumped around the circulatory system; organs started to shut down and the last to go was the brain itself, followed by blackness as she went into a cardiac arrest.

The man sitting next to her went into a total panic mode, followed by shock, just as the driver of the Ford was being released from his car. All of this took place simultaneously, each group experiencing their own problems and fighting against time to cope.

The second ambulance crew went to the aid of the two in the Toyota, one looking after the driver, who was now in an advance state of shock, whilst the other paramedic worked with Tom on the lady who had arrested. They worked flat out to get the woman back. As the seconds passed Tom's mouth became dry and bland, the clamminess of his hands gave away to the inner fear that he tried to hide. The cool exterior he displayed as he worked was a sham, for inwardly he felt the panic rise up gripping at his throat. He tried to find a carotid pulse, but there was no sign of any movement beneath his fingers.

Tom struck one blow to her chest with the palm of his hand, still no response.

Using the inflatable bag and mask, he inflated her lungs while Dave, the paramedic from the second vehicle, began chest compressions. On completing every fifth compression, Tom squeezed the bag to inflate the lungs.

He spoke in a soft whisper, 'I think we are going to lose her, she is just not responding.' They continued on for a couple of minutes, then Tom took over both operations to give Dave time to set up the defibrillator. Paddles in position the monitor of the Electrocardiogram showed a reading on its tiny screen. Unfortunately it showed an (Asystole rhythm) long, straight and flat not even a slight blip broke the ruled line. Dave passed the rhythm strip over to Tom who took one glance and responded "Ok, let's go for it." He abandoned his part in the resuscitation, leaving Dave to continue with the CPR.

Tom positioned the woman's head to give him the best access. With a Laryngoscope in one hand and an 8.5 endotracheal tube in the other he bent forward to insert the Laryngoscope, searching out the familiar landmarks as he went. The endotracheal tube slipped neatly into position between the vocal cords and was tied off and connected to the resuscitation bag. Now that they had secured a clear airway, the 'Asystole' protocol could proceed. The two paramedics worked quickly, first the airway, then drugs, followed by CPR and finally the monitor. Two more circuits and the monitor changed to a ventricular rhythm. Now they had a slim chance. Dave picked up the defibrillator paddles and set them for the required shock sequence.

Ready to start, he shouted "STAND CLEAR." He looked about, making sure that Tom, himself and anyone else was not in contact with the woman's body. "SHOCKING NOW," he shouted in a strong clear voice as he hit the buttons on the paddles.

As the shock waves surged through the woman's body it arched once before settling back into position. Heart massage assisted breathing; adrenaline, atropine and the external defibrillation had all played their part in the hearts reactivation. Now they could concentrate on the airway. Her heart slowly responded picking up a little then a normal rhythm appeared on the monitor screen.

The man in shock was still very upset but now stable, which was just as well, for at this moment the Fire Officer came forward and told them that they all needed to move away from the area very quickly, as the situation with the lorry's load was now very serious. He could not guarantee their safety any longer.

"We were just about to get the lady off to hospital; can we just tie up with the other paramedic first? It will be easier if we can get the two drivers into the same ambulance, as this woman is not very good. She will need a lot more work on her before we get her there."

The Fire Officer agreed but stressed the urgency in evacuating the area extremely fast. "I just don't know what time we have, or what we can expect. Just move as quick as you can and if we shout go, get the hell out. No matter what you are doing. We don't want any heros."

The second ambulance crew loaded the woman with cardiac problems, then set off to the local hospital. They had not gone more than one mile, when the lady's heart rate started to increase and become rapid. The paramedic knew that if the heart kept on increasing its rate, it would only be a question of time before she went into 'Ventricular Fibrillation' and soon after that, full blown cardiac arrest again. Treatment for this was to shock the patient with 200j with the defibrillator, to try and convert the heart back to normal rhythm. As was the case with this woman, the paramedic had prepared for the inevitable and with one shock from the defibrillator, had successfully converted the heart rate back to normal. This was lucky for her, as it is not very often that conversion is so easy. Most of the time it will not work. She was not out of the woods yet, still very unstable and in need of urgent hospitalisation. The paramedic leaned forward into the front cab and picked up the radio mike. He gave his controllers a run down on the condition of the patient, requesting that the hospitals accident unit be put on stand-by alert ...

The current admissions coming into the casualty department had slowed to a trickle, the hospital had an awkward stillness and only the soft, muted squeak of a drug trolley interrupted the silence. There was an odour of stale body waste about the place so strong that it attacked nasal passages with gusto, making the olfactory nerves work overtime and as usual the smell was disguised by hospital disinfectant. Sharp ears picked up the sound of an ambulance arriving outside and the whole department seemed to spring back into life with a sudden urgency. Staff seemed to appear from all directions, picking up bits of equipment as they moved forward, each knowing exactly where they were to be positioned. Doctors and nurses stood around the receiving trolley waiting for the medical emergency to burst through the plastic doors of the resuscitation unit. The room was suddenly

251

illuminated as light switches were activated, throwing silhouetted shadows around the walls. Each member of the medical team stood in their allotted positions, opening draws and cupboards that housed the drugs and intubation sets. Drip stands with intravenous fluids attached to giving sets stood waiting for the expected patient to arrive. Cardiac care were notified and put on alert; everything was prepared for any eventuality and any second now everyone would act like the precision parts of a Swiss timepiece.

On arrival at the hospital, they wheeled her into the resuscitation room where the team of doctors and nurses quickly took over from the ambulance crew.

A second intravenous access was put into place, the steel needle eased forward with deft fingers until a flash of blood appeared in the chamber marking a successful entry into the vein. The senior resident began to issue his orders, blood samples were taken for examination and drugs inserted into the porthole of cannula. Whilst continuously working on the patient, the hospital team were firing questions at the ambulance crew trying to extract all the information possible to help them build a history firmly in their minds ...

Many road accidents that include two or more vehicles tend to produce more carnage. You cannot imagine some of the grotesque scenes that greet ambulance crews. Working amongst broken glass, hot engine oil, petrol and fresh blood creates a special kind of aroma, not forgetting the smell of fear coming from the rescue workers.

The driver of the Ford had a prodigious open wound to his right leg where the metal frame of the car had wrapped itself around it. The torn flesh in his leg had been gouged open by the sharp metal and this had been the reason why it had taken time to release him from the wreck. Although he was complaining of pains to his lower back, it was thought to be more muscular than spinal. But he was treated for the worst possible injury just to be on the safe side. His treatment had been to dress the wound and immobilise the leg in case of any underlying fractures.

Getting the Ford driver out of the vehicle was slow and laborious, having to take him out an inch at a time just in case anything else showed up. Halfway out, with many caring hands courtesy of the Fire Brigade, they took the strain and eased him clear. Then he was placed onto the spinal board and strapped down; with the low-neck collar already in position around his neck, he was completely immobilised from any movement. To assess fully the injuries Jason would have needed x-ray eyes. It was not just a question of treating what was found: they had to think of all the possibilities that could have resulted from the impact. This was a tried and tested procedure: always treat the patient for the worse possible injuries in the situation found.

Their other patient was in a similar state, suffering a fractured, right leg, possible spinal injury and of course, still in a state of shock from seeing his wife having a heart attack. The treatment for this man was to be the same as the other, but this one was demanding much more attention from the crew in the way of reassurance. He was anxious, constantly asking questions about his wife's condition, which of course the crew did not have the answers to. They just had to keep reassuring him that she was going to be fine, praying they were right.

Tom reflected on the woman passenger and wondered about her progress. He had felt much easier when Dave had turned up to help with the resuscitation; it had not been pleasant trying to save her life on his own. He had been sure that they would be dealing with a fatality, needing a Doctor to certify death on arrival.

Tom and Jason straightened their backs as they heaved the two stretchers into the rear of their ambulance and made both drivers as comfortable as conditions would allow. It was at this

253

time that Jason experienced the first sharp pains that cut into his brain. Lasting only seconds, he dismissed the episode and continued with the task at hand.

Being forced to disregard the standard practice of not carrying two drivers that had been involved in the same traffic accident in one vehicle was not ideal, but because of the situation with the lorry load, they had no choice. The crews were able to get away from the crash site without any explosions taking place. The Fire Brigade had managed to keep the lid on things. Their quick action had prevented any major disastrous events from happening and they would remain to contain the crash site.

As the driver of the Ford was now under arrest for drink driving, he had the pleasure of a police officer to accompany him to the hospital until he was fit enough to be charged. Even though he could not physically get up and run off, he was now under the control of the boys in blue.

Now came the job of getting clear of the crash site. You have to look out for yourself after a major road accident because the traffic builds up fast. Drivers attempting to get a closer look at the mangled vehicles tend to drive far too slow and this frustrates others who get caught up in the queues. This in turn causes some drivers to make silly manoeuvres and create more accidents. Most crews wonder what drives people to gather at the site of a car or plane crash. Is it just curiosity or the ghoulish nature that drives man to relish in the misfortunes of others?

The journey into the hospital was uneventful and they arrived just as the other crew was coming out of the accident unit. They unloaded the ambulance, using all four crewmembers, making life much easier to wheel in the two stretchers together. Both the drivers were handed over with a complete breakdown on conditions and treatment given, on scene and on route to the hospital.

Jason took one of the staff nurses to one side and let her know that the Toyota driver was the husband of the cardiac arrest woman brought in by the other crew. Also, that the other driver was under arrest and the police wanted to remain close by.

She whispered softly that the lady was not expected to make a full recovery and that the casualty team were still working on her in the resuscitation unit. The pain returned, attacking Jason's head with such ferocity that it caused him to cry out, but then subsided just as quickly and was soon forgotten. After they dispatched their charges into the care of the casualty staff, they took leave from the situation and made for the exit doors and out into the cool fresh air.

Every effort, every trick in the book had been used to stabilise the woman's condition and although the hospital staff had worked hard, the end result was failure, for she had suffered a third arrest while on the resuscitation table and died...

Jason was not feeling well, his head was like a pressure pot waiting to boil over and he felt like death warmed up.

"You look bloody awful, Jay, you can't keep working if you are feeling ill. For God's sake go sick," exclaimed Tom.

For once he had no doubts that his partner was right, as another sharp pain attacked his skull.

Tom picked up the radio and informed control that 'Jason was reporting sick for the rest of his duty and would see his own doctor later that day'.

"Drop me off at home, Tom, I'll pick the car up later. The way I feel at the moment could make driving a bit risky."...

Jason was halfway down the hallway of his house when the pain erupted inside his skull. He clasped at his head with both hands before staggering forward. The pain showed no mercy. causing him to cry out. Then terror swept through his medically trained brain with the realisation of what was happening. His pounding heart increased its beat and the unrelenting pain intensified. The

255

walls seemed to be spinning as he tried hard to focus his tormented eyes. Somehow he managed to reach the kitchen door before the ticking bomb inside his head detonated, causing an explosion of bright illuminated light that filled his vision. His legs gave way and he crashed forward falling onto the stone tiled floor as if pole - axed. For a few minutes his body shook and convulsed in a spasmodic rhythm before he lost consciousness and was still...

As Olive turned her key in the lock she had a sense of foreboding. Unaware that Jason was home, she could not comprehend the overwhelming fear that twisted and knotted her stomach. She walked into the kitchen and screamed, dropping the bag of shopping onto the floor. The shock of seeing her husband prostrate and motionless on the ground was unmerciful. At first she thought he was dead; he looked awfully pale, almost grey and his skin was wet with perspiration.

It took her a few seconds to compose herself before she attempted to tend to her husband. She knew instantly what was wrong; all those years in the ambulance service had taught her what the signs of a stroke were. He was alive, that was a blessing and she thanked God aloud. Instinctively she made sure that his airway was clear before picking up the phone to call for help...

WHEN THE CALL CAME IN, THE AMBULANCE CREW KNEW IMMEDIATELY THAT IT WAS JASON'S ADDRESS AND SPURRED ON BY THAT KNOWLEDGE, THEY WERE PARKED OUTSIDE HIS HOUSE WITHIN MINUTES.

Tom found Olive sitting crying on a bench outside the casualty unit and she looked to be in a terrible state. "How is he progressing?" he asked almost dreading her reply.

She wiped her eyes and looked directly at Tom before she answered.

"He's regained consciousness, but his left side is badly affected. The consultant was very blunt: he stressed that although Jason had survived one stroke he may not be so lucky the next time." At this point she burst into floods of tears before continuing. "They say that he should get his mobility back after a while but it will be quite a long haul."

"At least it will make the silly old bugger take things easy for while." Tom was trying hard to make light of the situation but his own thoughts were uttered by Olive's remarks seconds later.

"Don't you worry, he won't be coming back to work. I'll make damn sure of that. Another attack like this could finish him. I love him and always have."...

Jason lay in the darkness of the ward in silence except for the soft bleeping of his monitor. He tried to work out the strange surroundings and the reasons why the left side of his body would not function. He closed his eyes again as if waiting for the divine voice of God to give him the answers. Then slowly things became clearer and he started to remember some of the events leading up to the collapse.

After a few minutes he opened his eyes and tried to focus on the misshapen silhouette sitting alongside the bed. Olive looked across at her husband with a concerned look on her face. Then she reached over and took his hand into hers. "I really thought I had lost you, I love you so much."...

Week's later Tom called round to check on his partner's condition. He had heard various accounts of Jason's progress but wanted to see for himself. Jason was sitting in the conservatory watching two birds fighting over the same worm. The first blossoms of spring filled the fruit trees with their magnificent displays as the sun kissed each tiny petal with its warmth.

"Hello, you old bugger, lazing about again?" Tom exclaimed.

There seemed to be a strange calmness about the man propped up by pillows that gave support to weakened limbs. The sleepless nights had stopped and the dreams had faded away; hopefully they would never return.

The Ambulance service had declared him unfit for work and was arranging early retirement on medical grounds. When he first saw the letter stating that he was to be pensioned out of the service, he was filled with deep depressions. Being told that after twenty-two years you are no longer wanted or capable of doing the job you once loved was hard to except. Then, after the initial shock had passed, he realised that after all those years of praying for a way out of the stress and responsibilities God had granted his wish.

But most of all he had helped Jason survive his own personal 'NIGHTMARE.'